Our
SONG

ISBN: 9781691485864

To all my music lovers out there.
Keep rockin'!

Prologue

Sarah

"I've never felt so alive!" I jump into the arms of Donnie, our drummer, as applause rings out in front of us.

"You killed it tonight! Biggest crowd yet!" he replies.

My eyes widen in disbelief when I pull back. "You noticed that too?" I jump on the balls of my feet as we run offstage.

"All of us noticed," Tony says as he joins us in the backstage hallway, his guitar slung over his shoulder. "The owner said it was a sold-out crowd."

I squeal and do a happy dance, spinning around. I can't believe all our dreams are coming true.

Tonight, my band, Endless Hope, played at the most happening bar on Bleecker Street. It's hard to tell when you're onstage with the lights shining in your eyes how many people are there, but the noise and vibe were more intense than any other show. Everyone was engaged with our performance, and I even heard people singing along.

Having a crowd sing the words you wrote is beyond anything I've ever imagined!

Tony wraps his arm around me. "You've done us proud, Ms. Hart." He laughs, and I know he's teasing me about my name.

I moved to New York from a small, country-living, religious

Our SONG

Northern California town to follow my dreams. My parents think I'm only here to attend college. Yes, I've been going to classes for my degree in education, but all of my spare time is spent trying to make a name for myself in the music industry.

Well, except I don't dare use my real name.

If my parents found out, they'd be here in a heartbeat, dragging me back home where my dad would cleanse my soul in holy water for a month.

To say he disapproves of my music is an understatement. As the pastor of our small town that is seemingly stuck in the 1950s, he points his nose down on anything that uses profanity, loud guitar strings, or the pounding of a drum solo.

He won't take the time to actually *listen* to the lyrics and how they're more powerful and meaningful than some of the ones he sings in his beloved church. I've made it my goal in life to make him see what rock music is all about, so he will be okay with me following my dreams. I've given myself the four years while I'm here to try to make it. When I do, I pray he'll be able to accept my passion.

I try not to think about what will happen if I can't change his mind at that point. I keep reminding myself that, if I've already made it in the industry, it wouldn't matter, but deep down, that little girl inside me still wants the approval of her father.

"Okay, you guys, ready to head out?" Donnie asks after he loads the last of his drum set into our rental van.

"I can't just go home." I throw my arms in the air. "I'm still flying high from tonight! Want to go to the diner to get some food?"

Tony glances at his watch. I'm sure it's almost four in the morning.

Before I moved to New York, I'd drive to San Francisco, trying to get a taste of the life I wanted outside of my small town. The clubs closed at two in the morning but not here. Living the nightlife has a totally different meaning in the Big Apple.

"I could go for some breakfast. I have to work in a few hours, so as long as they have fresh coffee, too, I'm game. No reason to try to sleep now," Donnie says.

I wrap my arms around his neck, tightly hugging him.

I don't know what I'd do without these guys. When I found their flyer, looking for a lead singer, at a local bar, I took a chance and made the call. I never would have imagined they'd become like family to me. While I have my parents paying my way, these guys both work

2

two jobs, plus our gigs, to make ends meet. They see the end goal and have the same dream of making it big someday.

We walk the block to a diner on the corner. It's a beautiful night in Manhattan, and the cool breeze washes away the last of the sweat on my brow from bouncing around the stage. While Tony goes over tonight's set, discussing which song was received better and if we should switch up the order, I take in the calmness of the last hours of dusk before dawn. Even with the majority of stores and shops closed at this hour, there's still an energy, about this city that lives when everyone else is asleep.

I feel that buzz in my toes.

It's a bright light glaring in the midnight hours.

Except that light is no longer a metaphor.

I turn around just in time to hear the screech of tires, the headlights glaring in our eyes brighter than any stage I've been on.

Screams yell out.

There's a loud pounding as the car hits the curb.

Donnie covers me with his large frame, taking me to the ground with such force that my shoulder comes down with a shooting pain.

My head throbs, and then there's darkness.

Total *darkness* is all I know after that.

And my dreams … they fade away just as fast.

Chapter 1

Sarah
Seven Years Later

"Morning, sweetheart. Just calling to wish you good luck on your first day. Is your classroom all set up?" Mom asks over the phone as I walk out the door of my small apartment.

I grin at the memories of helping her set up her classroom over the years.

"Yes. I finished everything last week and prepped the next few weeks until I'm able to get some parent volunteers."

I can only imagine her smile when she says, "I'm so proud of you, Sarah."

Hearing these words is bittersweet.

My mother retired from being a kindergarten teacher five years ago, and I know she misses it every day. I took the reins, stepping seamlessly into her classroom and keeping the traditions going. It wasn't my first choice, but following in her footsteps definitely helped the sting of not being able to follow my own dreams—or rather, having my dreams ripped from me.

"You know you're welcome to stop by anytime you want. Principal McAllister was asking if he'd see you this year," I say as I head toward my car.

I hear her slight laugh under her breath. "You know I can't stay away, but I'll wait a few weeks to let everyone get in the groove of things. Then, I'll see if anyone needs help."

I open the car door, juggling my coffee and purse while holding my phone up to my ear. "What's on your schedule today? Has Dad finished prepping this Sunday's sermon?"

My father, Pastor Russo, spends every morning working on his weekly message. He studies and reads scripture daily until it's perfect. If only, somewhere in that scripture, there were something that taught him to not be so harsh on his own daughter.

"He'll spend a few more hours on it this morning, so I'm just sitting here on the back deck, sipping my coffee. I'll probably read or crochet for a bit." Her tone leaves nothing to the imagination.

I know, to some people, that would sound like heaven but not my mom. She's bored spending day to day with nothing really big to do. Besides teaching, tending to my dad, or caring for me and my sister, Emily, she's never had a hobby that she was passionate about. Now that she's retired, I can tell she questions things a little more and is looking for that next something in her life.

"Call Emily. I'm sure she could use the help with Emma," I suggest. I know my niece, Emma, lights up her world like she does mine.

"She already has a playdate set up, but I'll find something to do; don't worry."

I slide into my Honda Civic, juggling the phone and my stuff as I do. "Sorry to cut this short, but I have to get going, or I'll be late."

"Okay, honey. Have a great day. I know the kids will love you. Call me when the day is over."

"I will. Bye."

I start the car, loving the new system that automatically hooks up my phone's playlist to feed through the speakers. Morning talk shows are fine, but I want music to get my day started off right. It helps calm the anxiety twirling in my stomach.

The first song to pump out is a high-velocity rock song by Devil's Breed. They're a popular band among the rock circuit, known for heavy bass lines, powerful drum solos, and the enigmatic, deep, and somehow soulful vibrato of their lead singer, Adam Jacobson.

I dance my fingers on the steering wheel as I belt out the lyrics

Our SONG

to their song *Don't Need You*. Of course this is at the same time I drive past my father's church where he's set the weekly inspirational billboard to say, *The Lord hears you, even when you sin quietly*.

Way to take the joy out of life, as always, Dad.

I arrive at school thirty minutes before the bell rings, and already, families are playing on the swings and blacktop. I pause for a minute to take in the new parents, wondering who will be in my class. And yes, I said parents, not kids. At this age, a lot of their tendencies are learned from their parents, so I can get a good gauge on the kids just by watching their interactions. And this group looks good ... so far.

The first day is always a little nerve-racking, even for us teachers. Kindergarten can be a very exciting time in a child's life, but at the same time, it can be a challenging one. With the bad also comes the good.

Though teaching isn't my dream, I love the innocence of kindergarten. There's nothing better than seeing a child's eyes light up when they read their first sentence or the excitement of making new friends and gaining their first taste of independence.

"Hey, girl," Cindy, a fifth grade teacher I've known almost my entire life, says as I enter the building.

"Hi. How was your summer?" I ask, knowing what the answer is gonna be.

We were close in high school, but when I left for college, we drifted apart. She was completely satisfied with staying in our small town while I wanted out. Now, she's married to her high school sweetheart with two kids, and as she says, she's "living the dream."

"It was great. The kids are getting so big. We took them to the beach a few times and were just lazy, watching movies and being bums the rest of the time. I'm sad to be back." She wraps her arms around the folder she's carrying with a frown covering her face.

I don't expect her to ask me about my summer because I know she doesn't care. In this town, if you don't have kids and a family at our age, there's something wrong with you.

My summer break is the only time I get to try to get a piece of me back again. Maggie, my best friend who lives in New York, and I took a trip to Austin, Texas, where we listened to some amazing new bands. We stayed up late every night, having a good time and not wanting the nights to end.

Of course I'd love to have a family someday, but I'd take them with me to shows and introduce them to music, hoping they had the same love I did. Every time I see a family dancing with their young kids, my heart melts.

That's the life I want.

Too bad I know I won't find it here.

When I was left without a choice, I moved back home, and I feel like I've been wandering aimlessly around ever since. I'd like to leave, but I have no clue where I would go.

After my first attempt at a new life ended in a tragedy that led my father down a secret path of both ridicule and resentment toward his own daughter, I'm not sure I have the strength to go through that again.

When my sister announced she was pregnant and then my mom's position opened up at the school, it seemed fitting I should stay. Yet, as the days turned into years, I'm not so sure staying here is in my best interest anymore, but then I see my niece, and I wonder how I could ever leave, especially when I don't have a good reason or anywhere to go.

"Well, I have to get ready. Here we go; another year is about to begin." I bring my shoulders up to my ears, displaying my anticipation.

"Yep, good luck with those kindergarteners!" She waves as she heads toward her classroom.

After getting my things situated and setting up the name sheets I printed for each kid, I check around the room to make sure everything is set for the storm of kids and parents who are about to come in. After all, first impressions are everything, and I know they're checking me out the same as I'm checking them.

I glance in the mirror one last time. Half of my blonde hair is pulled up, and I curled big ringlets in the back. I run my finger over my scar on the back of my head as I take in the person I am now.

A part of me misses my brown hair, but that was the old me who died in New York. Now, I'm a blonde-haired kindergarten teacher in the suburbs.

I make sure the tattoo that wraps around my shoulder is completely covered with my cap-sleeved shirt. It'll be hard to keep a secret all year, but hopefully, by then, the parents will be happy with me as a teacher and not judgmental like some people in this community are.

Our SONG

When the bell rings, I head toward the playground where my students are lining up.

The blacktop is covered in parents standing next to their children. Some appear excited to have a kid-free day while others have tears in their eyes as they stare down at the precious life they created who's grown up too fast.

As I approach the line for my classroom, I crouch down to the level of the little girl at the front who I don't recognize from orientation. Whoever makes it to the front of the line gets to be our leader for the day as I walk them back to the classroom, which is a pretty coveted spot as the weeks progress.

"Hello there. My name is Miss Russo. What's your name?"

The sweet little girl with sandy-blonde pigtails and curls stands tall and proud. "My name is Cailin. You look like Cinderella."

I smile brightly as we shake hands. "Well, you're not the only one who thinks that. Just wait until you see my Halloween costume. Then, I'll really look like her."

Every year, I dress up as Cinderella. The kids love it, and the parents even comment on how much I resemble the Disney character.

"Did you hear that, Linda? I have Cinderella for my teacher!" Cailin says as she bounces on her feet, turning toward a woman that I've seen around town for a few years, albeit never with a child.

"I did, dear. I knew this would be the perfect place for you," Linda replies, running her fingers through Cailin's curls and twirling them around.

"Morning, everyone. Are we ready to go?" I say to the rest of the class standing behind Cailin.

They all nod in different levels of excitement, some already crying or clutching their parents for dear life.

I hold out my hand for Cailin. "You're my line leader today. Shall we head toward the classroom?"

Cailin places her tiny fingers in mine and does a happy skip and jump as we walk toward the hallway. She turns back to Linda, waving. "Bye, Linda. Have a good day."

I pause and turn to the group. "Parents, you're welcome to join us for a few minutes as we get settled in."

Cailin holds her arm out wide. "Yes, come here. You can hold my other hand."

Linda looks around at the other parents, whom she's much older than, and then down at Cailin with a sideways smile. It's obvious Linda isn't sure what her role is, but after a beat, she joins us as we head back to my classroom.

After we enter, I tell the kids to find the seat where their name is written. I go over our daily routine of the calendar, the pledge, and our counting of how many days we've been in school. As the days add up, we'll count them in fives and tens, helping them with bundling numbers.

I like teaching kindergarten because we have more freedom with our curriculum than the other grades, and I'm the only teacher who includes music in our free time. Every morning, we'll work on a song, and at the end of the year, we'll sing them for the parents.

Our first one is *God Bless America*, so I ask the parents to sing with me as we introduce the students to the song for the first time. When we're finished, I excuse them all, making sure to recognize who's with which child, as we don't allow them to leave the school until we see a ride is there, waiting for them.

The weeks fly by as summer turns to fall. My students have gotten the hang of our daily routine, and some are starting to test the limits of how they can act, which is very normal. With comfort comes misbehaving.

Now is when I have to turn up the sternness while not losing my Cinderella status with the kids. It's a delicate line of being their friend but also their teacher. They need to respect me and know that when they're in the classroom, they are to act a certain way.

I say, "No, thank you," more times than I ever thought possible to kids as they do things they aren't supposed to.

Some kids react and obviously don't want to get in trouble while some need the constant reminder.

We're discussing family trees and the difference between siblings, cousins, grandparents, and more. Each kid was to draw a picture of their family along with their favorite place in their house to give the art piece more depth. Now, each student stands to describe it to the class.

Our SONG

Timmy shows us a picture of his mom, dad, and sister in their kitchen. I love the way kids this age draw stick figures for people with fingers as straight lines, which take up more than fifty percent of their body size. I have a feeling it's drawings like this that influenced the movie *Edward Scissorhands*.

"Very nice, Timmy. And why did you choose the kitchen for your drawing?" I ask.

"My mommy cooks really good food. She says I'm in the kitchen too much and I eat a lot because I'm a growing boy."

The kids all laugh as he stands up taller to show how big he is.

"That you are," I say. "What a wonderful picture. Okay, Cailin, why don't you go next?"

Cailin steps to the front of the class where she holds up a picture of only her and who I assume is her dad, though I've only ever seen Linda drop her off or pick her up. The two of them are next to an airplane.

"This is me and my dad," she says with a huge smile on her face. "He's on the road a lot, so we fly to some really cool places."

"How lucky! You've been on a plane before?" Devin, a student, asks.

I try to put the focus back on Cailin's picture. "You did a fabulous job, but you were supposed to draw something from your house," I say, reminding her about what the assignment was.

Her shoulders sag. "I know, Miss Russo, but I haven't seen our new home yet. It's being worked on, and my dad hasn't been to Linda's house that much, so I drew my favorite place to be with my dad instead." Cailin joins the rest of the kids on the carpet after handing me her drawing.

As a teacher, you have to be very careful with each kid's family situation, and I must say, a plane is a new one for me. Still, I'm quick to make sure she feels secure. "How fun that you're getting a new place remodeled. Well then, I think you did a great job in choosing the plane. Thank you, Cailin. Lisa, why don't you go next?"

I noticed when I filed her paperwork the first week of school that there was no mom listed on her emergency forms, and this drawing solidifies that there's not one in the picture. Linda signed all the forms, and in the column where it asked for the relationship to the child, she simply stated, *Friend of the family.*

I haven't seen or heard anything else about Cailin's dad, and I wonder if he'll make the father-daughter dance coming up. It's my favorite event at the school, and I'd hate for Cailin to miss it.

Something I thought was cute at first but is starting to cause issues in class is Cailin's singing during times when everyone is quiet. When other kids want to know what she's singing, she starts to explain the song, and the cycle continues. How this little girl knows so many lyrics is beyond me.

I've broken up the kids into groups, and with the help of two parent volunteers, the groups rotate between stations, all working on different projects. This is when I get my one-on-one time with students as I pull them up to see where they are in their reading skills.

I ask the volunteers not to talk to the students since they're supposed to be quietly working, but no matter how much I stress this rule, they always engage the kids.

As Cailin cuts out shapes, she starts to sing, "Somebody once told me the world was macaroni, so I took a bite of the cheese."

"What's the song you're singing?" I hear Alicia, Brandon's mom, ask.

"It's *All Star*. It's from the movie *Shrek*."

Cailin repeats the lyrics, and Alicia laughs.

"Sweetheart, those aren't the words to the song."

"I know! My daddy and I like to make up silly lyrics. I think that one's my favorite."

"Cailin," I announce from across the classroom. "Please, no more singing."

"Yes, Miss Russo. Sorry," she responds, turning her head back down and focusing on her project.

When the last bell rings, I have the kids line up outside the door, waiting to be excused until I see their parents. When I notice Linda, I ask her to step inside briefly.

After setting Cailin up to play on the carpet, I turn to Linda.

"Is everything okay with Cailin?" she asks before I can say anything, worry evident in her tone and expression.

Our SONG

"Oh, yes. I'm sorry. I didn't mean to concern you. I just wanted to mention her singing. I've asked her to stop multiple times, but it's becoming a bit of a problem. I was hoping you could reiterate at home that there's a time and a place for everything, including singing."

I've had parents act surprised, like they think there's no way their children could do what I'm saying, and I've had parents look ashamed at their child's actions, but I've never had someone laugh like Linda does.

She holds up her hand, trying to hide her reaction. "I'm sorry. I shouldn't laugh. I know it's not funny. It's just …" She pauses, taking in a breath. "She wants to be like her dad; that's all. It's pretty cute."

"Does he like to sing, too?" I ask, curious why this is funny to her.

Linda bites her lower lip, obviously thinking about what to say next. "I guess, as her teacher, it's okay for you to find out early. He'll be home in a few weeks, and when the news does break, we might need your help, but please, keep this to yourself. I would assume there is some kind of oath to keep the privacy of your students between you and the family, correct?"

I smile in reassurance. "Of course. I keep everything private. Is there something I should be concerned about?"

"Oh no, dear. It's nothing like that. Cailin has spoken very highly of you. I know as soon as he's back in town, he'll stop in to meet you, so that's why I think it's okay to tell you now."

I nod my head, letting her know she can continue even though I'm really not following.

"Her father is Adam Jacobson." She stares at me, waiting to see if what she just said means anything to me.

My eyes narrow in disbelief. "You mean …"

She inhales as she nods. "Yes, the lead singer of Devil's Breed."

"Um …" My mind goes blank while my heart starts to pound.

Adam Jacobson is a media gold mine—or nightmare, depending on how you look at it. As the lead singer of the hottest rock band alive, he's all over the news for his wild antics during shows, setting things on fire and mosh pits so big that smaller venues can't hold their concerts anymore.

I've followed them since the start of their career, and never once have I heard about him having a daughter.

We live in a small Christian town of only seventeen thousand people. Everyone knows everyone, and if someone, God forbid, bounces a check at the local grocery store, it's town news for weeks.

How does a mega rock star live here and no one knows about it?

I look toward my bulletin board where every kid's name is spelled out, and I notice something. "But her last name is Tyler?" I ask, still a little confused. Then, it clicks—Linda's last name. "Isn't your last name—"

"Jacobson." She nods. "But he's not my son." She wrings her fingers together with a concerned expression gracing her face. "It's not my story to tell. Adam Jacobson is his stage name. His real name is Adam Tyler. He's worked really hard to keep her a secret from the media. We knew enrolling her in school would change that, but he wants her to have a normal life, and missing kindergarten wasn't an option. We haven't said anything yet because he wanted her to be known as just Cailin and not his daughter for as long as possible. Especially since he's on tour and not here to help guide her through any media issues. Or, as Adam says, 'haters,' when people find out."

I slowly nod my head, letting everything sink in. My palms start to sweat as nerves take over, but I try to act unaffected by the news. She might think it's because of his fame, but there's so much more to the news she just dropped than she would ever understand.

After a few breaths, I'm able to speak. "May I ask what your relationship is to Cailin?"

She smiles fondly while turning toward Cailin. "I'm someone who loves them both dearly."

Cailin stacks some blocks on the carpet. I try to see any resemblance to Adam in her, but it's hard to tell. She's sweet and innocent, and he's anything *but*.

Her tiny voice starts to sing again, "*Whoa, ohhhhhh-oh, it's still Tuesday. Whoa, ohhhhhh-oh, it's still Tuesday.*"

I raise my eyebrows to Linda in question, and she laughs out loud.

"It's a game they play. Every night when Adam calls, they discuss songs and make up lyrics. She's singing the song *Listen to the Music* by The Doobie Brothers—you know, *Whoa, ohhhhhh-oh, listen to the—*"

"*Music,*" I finish, trying to hide my smile.

"It's how they connect. She looks forward to every call, and he's never missed one. Don't worry though. I'll talk to her. Thanks for letting me know."

She steps toward Cailin, grabbing her bag and pointing her toward the exit.

Cailin stops and turns back toward me. "Bye, Miss Russo. Have a good day!"

I wave. "You too, Cailin."

Once the door closes, I'm not sure if I should scream or faint from the bomb that was just dropped. *After all these years, after everything I'd been through, did that really just happen? Is fate biting me in the ass again?*

I don't believe in coincidences—not anymore. *But how in the world is my life about to collide with his, especially here, in this small-ass, nothing town, so far away from that world I once knew?*

Chapter 2

Adam

"Fifteen minutes until showtime," my PA hollers as he sticks his head in my dressing room.

I search for my phone to call my daughter. No matter where I am in the world, my watch keeps the time of home, Northern California, where my heart really is.

My painted pinkie fingernail comes into view, putting the biggest smile on my face. Mine is black, and Cailin's is purple. It's a reminder we constantly have of each other, no matter how far apart we are.

People think it's my way of being hard or a drug reference. I'd die to see their faces if they found out it was actually my five-year-old daughter wanting to do my makeup, and that was our compromise. We liked it so much that it's stayed.

"Thanks. I'll be ready," I say over my shoulder with my feet kicked up on the dresser.

He nods and then shuts the door, closing out the chaos that is my life. I used to live for this shit. I still love it, but every day I'm away from my daughter, it gets harder and harder.

I dial Linda's number.

"Daddy!" Cailin yells into the phone as my angel comes into view for our FaceTime call.

Thankfully, she has my eyes, and the freckles that line her nose remind me of baby pictures I've seen of myself.

"Where are you tonight?" she asks.

Hearing her voice lifts my spirits up to where I'm flying high in the sky.

"I'm in Texas," I respond.

She sets the phone on the counter, so all I see is the ceiling while she starts her search. I can picture her tiny finger circling over the map I gave her, looking for the state. She puts a sticker over every one I visit, so she can keep track of me.

"Is that spelled T-E-X-A-S?" she yells out, taking her time in telling me every letter.

"Sure is." I sit back, closing my eyes to enjoy this moment.

"That's the biggest state yet!" she exclaims as she picks the phone back up, so I can see her again.

God, she's beautiful.

"You got that right. We have four shows across the state. Tell me about your day, Sugarplum." I use the nickname she said I should call if I was around someone who didn't know who she was. Even though I'm alone, I still use it.

She thought having nicknames would be fun, and I'm pretty much game for anything she suggests, especially if it means I get secret things to share with just the two of us.

"Well, Chestnut," she says excitedly because I remembered, but her tone changes quickly, and she frowns into the phone. "You know my teacher, right?"

"Yeah, Miss Russo. I thought you liked her. Did something happen?" My heart pangs at the thought of my little girl not having a good day at school.

"She doesn't like my singing," she says all grown-up and matter-of-factly.

A sharp laugh escapes my lips. "Are you singing when you shouldn't be?"

There's silence over the phone, and I know I've hit the issue on the head. Her eyes search the room and then land back on me.

"You know I love to hear you sing, but you can't sing whenever you feel like it, especially if she's trying to keep the class quiet," I say in my best parental voice.

She breathes heavily into the phone, and her bottom lip pouts out. "Linda said the same thing."

"And you listen to Linda, right? And Daddy too?"

"Yes, Daddy," she sighs.

"We'll have plenty of time to sing when I get back. Only a few more weeks, okay?"

Her little face turns even sadder, and I sit up in question.

"What's that face about?"

"It's nothing." She slumps back in her chair.

"Cailin, obviously, it's something. What's up?"

"They're having a father-daughter dance. Linda said it's while you're gone."

My heart breaks in two. I'd give anything to have that dance with my daughter. Linda has my schedule, and if she says I can't make it, then I can't.

"I'm sorry, Sugarplum. I'll make it up to you, I promise. Next year, I'll make sure my manager checks with your school before making our schedule, so I can be home for the dance, okay?"

She nods slowly, trying to put on a brave face, but the way her lip trembles does wonders on my soul. "Okay, Daddy. I know."

There's a knock on the door.

"One more minute," I yell back. "I love you, little girl," I say into the screen.

"I love you too, Chestnut." She makes a big kissy face and then wraps her arms around her tiny body like I'm hugging her.

I do the same before saying good night and hanging up the phone. Whenever I talk to her, it both lights up my world and rips it apart. I want to be with her, but right now, I have a stadium with thousands of people screaming my band's name.

I step into the hallway with chants of, "Devil, Devil, Devil," seeping through the walls.

Loud stomps rumble around us, making the lights quake like we're on the San Andreas Fault. The thunder of cheers echoes around us. It's absolutely exhilarating.

Music is my life just as much as Cailin is. Until now, I was able to have both, but I knew it wouldn't last. Normally, I'd have my own bus with just her and me while the guys traveled in their own bus. This is the first tour she hasn't come along with me.

Our SONG

In the past, I hired nannies to keep her happy, safe and, more importantly, out of the media. We never arrived or left with each other, but behind closed doors, the nannies would go back to their rooms, and it'd be just the two of us. I try to be a hands-on dad as much as I possibly can.

I knew this tour would be hard, but seeing her joy for her class and all she's learning reminds me that we made the best decision. I couldn't do it without Linda though. Yet again, she's come through for me in more ways than one.

"We'd better get out there. Things are wilder than normal," Jack, our bassist, says as he slaps my shoulder.

I nod with a shit-eating grin covering my face.

Max runs by us, screaming like a madman. He always acts a fool before we go onstage. People working the venue freak out every time, but Jack and I don't even notice.

I turn to see if Noah, our drummer, is coming—and I mean, in the physical sense, not the sexual. The man will stick his dick in any woman who has a pulse and is an exhibitionist, so it's not uncommon to find him fucking some chick before and after the show.

When he turns the corner with a female draped over his arm, looking a mess, I know he's had his fix. Every one of us has something that keeps us going. Noah's is sex, and Max and Jack love the alcohol and drug options while the music is the only fix I need.

Nothing can feed my soul or fill my veins like the strum of an electric guitar or the thump of the bass drum.

Once we're all backstage, we pause, in a circle. No words are ever said, but it's become a ritual we all need. Each one of us breathes deeply, readying ourselves for the next few hours where we push our bodies to our limit.

Our shows have been reviewed using words like *anarchy*, *pandemonium*, and—my favorite—*lawlessness*. Our antics are a little over the top and really have an *anything goes* mentality. One thing is for sure though—we put on one hell of a party.

I'd like to say no one gets hurt, but mosh pits are known for injuries. I've stopped the show a few times, making sure the crowd is okay and everyone is taking care of one another. You can slam into your fellow concertgoers all you want, but if they fall down, the number one rule is you have to pick them back up.

The walls start to shake as the noise gets louder. I see the eyes of the venue staff widen, but I brush it off. This isn't our first go-around.

At the start of every show, we cut all the lights. We always know the second it happens due to the screams that follow.

We wait, and nothing happens. I turn to the head of our security who isn't there. Questions swarm my mind before people come running backstage.

"We have to get you out of here. A riot has broken out. It's not safe out there."

Arms wrap around me, trying to move me back to my dressing room, but I stand firm. "Fuck that. They're rioting because we aren't out there yet. Let me by."

"Adam"—Nick, the head of security, comes around the corner—"not today, bro. Shit's out of control. We're calling the police in."

I eye each one of my bandmates, making sure they're on board before I step up to the man I hired to protect me against all odds. He's as tall as I am, but he must have one hundred pounds on me. I'm lean and mean, whereas he's just straight mean. I know he has my best interest in heart, but when it comes to my shows, no one fucks with me and my fans.

"No police. We got this. Let us by." I puff my chest, making sure he knows I'm the one who writes his paychecks.

"Fuck, Adam, you go out there, and I might not be able to protect your ass."

"If we don't go out there, we might not be able to protect the fans who just came for a show. If it doesn't work, then you can call for backup. Now. Let. Me. By."

Nick moves to the side, and we all run out onstage. The stadium lights are on, and it's pure chaos. People are climbing the rafters, trying to get away from the mob of people throwing punches at each other.

The noise is deafening, and there's no rhyme or reason to the screams coming from all around us.

We normally close the show with our song *Riot*, but the irony is too much to not take full advantage. The song starts with one of the best guitar riffs that Max, our lead guitarist, has ever come up with.

I turn to the guys. "Grab your guitars and follow me."

We head up to the drum stage that sits high above the floor. Noah likes to be ten feet up in the air like the badass he is. It's pretty tight, having flames shoot off below him during his drum solo, but I've never been happier for its height than I am right now.

Once we're all in place, I nod to Max. "Start *Riot* off but continue to play the riff until we join in."

He sets the guitar low on his hip and begins to play, picking each individual chord over and over again. I keep my eye on the crowd, encouraging him to continue to play while I motion to our sound guy to turn it up some more.

Slowly, the crowd turns their attention toward us instead of at each other. Once I feel things are getting under control, I nod to my guy, telling him to cut the lights.

Once he does, flames shoot up around the stage as a devilish laugh radiates around the venue, and we all join in on the song, starting off one hell of a show that won't be forgotten anytime soon.

Chapter 3

Sarah

"I'm sure you saw the news this morning," Dad says when I enter his office at our church to say good morning and put my stuff down.

"No. Did something happen?" Worry creeps up my spine.

My dad might only be a pastor, but in this town, he might as well be the President of the United States.

The community looks up to him for both guidance and healing. Yes, we have a mayor and a city council, but everyone knows it's really what *he* thinks that guides the city. The only reason we have the other positions is because of the separation of church and state. It's no coincidence that he meets weekly with them all.

His jaw clenches, and I have a feeling this is about me rather than something involved with the city. His eyes roam over my outfit, which I'm sure he doesn't approve of since it's not a long skirt like most women wear here, and then to my shoulder, making me *almost* reach up to make sure my tattoo is covered.

He's ridiculed me for it, saying I have to get it removed but I refuse. It's the only thing I have that's left of the old me, and I'll never get rid of it even if I have to spend my life covering it up.

"That awful music you listen to had a riot break out at a concert last night. Some band called Devil's Breed," he spits out once his eyes reach mine again.

My chest tightens for completely different reasons than before as my thoughts instantly go to Cailin. "Is everyone okay?"

"No, they aren't. A few people even had to be taken to the hospital. When will these people realize what they're doing is wrong? Their name states it clear as day—*Devil's Breed*." He shakes his head in disgust.

"But the band … are they okay?" I ask, placing my hand over my chest.

"Honestly, Sarah, why would you care about them? It's people like that who are ruining this world and almost …" He thankfully doesn't finish that thought. Instead, he tsks when he tosses me the paper as he heads out of his office.

The concert was Friday night in Texas. Pictures of torn speakers and broken railings with the headline "Rock Show Riot" shines across the front page.

It was obviously taken during the show. Adam is screaming into the microphone as people swarm the foot of the stage. Lights flash all around as fire falls from the drum set perched high. His hair is sweaty, and his shirt is ripped from a woman reaching up, trying to get a piece of him, but he doesn't seem to mind.

The passion he feels for the music is as evident as ever.

I've seen so many pictures of him, but looking at this picture now, I try to find any part of Cailin I can. He's aggressive and raw, as she's frills and bows, yet from what Linda said, they have a close relationship.

It's hard to imagine.

I scan the article. Glad to see the only injuries were minor, and the band was never in harm's way. As I read, I learn the band actually helped to halt the riot instead of caused it, like my dad implied. They even visited the injured in the hospital before heading back on the road.

Of course, I don't go after my dad to try to point that out to him. He will never see the other side, so there's no point in trying.

I breathe a sigh of relief that Adam is okay and put my things down before taking my post at the front doors, so I can greet the people who enter my dad's church.

I stop to say hello to my four-year-old niece, Emma, who's playing in the pews before people arrive. "How's my baby girl?" I hold out my arms wide as I crouch down.

"Auntie!" She comes running.

She always fills my world with that special happiness I thought I'd lost.

"Where's your mommy?" I ask, smoothing the hair from her forehead.

"Over there." She points to Emily, who's slowly approaching us due to being six months pregnant.

I'm hoping my nephew fills the rest of the holes in my heart—at least until I can figure things out in my head.

"You okay there, sis?" I stand up, holding Emma in my arms.

"No, this boy is going to be the death of me. How I let Chris talk me in to having another child is still beyond me. I can already tell he's going to be crazy like the Samson boy who's constantly jumping during the service."

I give her a side hug before rubbing my hand over her belly. "You'll be fine. Only a few more mon—"

"Don't say it." She points her finger at me like hearing how much longer will be the death of her. "Come on, Emma. Mama needs to sit down."

I try not to laugh as she takes Emma before heading toward her husband Chris. He's the perfect son-in-law in my dad's eyes. He's faithful to both Emily and God, has a great job and is as clean cut as they come. His everyday wear is khakis with a polo shirt, and he doesn't listen to anything but jazz music. He's perfect for Emily but is someone nowhere near who I would want to spend the rest of my life with.

I walk toward the door, ready to greet our parishioners.

"Hello, Sarah dear. Are we going to get a solo again this morning?" Mrs. Osborn asks as she grips my hand in hers.

"Yes, Mrs. Osborn. I plan on singing *I Can Only Imagine*," I respond, smiling sweetly.

She lets out a gleeful cheer as she turns to inform her husband, who is hard of hearing.

I've been singing in this church since I was six years old. What started out as singing in the children's choir quickly turned into solos every Sunday by the time I was sixteen years old.

Even though being here isn't what I truly want, seeing my father's proud grin as I sing words of the Lord fills that emptiness inside me—at least for the hours I'm here. He says his church has grown three times the size because of my songs, but I know he's just praising his "little girl," as he still calls me. No matter how much not having his approval for the life I want hurts, seeing he's proud of me here helps that tiny bit.

To him, I'll always be his baby. He'll never see me as the person I want to be.

I take my place off to the side once everyone is seated as music plays, and we wait for my dad to begin. When the door opens, I'm surprised to see Cailin and Linda enter.

I have a lot of students who attend this church, but this is the first time I've seen either of them here. I stand up and quietly make my way to them, welcoming them into our church.

Linda wears a sorry expression, apologizing for disrupting things with her eyes, and I make sure to motion that it's okay, as they are always welcome. The music will play for a few minutes to make sure the people who are running late can enter.

I crouch down to greet Cailin first. "Don't you look cute in your Sunday best?" I say, pointing down at her pink dress.

"Thank you," she whispers. "My daddy told Linda to buy me the best dress she could find. It's for the father-daughter dance next week." She twirls around, showing it off.

"Is your daddy going to be able to make it to the dance?" I look up to Linda for confirmation.

Her face says it all as she slightly shakes her head.

Cailin's face falls. "No, but Linda's husband, Wayne, is taking me. I figured since I wasn't going with my daddy, it was okay to wear the dress today too."

"It sure is. I'm glad you came. Let's find you guys a seat." I take her by the hand and lead them to an open seat right before my father begins.

When it's time to start the songs, I head toward the front with a microphone in my hand and start the words to *I Can Only Imagine*. Our church is known for our music, and when the guitar and drums join in with a soft beat, people's faces light up but not as much as Cailin's.

Her expression resembles the excitement of a little girl meeting her favorite Disney character, not one who's listening to a gospel song.

After church, I notice them both waiting to talk to me. "Did you enjoy yourself?" I ask as I approach.

"You sing like an angel," Cailin says, her tiny voice rising in joy as her face brightens.

I grin, looking at her and then Linda before saying, "Thank you, sweetie. Is this your first time coming to this church?"

Linda seems to blush in embarrassment. "I'm sorry; it is."

I touch her elbow in reassurance. I know most people feel like if you live here, you have to attend this church, but I know not everyone feels that way. I'm one who thinks people have the right to not attend if they choose so.

"There's no reason to be sorry. I'm glad you made it."

"I was telling a friend how Cailin has you as a teacher. When they told us about your singing, Cailin begged to come."

I lean down to be level with Cailin. "That's very sweet. Maybe you can sing with me someday. Just like I tell you in class, there's a time and a place. Here's a perfect place."

Cailin jumps up and down in excitement, pulling on Linda's arm. "Can I, Linda? Can I?"

She laughs at her joy. "Of course, sweetheart. I'm sure your father would love to hear you sing one day."

My heart skips a beat at the thought of Adam Jacobson entering our church. My father is very old school and expects his congregation to keep up that mentality of wearing their Sunday best when you come to praise the Lord.

Add in everything that's happened in the past, and I can hear it now, the sound of a record screeching to a halt as Adam walks into my dad's place of worship. His head would turn in shock and—I hate to say it—disgust of the man covered in tattoos.

We'll have to do this *before* his tour ends, so we can avoid the awkwardness.

"I'll tell you what. We'll set up a time very soon for you to stay with me and practice."

Cailin dramatically nods her head as she bounces on the heels of her feet. "Thank you so much, Miss Russo."

Linda wraps her hand around Cailin. "Come on, sweetie. We have to get home. Thank you, Miss Russo."

"My pleasure. I'll see you on Monday, Cailin."

25

Our SONG

"Bye," her tiny voice calls out as she waves while walking away.

My mind has been wandering ever since I found out Adam Jacobson has a daughter.

Every female has her eye on a certain bad boy, that one guy she wouldn't dream of actually doing anything with but loves to admire from afar. Adam always caught my attention when I passed a magazine rack or his picture flashed across my Instagram—because, yes, I follow him and have for years.

No matter the tattoos that run up his neck or the way his hair always looks messy yet perfect, every picture of him spikes my heart rate.

I used to sneak rock music when I was younger, keeping it down really low in my room, listening to the hard guitar riffs with hearts in my eyes. At the time, my fourteen-year-old self wanted to defy my parents strict, clean living lifestyle and run off with the first bad boy I met.

I might be a kindergarten teacher, but inside is someone dying to be heard, to make a difference, the way Adam has through music. Knowing that he has secrets that might change his bad-boy image intrigues me even more.

I pull up my playlist on my phone and click through until I get to Devil's Breed. Scrolling through the songs, I search for one that might stand out, giving me clues to who Adam really is.

I decide on their first album and run through the songs—not listening to every one entirely, but trying to get more of a feeling to his words.

Their first album is raw and gritty with a lot of pent-up anger. As the albums switch, I can feel a healing that he was achieving through his art. The anger is gone, and questioning now stands in its place.

This was the album that got me through *my* hard times. My parents think I turned solely to the Bible and God to help heal me, but really, it was just as much music as it was my faith. Music might have been the cause of my pain, but it was still my doctor, my therapy, and my lifeline.

The cover of the next album pops up on my screen, and I pause, taking in the pink heart that graces the cover. It's a collage of music notes, guitars, and even flames all around. But it's unmistakable that the core of the design is a pink heart.

It was released five years ago—the year Cailin was born.

Each song has a different tone. There are songs of forgiveness, inner peace, and even love.

He wasn't keeping her a secret from his world; she was there, in plain sight, just no one thought to pay attention.

I'm paying attention now, Adam, and I like what I'm hearing.

Chapter 4

Adam

As much as concerts are my entire world, the after-parties are the entire demise of the high I had merely an hour before.

My manager knows not to plan one after every show, but some are a required part of the gig. Radio stations want to give away tickets, and fans pay big money to party with us.

It's at these events that I feel like I can't be myself. Here, I'm the rock star, putting on a show for everyone, trying to act like the rest of my band.

Onstage is the *real* me—music being the only thing that makes me feel absolutely alive. Back here, partying, is not and never really has been me.

The best parties are the ones where the fans talk about our songs and how they've helped them through certain parts of their lives. I've been there, turning to music for healing, and hearing that I've helped them affirms my purpose in life while making these parties tolerable.

I lean against the doorframe as I glance around the room, noticing most of the radio personnel and record label suits have left. Remaining are more of the groupie fans who are dying to party like rock stars—whatever that means. These parties aren't much different than ones I attended ten years ago—before I had a pot to piss in.

Noah is making out with some chick on the couch, and the two women sitting next to them keep trying not to notice. I feel like I should warn them that, any minute, she'll either be sucking his dick or they'll be fucking, but I decide against it, hoping when they figure it out, their faces will at least provide some entertainment tonight.

They're talking to a few guys from our crew who I've seen try this tactic before to get laid. Some girls get turned on by watching others go at it. Unfortunately, I don't think these two are those types of girls.

The guys are hoping to get in on the action, turning Noah and his chick into an orgy once he makes his final move. It's a puss move on their part, but as they're roadies, I can understand them just wanting to get some action before we move on to the next city.

Too bad these guys aren't paying close enough attention to the girls, as it's written all over their faces that they aren't okay with the couple next to them, no matter who Noah is.

I have to cover my laugh when the girls have finally had enough and decide to leave. Disappointment covers the roadies' faces when they realize they probably aren't getting any tonight and that all the effort was for nothing.

I turn my attention to Jack, who's taking a shot from some chick's boobs, while Max is licking down the stomach of a girl lying on a table before pouring liquor into her belly button. Giggles from the girls fill the room as hoots and hollers follow from the groups of guys who surround them, watching the show, wishing they were them.

A guy I don't recognize in the corner catches my eye. The girl he's with keeps swaying from side to side, and her eyes are glazed over. If he wasn't pressing her against the wall, I doubt she'd be standing at all.

My dad mode clicks into high gear.

I nudge the crew member next to me. "Hey, is this guy with us?" I point to the couple.

He glances and then says, "Nah, he's part of the local crowd."

The way he keeps trying to feel up on the girl, pushing his body into hers, as he kisses her neck isn't sitting right with me, so I make my way toward them.

Once he sees me walk by, he stops, happily taking advantage of his chance to talk to me. "Adam, dude, you're my fucking hero."

We slap hands, and I nod. "Thanks for coming. Is your friend okay?"

Our SONG

The girl stumbles, just like I suspected she would, when he's not holding her up anymore.

"What's her name?"

He shrugs. "Haven't even gotten it yet. Won't matter tomorrow though, if you know what I mean." He playfully hits my arm like that's supposed to make me laugh.

It doesn't.

I turn to her, holding my hand out to shake hers. "I'm Adam. What's your name?"

"Sheila," she says, smiling and pressing out her chest to me. The motion is too much for her to handle, and she falls into me instead.

"Who are you here with?" I ask, searching the room to see if anyone is paying attention to her.

She steps up to me again, placing her hand on my chest to keep herself steady, alcohol reeking from her breath. "I'm here all by myself. My friends were too afraid to come party with y'all, but I wasn't going to miss out on the chance."

I run my eyes down her outfit with the short miniskirt and tight leather top that pushes her boobs out more than necessary. No wonder this guy was all over her. She looks like she's here to find someone to go home with, but the fact that she's as drunk as she is makes me pause.

The guy she was talking to nods his head and raises his eyebrows when he notices I just checked out her goods. He thinks we're thinking the same thing, but we're *not*.

"So, tell me, Adam, do you like to party?" Her words slur out.

"Hell yeah, he does!" the guy hollers, and I decide to play along.

I don't see tonight ending well for her, especially if she's here alone.

I grab her hand. "Come with me," I say, trying not to sound too sexual, but making sure she follows me just in case.

"Yeah, Adam," the guy cheers.

I nod my head as I slide my arm around her waist, more to make sure she can walk straight than for anything else. I get Nick's attention, the head of our security, so he follows me.

The after-party is at the hotel where we're staying, so I hit the elevator button and bring her inside. Her eyes are getting heavier by the minute now that we're away from the other partygoers who were keeping her semi-awake.

"Whatcha got here?" Nick asks as he steps into the elevator with us. He knows I'm not one to take almost-passed-out girls up to my hotel room.

"She's wasted and here alone." I press the button to the top floor and wrap my arm around her shoulders, bringing her into me.

"And you thought it'd be a good idea to bring her up to your room?" Nick questions with his brows furrowed and a tilt to his head.

"I can't get her a room. Some of the guys are crashing on the bus because the hotel is full. I didn't like the way a guy was trying to get on her, so what was I to do? I'll crash in Max's room."

"Yep, you're definitely the dad of a daughter," he teases with a grin on his face.

"Fuck off. Just help me get her situated. She can crash in my room, sleep it off."

Riding to the forty-ninth floor takes a while, and I'm not sure if she can even walk, so I lean down to pick her up and carry her to my room while Nick opens my suite.

Inside, I make my way to the bedroom, remove her shoes, and slide her under the covers. There's no way a phone is hidden in her tight outfit, so I turn to Nick. "Can you check to see if she had a purse down there and make sure we get it up here?"

He slaps my back. "Sure, man."

He turns to leave, but before I walk away, I take in the woman who's sleeping in my bed tonight, forcing me to move to Max's room next door. She looks more peaceful in her sleep, and I can't help but imagine Cailin at this age. I can only hope she never puts herself in anywhere near this type of situation like this girl did tonight.

Thoughts of Cailin's mom come blaring back, but I force them away. The two situations are not the same.

I leave a note, telling her to come to the next room over to get her purse in the morning. After closing the door, I head to the living room where Nick is pillaging through the gift basket the hotel left for me.

He grabs the alcohol bottles, knowing I won't use them. "Thank you very much," he says as he nods his head and makes his way toward the door.

I laugh at his antics as I call down to security to get them to open Max's room for me. "Have a fun night," I say as he leaves.

"You know I will."

Our SONG

I'm woken up to the sounds of someone knocking on the door. I didn't want Max to come back to his room and find me sleeping in his bed, so I slept on the couch. My feet hung over the ends, and the blanket I had barely covered my tall frame. Let's just say, I didn't get the best night's sleep, especially since Max came back with some chick an hour ago.

"Hi." Sheila waves shyly when she sees me open the door. "You have my purse, I take it?"

I yawn as I run my fingers through my hair. "Morning."

"Whose room was that?" She bites her lip as she covers her body by wrapping her arms around her center, obviously questioning what's going on.

I rub the sleep from my eyes before I say anything.

"Wait. Holy fucking shit. Adam Jacobson?" She glances around the room and then stares at me again in disbelief.

I try not to laugh. "Yeah. Nice to meet you more officially."

I raise my arms above my head, trying to stretch the aches away from my body.

Her eyes widen as she takes in my bare chest, turning red when I notice. "How the hell did I end up there?" She turns toward the room she just came from and then back to me.

I give her the same expression I give Cailin when she's done something wrong, which feels weird, so I quickly wipe it away and try to act nonchalant. "You were pretty drunk, and I didn't like the way a guy was treating you. So, I brought you back to my room, and then I came here."

Her posture stiffens when she realizes what I just said. "What guy?"

I briefly close my eyes, inhaling a deep breath. "Exactly. That's why you're here, and I slept there." I point to the small couch behind me.

"But you didn't try …" She points back and forth between us, seeing if I'll get her drift.

I glare at her. "Of course I didn't. I brought you up here to protect you."

Her head falls to the side with a small grin gracing her face. "So, you were my hero last night."

I let out a quick laugh. "Hardly. I just wanted to make sure you didn't end up in the wrong place since you weren't there with anyone."

A full smile builds on her face. "Wow, so you're, like, a good guy then."

"Yeah, don't tell anyone." I wink, trying to keep the mood playful.

A girl moans from the bedroom before I hear Max saying, "Yeah, take that dick. Take it all."

I turn to Sheila. "I'm hungry. Want to get some food?"

She covers her mouth, not sure how to react from what we just heard, and nods slowly. She's obviously in shock from the morning's events, but it's just another day in my crazy life.

Holding her hands out to her sides, she says, "Why not? Adam Jacobson, let's go get some food."

"You can just call me Adam." I grin before I slip my shirt back over my head.

She inhales and tries not to laugh. "Okay … Adam."

Chapter 5

Sarah

I enter the multipurpose room that's lined in pink and white streamers and balloons for the father-daughter dance.

This is my favorite school event, and I offered to help make sure things run smoothly just so I could take part.

I remember attending this same dance with my father. It was my best memory as a little girl. Every year, my mom would buy me a dress that I could twirl around in and even take me to get my hair professionally styled.

I make my way to the registration desk, lining up the papers that list who has paid before people start to arrive.

"Do you need any help?" Cindy asks as she approaches the table.

I hand her half the stack of papers. "Do you want to help me check people in?"

"Sure." She sits down next to me. "I think we need to start a mother-son dance." Since she has two boys, the statement makes sense.

"I don't see why you can't organize something like that. Do you think your boys would want to come, all dressed up?"

Her head drops back in laughter. "No way. We'd have to do a glow night or a carnival or something like that. But I think it'd be fun."

"You should do it. Let me know if I can assist."

She brightens up, proud that I agreed with her suggestion. It's not often that we see eye to eye on things.

As people enter, I admire every dress worn by some of the sweetest girls around. Some even have corsages on their wrists.

When Cailin steps up, she introduces me to Linda's husband, Wayne. I don't bring up anything about how it's nice that he could bring her or the fact that her own father isn't here. That little spark I normally see in her eyes is gone.

By six thirty, the place is full. Our PE teacher tries his best to DJ. Sights of dresses twirling around on the dance floor bring me so many happy memories.

A father dressed in a form-fitting gray suit holds his hand up high as his daughter spins. His expression is priceless as he watches his little angel having a fun time.

Wayne is doing the best to accommodate Cailin, but I get the feeling he's out of his element. When they dance, he's not holding her like the other fathers do. He's questioning where to put his arm, and his posture is stiff.

As I walk around the room, making sure everything is going okay, I catch Cailin doing a little dance that signifies she has to go potty. Wayne's eyes widen as he nervously looks around, so I swoop in and offer to take her.

The night progresses, and poor Wayne doesn't fit in the groups of young fathers who begin to line the walls as the girls start to play with their friends. He's tucked in the corner on his phone, but when he hangs up, he heads straight to Cailin, leaning down and pointing to the door.

I follow his finger and am shocked when I see Adam—*the* Adam Jacobson—standing at the door in tight jeans with holes and a black shirt that clings to his body, revealing tattoos that cover both arms. His hair sticks up straight, and the black gauges in his ears stand out in our clean-cut, country community.

Cindy is talking to him, and by her expression, I can tell she doesn't recognize him.

Why am I not surprised?

When she motions to Principal McAllister, I rush to the door, making sure he doesn't say something he'll regret before he realizes who just crashed our party. He's close to his seventies, so I wouldn't expect him to recognize Adam.

He takes pride in knowing who all the parents are here at Markham Elementary and is quick to make it known when people aren't welcome. Since he doesn't know Cailin's father is a rock star who's on tour, he has no clue who the man is that just walked in without a student on his arm.

Cailin is making her way to us as I step in front of Principal McAllister.

"Hi. You're Cailin's father, right? So glad you could join us." I reach my hand out to him.

Principal McAllister gives me the side-eye for cutting him off but thankfully keeps his mouth shut once he hears me say it's Cailin's father.

Adam reaches his hand out to mine, securely gripping it. "You must be Miss Russo." His crystal-blue eyes stay locked to mine, and his lips tilt up into a slight grin.

I'm glad Cailin jumping into his arms breaks our moment, so I can gather myself better.

"Daddy, how are you here?"

He wraps his arms around her, hugging her so tightly that she giggles his name as he bounces her up and down. "I couldn't miss my little girl's first dance," he says when he pulls back to look at her in the face. He sets her down. "And this dress!" He motions for her to turn around.

"Do you like it?" she says, holding out the sides for him to see better.

"I love it, but you're missing one thing." He takes the small box he's holding and opens it for her, revealing a beautiful dahlia corsage.

Cailin jumps up and down, clapping her hands. "Is that for me?"

Adam removes it from the box and places it around her wrist. "Now, it's perfect. So, my lady"—he holds out his elbow to her—"may I have this dance?"

I turn to the rest of the crowd, only to see the spectacle they've created. Most of the parents here are my age, and though they might not like rock music, thanks to apps like TMZ, they know exactly who Adam is, especially after the riot that just occurred.

Adam seems unfazed by the buzz around him. I'm amazed he can act like no one cares that a huge rock star just entered our small-town elementary gymnasium. He swings his daughter around, holding his hands out to her as she steps on his feet, and they dance like it's something they've done a thousand times before.

Whispers progress, and before long, cell phones are removed from coat pockets, and pictures are snapped. Worry of his secret getting out grips at my stomach, but when I see the way he's looking at Cailin, it calms my nerves.

Right now, he's just a normal dad who wants to dance with his little girl. Nothing should stop him from having this memory with his daughter.

"Who is this guy, and why are people freaking out that he's here?" Cindy ruins the sweet moment when she snidely crosses her arms in front of herself.

"You don't recognize him?"

She scrunches her face. "Why would I know *what* that is?"

Yep, that's why we aren't friends anymore. I need that reminder of how judgmental and snobby she really is every once in a while. The whole town is like this. My sister, Emily, is the only friend I have who lives here. She's not as bad as some of the people, but she definitely has her moments.

This is just another reason why I need to make a plan for something else in my life—quickly. Thank God I have Maggie even though she lives on the opposite coast. I vent to her often, and she keeps me sane. I promised her this was my last year teaching here, and I plan on keeping that promise. I'm ready for what's next.

I try to hide my irritation. "He's a famous rock star. You should look him up. He's the lead singer of the band Devil's Breed."

She flips her hair my way in an instant. "You really think I'd listen to a band with the word *devil* in it? Please don't tell me that's his daughter. How did we let someone like that in this school?"

I open my eyes wide to her. "In this *public* school, where everyone and anyone in our city is welcome to attend? You don't have to be so rude. You don't even know the guy, and his daughter is a sweetheart."

She rolls her eyes. "Of course you would stand up for something like that. When will you grow up, Sarah?"

With a huff, she storms off to talk to the other teachers and, I'm sure, to try to start a gossip train.

I shake off her negative energy and turn my attention back to the sweet dance happening in front of me.

The song ends, and Cailin pulls her father by the hand over to where I'm standing. "Daddy, this is my teacher, Miss Russo," Cailin says with so much pride that I can't help but smile.

He picks her up with his left arm and sticks out his right one to me again. Tingles fly through my body when our skin meets.

"Yes, we met when I first got here. Thanks for taking care of my little girl." He tickles her after he drops my hand.

"Please, call me Sarah." I kick myself internally.

Adam looks back to me, pausing for a brief moment before repeating my name breathlessly, "*Sarah.*"

It rolls off his tongue in a raspy baritone that makes it sound more like a song lyric than just five letters, and I swear, my heart skips a beat.

I've never asked a parent to call me by my first name, and the expression on Principal McAllister's face proves he heard me. I know he's waiting patiently for me to fill him in on why people are taking pictures and acting weird toward this man, but he'll have to wait a little longer because I'm currently being held hostage by the smoldering stare of a rock star.

This man, who has seen the world, is looking at me like I just might be the bluest ocean or the brightest star and he's mesmerized by my existence. It's intense and hypnotic, and if I'm not careful, I might just believe it's more than what it is.

Adam turns back to Cailin. "Thank you for the dance, Sugarplum, but I have to get going."

She pouts, and I can't help it when I ask, "You can only stay for one song?"

He sighs as he places her down on the ground. "I have a show in"—he checks his watch—"two hours in Arizona."

"Arizona?" I spit out in surprise.

A grin covers his face, and he glances down at his daughter. "Yep. I couldn't miss this beautiful girl's first dance, so I hired another band to perform before me to buy time. I have a private jet waiting to get me back in time."

My eyes open wide in both shock and awe. The love this man has for his daughter has no boundaries.

"But only ten more days, right?" Cailin asks.

"That's right. We have a few shows in Arizona, then LA and Vegas, and then I'm home." He leans down to give her a hug.

"Yay!" She holds her arms up in celebration.

"Give me some love," he says, and the two rub noses.

"I love you, Chestnut," Cailin says with their faces inches apart.

He laughs before saying, "I love you too, Sugarplum."

He holds up his pinkie finger to show his nail painted black, and Cailin matches his movements, showing her purple one.

Witnessing such a personal moment warms my heart.

"And you"—he stands, facing me, making me feel bad for invading their personal time—"Sarah … it was nice to meet you."

"It's my pleasure, Adam. I mean, Mr. Jacobson. I mean—"

He smirks. "Just Adam is fine." He turns to the people still staring at us before turning to me and whispering, "I guess the cat's out of the bag." He glances down at Cailin in admiration. "Totally worth it. I couldn't miss her first father-daughter dance. There wasn't a better way for everyone to find out anyway. Bye, baby girl." He rubs his finger under her chin.

"Bye, Daddy. Love you mucho."

"Love you mucho more!" he yells back as he walks away, making Cailin laugh as she waves her tiny hand good-bye.

I inhale a deep breath, calming my nerves.

I knew his tour was ending soon, but hearing it's only ten days away makes my stomach flip.

Will he be bringing her to school every day? How will the community react to having him here?

So many things fly through my mind.

But the biggest one of all is, *How am I going to breathe knowing my own broken dreams are living just down the street?*

I've been able to survive here, going about my life, with no memories or reminders of what was lost. It's such a different world that I've tried to forget it even exists. *How am I going to deal with it smacking me across the face every day?*

I turn to Cailin, who's still grinning from ear to ear as she watches her dad hop in a car waiting for him.

I guess only time will tell what happens. I just hope I have enough strength to pull through again.

Chapter 6

Sarah

My mom greets me at the door when I enter the church. "How did last night go?" Her hands are clasped in front of her chest in excitement. The father-daughter dance was always her favorite too.

"So cute." I sigh. "All the girls in their fancy dresses still make me smile."

"Me too! I think I miss that dance most of all."

We walk to the back to put my stuff down as I tell her all about the night, leaving out the part of our famous visitor. That could open up a can of worms, so it's not worth even bringing up.

When we make our way back, Cailin comes running up, giving me a hug.

"Well, good morning," I say. "Did you have fun last night?"

"I did!" She grins when she pulls back. "I still can't believe my daddy made it. Best surprise ever!" She swings her arms out wide to the sides in celebration.

Linda makes her way over to us. "Good morning, Miss Russo."

"Hello. I'd like to introduce you to my mom, Sandra."

They exchange pleasantries before I turn my attention toward Cailin.

"Would you like to stay after church today and work on a song with me to sing next week?"

Her eyes light up, and when she turns to Linda in shock, my heart melts.

She folds her hands in front of her as she asks for permission, "Can I?"

Linda's lips spread into a huge smile. "I'm sure we can make that happen."

"Yay!" Cailin raises her hands above her head and cheers.

"Okay, take a seat, and I'll find you afterward."

After the service, Linda and Cailin are waiting by the back for me.

I approach her with my arm outstretched. "Here, come with me up onstage."

Cailin's quick to grip my hand and make her way up the two stairs to where a piano sits.

"Have you ever played?" I ask as I sit beside her.

"No, but I've seen my daddy play."

I look up to Linda, who's standing at the end of the piano for confirmation, and she nods.

"Oh, I didn't realize he could play piano."

"Yeah, he plays the guitar too," Cailin says nonchalantly like I wouldn't know the lead singer of the rock band everyone envies also plays guitar.

Memories of pictures I've seen of him with a guitar in his hands make my heart flutter. I think there's nothing sexier than a man with a low-slung guitar, playing so easily without even watching what he's doing. The talent he displays is something I've always admired.

"Have you ever listened to my daddy's music?" she asks, glancing up with her eyebrows raised.

I have to bite back my laugh. "Yes, I'm familiar with his music."

"You are?" Linda's surprise is written all over her face.

I try to shrug it off like it's no big deal. "I've been a fan of theirs for years."

Linda purses her lips and nods, almost as if she's impressed.

Devil's Breed's songs stood out when they first hit the radio. Adam writes all of their lyrics. His songs have meaning. They aren't just silly rhymes or talking about partying and girls. He touches people with his words, and those words mean more to me than anything else.

I place my fingers on the piano keys and say, "Let's start with an easy song. Have you ever heard *Jesus Loves Me*?"

41

Our SONG

Cailin bites her lip and turns her head down like she's embarrassed she doesn't know it.

"It's okay if you haven't. I'll teach you. It's easy." I play the notes on the piano keys and begin with, "*Jesus loves me. This I know.*"

Cailin's sweet voice chimes in as we go over the words, repeating them until she remembers all of the lyrics. I've heard her sing in class, but this moment is different. Tied with the piano notes, her voice is soft and in tune. Some kids tend to sing too loud or off-key but not Cailin.

The words slide off her tongue in a calming manner. She could sing any baby a lullaby, and they'd fall instantly asleep. The way she sits up tall, singing like she's serenading the angels, impresses me. Not many people can get the correct inflection of their voice purely because of posture, but she's a natural.

We go through the song a few times, and she quickly catches on.

She's something special, and I'd love to see her perform for our church.

"You're doing great. Let's do it one more time all the way through, and then maybe we can do a special performance next Sunday."

Her head pops in my direction as she squirms in her seat. "Really?"

"Really." I grin and start the notes.

Without me having to prompt her, she sings on cue.

When we finish, my eyes tilt up to where Linda's got her phone held high, pointed directly at us.

"Look over here, Cailin," she says.

Cailin does, and her face glows when she sees Linda holding the camera facing our direction. She jumps up and runs to Linda. "Did you record us? I want to see!"

I stand and head over to Linda as well. My heart swells when I see the vision of us singing together. We are staring at each other as we sing. It's a sweet moment, one I'd like to keep for myself as well.

"Would you mind sending that to me?" I ask.

"Of course." Linda pulls her phone closer to her. "What's your number, dear?"

I give her my number and then turn to Cailin. "Make sure to practice every night, and I'll set up a time for us to sing together next week."

Her arms wrap around my waist. "Thank you, Miss Russo."

I rub her back. "It's my pleasure, sweetie."

Linda stands up, grabbing her purse from the seat next to her. "Thank you so much for doing this for her. It really means a lot."

"It's nothing. I enjoy singing just as much as she does. Hopefully, this will teach her that it's okay to sing, but there's just a time and a place." I raise my eyebrow at her, making sure she gets my drift.

"I promise I won't sing anymore in class." She reaches her hand out to shake mine, like she's making a deal with me.

I meet her hand, and she gives me one firm shake before letting go. The gesture makes me chuckle, and Linda does the same.

"How about we go get some lunch?" Linda asks Cailin while running her fingers through the little girl's hair.

"Okay. Bye, Miss Russo." She waves, and I wave back.

"Bye."

I head to my dad's office where I keep my personal things. When I check my phone, there are multiple missed calls and texts from Maggie.

How did you not call me?

I'm guessing this is at your school, but why are you so dressed up, and who is this little girl?

Is she a student?

Please tell me what I'm reading is true.

He's her DAD?!?!?! How did no one know this?!

OMG, what does your dad think?

Each text message is sent a few seconds to a few minutes apart. She has to be talking about last night, but how does she already know?

I step out of the church and hide in between the building and parking lot, so I can talk in private. The phone only rings once, and she answers on FaceTime.

"That was the longest church service—ever!" she yells with her black hair falling down over her smoky eye shadow. "Now, spill it."

I laugh nervously. "Spill what?"

"Ha! Don't act all innocent with me. I've seen the photo and read the stories online. How are you photographed with Adam Jacobson?" The way she says his name makes my stomach flutter and my palms sweat.

Then, reality of what she's saying clicks in. "Wait, what photo?"

"You haven't seen?" she asks way too loudly, making me jump and almost drop the phone.

She ends our FaceTime call without another word, and two seconds later, my phone chimes with another incoming text message. I click the link, and there, plain as day, is a photo of Adam and me smiling at each other while Cailin stares up at her dad with the headline of:

THE DEVIL'S SECRET LIFE

My hand instantly covers my mouth as I inhale a deep breath when my phone rings again with another FaceTime call from Maggie.

"Yes, the article says lust-filled if you haven't let that sink in yet," she says with eyes wide open at me, her bright red lips perched together in question for a beat. "Now, as I said before, spill it."

"It's not what you think …" I trail off, my mind going twenty different directions at once.

Who sent the photos to these news sites? Oh my God, my dad will freak if he sees me even talking to Adam. He'll think I'm planning things all over again. I can't start that fight back up.

"Hello?" Maggie yells.

"Um, sorry. She's his—"

"Daughter," she finishes my sentence in shock. "How does the most eligible rock star, everyone's dreamy bad boy, have a daughter no one knew about?"

"She's my student. You know I can't say anything about my students. They told me they've kept it a secret, but they knew it would come out soon with her enrolled in school."

I have to cover the phone again when she screams, so people don't hear her.

"And you knew?"

I drop my head back in shock, wonder, hell, even amazement of the memories that plagued me for so long last night that I couldn't sleep.

His eyes had seemingly melted into mine. I thought I had been imagining things, but something about the way I'd felt made me pine for more. He'd spoken to me with his simple look, making me imagine the possibilities of being with someone I shouldn't want in this world.

Maybe I wasn't imagining it?

"Hello? Earth to Sarah. I've already had to wait all morning. Now, tell me."

I close my eyes, letting the chills run through my body, which create goose bumps all over, before I respond, "I already did. She's my student."

"Law or not, best-friend code trumps silly law code."

I laugh at her thought process. "I don't think it works that way. Plus, it's cool that he kept her a secret. I didn't want to be the one to change her life and let their secret out."

"Why? Why does my best friend have to be the one person on earth to actually follow the golden rule and have such a big heart?" she teases.

She's back on the move, walking down the busy New York street, holding her arm out wide above her head, shouting up to God, looking like a crazy person and not having a care in the world about what people think. It's amazing how different our living situations are.

We met when the school randomly paired us as roommates. I was the goody-two-shoes virgin who wore Gap sweaters and ballet flats, looking to break out of my shell. Maggie was the miniskirt-wearing, flirting-with-any-guy-she-could girl from Queens. We were completely opposite yet perfect for each other.

Her craziness opened me up, and my virtue calmed her down. Neither one of us changed too much, yet we both grew to become smaller versions of one another.

I laugh out loud. "Because I'm the only person to tame your ass."

I hear her chuckle on the other end before she holds the phone up better for me to see her. "Yeah, you're probably right about that. And I'm glad to hear you didn't say *rear end* there. I am *not* going back to those days with you. You hear me, missy?"

I can't help the smile from the memories of her making fun of the way I used to speak. "Yes, *Mom*."

"So, at least tell me what he smelled like." She gives me a devilish grin.

Like manly heaven wrapped in a soft blanket placed around me. "I didn't get close enough to smell him."

"Liar!" she yells. "Your face can't hide shit. You totally did. But that's fine. Keep it to yourself. I won't hold a grudge or anything. But you haven't read what people are saying …"

My eyes open wide as I click to switch our call to a normal call. I pull up the article once again and start scanning.

"Are you reading now?" I hear her say through the speaker. "You see the speculation that you might be the little girl's mom?"

Shock fills my soul. *At least I know my dad won't believe that.* "No!"

"Actually, you might want to stay away from the comments people are posting. There are some haters out there but also people who want to share their knowledge. People from your small-ass town feel all big, knowing who you are, and were quick to rat you out."

"They did not," I say breathlessly.

"Um, yes, they did. You should make your Facebook and Instagram pages private because your life is being run through by jealous bitches."

I tightly close my eyes, praying I don't have anything too embarrassing on there.

"Miss Russo," I hear someone say and turn around to see Linda.

I quickly pull the phone up to my ear. "Maggie, I'll call you back."

Linda steps a bit closer, and I see the trepidation in her facial expression. Her lips turn down in a frown, and she sighs. "I take it, you know."

I stuff my phone down in my purse, not wanting to lie, but not sure what to say, so instead, I search for Cailin. "Where's …"

"She's in the car, talking to Adam. He asked that I check on you. He told me about the articles. He had expected something to get leaked, and he's sorry you got dragged into it."

I stand up a little straighter, trying to act cool even though I'm freaking out inside. *What if people recognize me? What if word gets out about my past?* I take a deep breath and put on my best acting role. "It's no big deal. I'm just sorry his secret is out. How is he handling it?"

She cups her hands together in front of her body. "He knew putting her in school would eventually let the cat out of the bag. He figured if he was going to tell the world, then what better way than at a father-daughter dance? He was prepared, and his PR people have been waiting for this since the day she was born. The photo of the two of you was never in that plan though."

"But we're just standing, talking to one another."

"Yeah, but when you're someone like Adam, all gloves are off. He's used to it. He even created his entire persona around it. People can be brutal, judgmental, and quick to state what they perceive as fact."

She turns to check on Cailin and then back to me. "But I think this is the best thing that could have happened."

My eyes widen in surprise. "You mean, um, the photos of—"

"Just as many people are wondering who you are as they are wondering who she is. You've helped take some of the focus off of her. There are millions of females who would die to be in your shoes. No one wants to be in hers; they can't relate to the story that way. People can relate to you; they want to be the one everyone is talking about."

"But I'm nobody." I shrug, biting my inner lip, hoping that's what people are thinking.

"Don't doubt yourself. Right now, you're everything to that little girl. What you did for her today, teaching her that song, is something she'll never forget. She's been surrounded by women who were hired to take care of her all her life. You taught her that song because you wanted to and for no other reason. Believe me, she knows the difference."

I stay silent, and Linda nods, like she's happy with our little talk.

"I should get her home before people start showing up at the church, looking for you. Thank you again for today. We'll see you tomorrow."

She heads back to the car, and when she opens it, I can hear Cailin singing at the top of her lungs the song I just taught her. I laugh out loud even though her voice lights the world around me.

47

Our SONG

Once I turn the corner, I pull up the photos again, seeing how visible my face is in them. I know I look different now, and the comments are saying my last name as Russo, but the thought of people finding out who I really am makes my heart pound and my hands sweat.

My father went to great lengths to keep my past a secret, saying no one would respect him if they knew his own daughter followed the path of the devil. I tried to help him see my side, showing him how different kinds of music could be just as healing as welcoming God into your life. I've felt them both and honestly believe it's the truth.

Let's just say, those words didn't go over very well. Seeing his face and how ashamed he was of me is not something I want to relive—ever.

Chapter 7

Adam

My face hurts from smiling so big. Hearing my little girl tell me about the song she just learned and then singing it for me is my absolute dream. The only downside is that she's at a church and singing a religious song. With my upbringing, there's no way I'd ever believe there was a God.

If there is, he has some explaining to do for the way I was raised.

I don't fault anyone who's religious, but believing in a higher power is something I absolutely don't do.

Cailin spoke fondly of her teacher, but no one told me anything about what she looked like, except her resemblance to Cinderella. I rolled my eyes at the notion of someone being like the cartoon character, but when I saw her, it was the first thing I thought.

Then, I really looked at her and saw so much more.

I saw a true woman. Someone so pure and wholehearted that any person who walked by couldn't help but smile in her presence.

I had been raised with the worst of the worst people around me. It wasn't until Linda had come into my life that I even knew a human being could show love. One glance at Miss Russo, and I saw so much more than love in her eyes.

I saw hope.

I hadn't expected other parents to take pictures the way they did, especially since they should have taken into consideration how they wouldn't want their own kids blasted the way they blasted Cailin all over the internet.

I'd learned early on to not be surprised by anything people do, especially in the company of someone famous. I'd seen it all—from people who passed out at my feet when I said hello to women who tried to rip off my clothes and suck my dick at the first chance they got.

Miss Russo was different though. She smiled sweetly and shook my hand. It was the first time in a while that I didn't feel like someone wanted something from me.

I saw the way her face flushed and her pulse rushed when we touched, and I couldn't stop my own heart from pounding too. I'd never had a woman affect me that way. I wanted to stay, I wanted to get to know her, but I knew I had to go.

Now, as I sit here, hearing how she went above and beyond for my daughter just because she wanted to, proves that my intuition was right. She *is* different.

Even though it's a religious song Cailin is singing, I'll remember this moment for the rest of my life—the day my daughter taught *me* a song—and I have Miss Russo to thank for it.

I hear the car door open, and Cailin shows me on FaceTime that Linda just got back in the car.

"What did she say?" I ask Linda.

Linda laughs as she grabs the phone from Cailin. "She must have just seen it when I approached her. She was a little in shock, but I think everything will be fine. *Miss* Russo seems to handle things in stride. I mean, she handles a room full of kindergarteners all day, so what's a few paparazzi compared to that?"

She laughs at her own joke, and I smile. Linda's always been able to find the bright side in every situation. Her optimism is what got me through life.

"*Miss* Russo is a kind soul, and I'm not concerned in any way that she'll help keep Cailin safe and away from any unwanted attention while at school. I'm positive *Miss* Russo is on our side."

"Is there a reason you keep saying *Miss* Russo, Linda? Are you trying to hint at something here?" I taunt, knowing Linda has something on her mind.

The grin that slowly spreads across her face proves I'm right, but she acts like I'm not.

"I'm just simply stating her name; that's all."

She grins, and I laugh out loud.

"Give me back to my daughter, *Mrs.* Jacobson."

"Good-bye, dear," she says as she hands Cailin back the phone.

My daughter's face fills the screen a little too close. "Tell me about the show last night," Cailin says. "Did you make it in time?"

"I was a little late, but no one noticed. It was worth every second. You looked so beautiful, Sugarplum."

Her face lights up, and when my favorite dimple on her left cheek shines brightly through the phone, I have to blink back the tear it brings me every time.

"Thanks, Chestnut. I had fun. The kids all asked who you were and why you left so fast."

"Did you tell them who I was?"

"Duuuuhhhhh," she draws out, like it's the stupidest question I ever asked. "I told them you were my daddy!"

I laugh out loud. Of course she did. To her, that's all I am. I hope that never changes.

Sarah

When I get home, I tell myself not to look at the news reports, not to search online, and to go about the rest of my day. Yeah, that lasts all of about ten minutes.

I start with the link Maggie sent me, and down the rabbit hole I go. Linda was right. Most of the comments are more focused on me. People wondering who I am, others wanting to be me. Some comments are mean, and some are positive.

Thankfully, nothing is mentioned about my past or who I really am—or rather, was—outside of this town. Ever since that fateful night, I've tried to forget that person ever existed. As far as my father's concerned, she died, lying on that asphalt.

People question if I'm Cailin's mom or if Adam is truly her dad.

Our SONG

I Google his name and click on pictures. Thousands of photos pop up, overwhelming me.

As I scroll, picture after picture shows a man with eyes so crystal blue, you wonder if you can see through them. His style is all his own as he stands out above the other guys in the band.

A small star tattoo shines to the side of his right eye in a photo, but what catches my attention is the way he has his hand up, showing his pinkie fingernail painted black. I've noticed Cailin only has her pinkie nail painted purple. I've questioned why, but remembering back to them holding both up together proves it's for each other and no one else.

Photos of him make my chest tighten. He's gorgeous in any outfit or any state of facial hair, clean-shaven or with a full beard. There is nothing this man can't wear or do to himself that will change the way his lips stand out or how his narrow face and chiseled jaw make you want to kiss him all over.

I've thought a few of my students' fathers were handsome, and I dated a few guys during college, but seeing my ultimate bad-boy rocker standing in front of me did something to my body I never expected.

It's been a year since I've been on a date. I get asked out, but no one has really done it for me. And, yes, I might be religious, but I'm not a virgin even though I'm not married. But the relationships I was in were just mediocre. Maggie would tease me that I was asexual, and I almost started to believe her.

Until I shook Adam's hand last night.

I keep trying to tell myself it's because he's the one I thought I'd never have a chance with—the guy who's on your bucket list. The one you grew up with, having a poster of him on your wall, dreaming you'd get a chance to kiss him.

Though I've followed his band and him on social media, I've never looked into him personally. I know nothing about the guy besides the fact that I love the lyrics he writes.

I put my cursor to the search bar and enter *Adam Jacobson's girlfriend*. To my surprise, photos of me pop up on multiple pages. I try not to absolutely freak out as I scroll through the pictures I've already seen.

There are stories of him being an eligible bachelor and pictures of him with girls draped over his arms, but none of them have names, and no female is repeated in any of the photos.

I search his Wikipedia page to see what I can learn. Surprisingly, it's pretty empty. It talks all about his music and his rise to fame, but stories of his past, his parents, or his upbringing are missing. I click the rest of his bandmates' names, and all of their info is there, some even with links to siblings who are trying to make it in the music business.

He seems to be a bit of a mystery, and all that does is make me want to know more, but I need to stop. Curiosity kills the cat every time. Him having these secrets are even more reasons I should stay far away.

I drop my phone and try to rid any thoughts of him from my mind. I'm not the same person I once was, and I definitely need to stay as far away from him as possible.

Chapter 8

Sarah

When I get to school the next day, a few paparazzi stand across the street with cameras around their necks, waiting to get shots of Cailin.

An uneasy sensation washes over me as I pull into the teacher parking lot directly next to my classroom. When I peek out my window, I see Principal McAllister approaching the two men. His demeanor should have the men scattering soon. He does not take lightly to strangers who don't belong hanging around.

To my surprise, I open my classroom door to see Cailin's already there, sipping on chocolate milk with a bagel and cream cheese in front of her that's big enough to feed three kids her size.

"I hope it's okay that they let us in early this morning," Linda says.

"Of course that's fine. I'm glad she's here." I walk to my desk and put my purse in a drawer along with my lunch.

"We got you a bagel too, Miss Russo," Cailin calls out.

"It's okay if you've already eaten," Linda quickly states.

I step over to where Cailin is sitting and pull out the tiny red seat next to her. "That's very thoughtful of you. Thank you."

They hand me a wrapped bagel.

"Linda wanted to get you an onion bagel, but I convinced her not to." She leans over to whisper, "You're welcome."

I cover my mouth when I can't help the laughter falling from my lips after I take a bite. "I love any bagels," I say once I've chewed and swallowed. "And the onion ones are actually pretty good, but you did fine with the cinnamon raisin. Is that what you got too?"

She holds up her bagel, so I can see the bottom of it. "Sure did. They're my favorite."

I glance up to Linda and notice the apprehension written all over her face. *Everything okay?* I mouth, so Cailin won't see.

She sighs before nodding her head toward the door. "Can we talk?"

I stand as Linda tells Cailin we'll be right back. Once we're outside, I turn toward her and wait for her to speak.

"I'm worried about people finding out more about her than they need to know. We knew it would happen, but I thought Adam would be back by then. It's important that no one knows where I live or who she lives with. Can we trust you to keep that a secret?"

I place my fingers over hers to calm the nervous way her hands are rubbing against one another. "My number one priority is to keep these kids safe. I understand why Adam kept her a secret. I admire him for it."

Her smile wavers. "People have no clue who I am, and I'd like to keep it that way. I can offer her a safe place. My concern is getting her to and from school. I don't want people following us. When news broke yesterday, we were able to get in touch with Principal McAllister. We actually met him at his house this morning and then drove with him."

Hearing that Principal McAllister helped them this morning makes me smile. That man has always been reasonable and, no matter what, puts the kids first. I wish there were more people like him in this community.

"He suggested getting doughnuts, but Cailin was raised with pretty clean eating, and Adam wouldn't want her having all that sugar before school, so I suggested the bagels instead."

Cailin holds up her bagel in celebration, brightening up the situation. I love the way she doesn't care about everyone trying to get pictures or info on her. She's as happy as can be with her bagel and cream cheese.

Linda looks around at the kids who have started to enter the school. "The problem is, he can't do that every day because he said he often has meetings off-site before school. I'm just not sure what the answer is. We don't want her treated differently than the other students. If there's a mob of cameramen posted out front, I'm sure other parents will start to complain."

Linda is a few inches shorter, so I lean down, making sure she hears me and knows I'm here to help. "So, we make sure they don't get any pictures. After a few days of nothing, they'll give up."

She sighs. From the bags under her eyes, this must've kept her up all night.

I try to put her at ease. "Why don't you bring her to my house tomorrow morning? My parking space is the first one right outside. The cameramen have to stay across the street, and from that angle, that big oak tree blocks their view." I point to the tree and then to where my car is.

"Oh, I'd feel bad, asking that of you." She purses her lips and shakes her head.

"Honestly, it's no trouble at all. I'm happy to help."

The interest in me was very short-lived. Thanks to some *helpful* people in our community, the idea of me being Adam's love interest was shot down pretty quickly. Now, it's all over the internet that I'm *just* her teacher. I know the truth shouldn't hurt, but the sting of it did a little.

Now, I'm happy about it. I can come and go without people questioning me. With my tinted back windows and Cailin's small frame, I can have her duck the few seconds we're in front of the school, and they won't know the difference.

"Well, um, I just …"

I softly place my hand on her arm. "Honestly, I'm happy to help. Let me give you my address. She can come home with me after school."

She nods hesitantly but follows me back to my desk. This might not be the best solution, but it will work until we figure something else out.

When the bell rings and the kids line up for class, I notice a few standing next to Cailin, so I approach with caution, making sure everything is okay.

"Is your dad really a famous rock star?" Mason, a boy in my class, asks.

Cailin smiles with pride. "Yes, that's my daddy."

"Have you been onstage with him during a concert?" Mason's excitement is barely contained.

"My parents would never take me because they say there's too much alcohol at those types of events."

"Not onstage, but I've been to his shows," she says as her eyes meet mine.

I can tell she's questioning if she should be talking about it. I smile, encouraging her to be proud of who he is.

Ashley walks up with her hand on her hip, obviously following a movement she's seen her mom do a thousand times, as she says snidely, "My mom says kids should be going to Disneyland, not vulgar rock concerts."

"Then, obviously, your mom hasn't been to a good rock concert. I've been to both, many times, and I like them equally," Cailin says flawlessly.

"Well, my mom said your dad is an awful human being, and she feels sorry for you."

Ashley turns to leave, and I instantly step in.

"Okay, everyone, let's get inside." I wrap my arm around Cailin, making sure she's not taking what was just said to heart.

Her smile greets my gaze, but I can tell it's not genuine when her eyes don't sparkle the way they normally do. I don't want to make a big deal of it or treat her any different than the other students, so I give her a quick hug as we enter the class, and she runs to her desk.

After school, we walk together to my car, and I help her get secured in the booster seat Linda left for me. Before I shut the door, I look her in the eye and can tell something's wrong, so I kneel down, seeing if she wants to talk.

"Can I ask you a question, Miss Russo?"

"Of course, sweetheart." I rub my hand over her tiny jean-covered knee.

"Do people really not like my daddy?" Her bottom lip quivers, and it takes all my power not to wrap my arms around her and block her from the hate in the world.

I take a deep breath, wondering how to approach this. "When someone is famous, like your daddy, they put their lives in the media for all to pick apart. The one thing you need to know is that not every person likes everyone. There are millions of people who love your daddy. But with that, there are some people who might not. That doesn't make him a bad person."

Her eyebrows bunch together, and I know I need to keep explaining.

"Is there a certain food you don't like?"

Her nose scrunches. "I hate broccoli."

I try not to chuckle at her admission. "Well, did you know I love broccoli?"

"How can you love broccoli? It's disgusting." She sticks out her tongue.

"Not everyone likes the same thing. But that's okay. Do you understand now?"

She sighs. "I guess. I'll never understand how you can like broccoli the same way that I'll never understand why someone wouldn't like my daddy."

Her innocence is so endearing.

"Exactly," I say, standing and closing the door before heading to my side of the car.

Chapter 9

Sarah

Church starts at ten, but I asked Linda to bring Cailin around nine, so we can practice and go through how the performance will go. As I sit in the entranceway, talking to my mom, Cailin comes dancing in the door, smiling from ear to ear.

"Good morning, Miss Russo," she says, swinging around to show me her outfit. "Do you like my new dress?"

I excuse myself from my mom and crouch down to her level. "Look how pretty you are. Did you pick it out yourself?"

She jumps up in excitement. "I did! Linda wanted me to get this boring yellow one, but this one has these ruffles, and when I twirl around, it looks so much better!"

I glance up to Linda, who's shaking her head and laughing. "She keeps me on my toes; that's for sure."

I reach out my hand to shake Linda's. "I can only imagine. Do you have children of your own?"

She covers my hand with her other one. "Oh, no, dear. The Lord had other plans for me. That's what led me to Adam, and now, I get to help raise this little angel." She lets me go as she stares down at Cailin with the love of a grandma even though I know she's not.

"Ready?" I say, holding my palm out for Cailin to grab.

"I'm so excited," she says as she skips to me.

Our SONG

I lead her to the open room and down the aisles to the front of the church.

Linda sits three rows back as Cailin sits next to me on the piano bench.

When my fingers press down on the first notes, Cailin doesn't hold back as she belts out the lyrics. Just like before, her ability to sing in tune blows me away. Each word is sung with the correct inflection, and she pauses at the right points with no direction.

"You've been practicing even more, haven't you?" I place my hands in my lap and turn to her in awe when we're finished.

She smiles brightly. "My dad worked with me last night on it. We sang it over and over until we thought it was perfect."

The idea of Adam Jacobson singing "Jesus Loves Me" over the phone with a little girl is something I'd never dream of him doing.

How is the guy I thought was the ultimate bad boy turning out to be anything but?

"That's very nice of him. Did you have to teach him the words?"

"I did. Can you believe he didn't know *any* words to this song? Thankfully, he caught on quick. I kept telling him I needed to practice, not teach him."

A sharp laugh escapes my lips. I love how this little girl is not afraid to tell him how it is. "Well, I'm glad he caught on. I'd say he has practice in doing so."

"He kept reminding me how, normally, he writes the lyrics, so there's no learning involved. I told him he was silly. Even though he wrote them, he still had to memorize them." She gives the best *duh* expression, and I have a hard time keeping my smile hidden.

When our time arrives during the service, my father announces that we have a special performance before Cailin and I walk to the stage, hand in hand.

I turn to see if she's nervous, but the smile spread wide and shoulders held high prove she's more than ready. I place my fingers on the keys, and she sings right on cue.

The sudden hush over the crowd surprises even me. I glance up from the piano to see everyone's attention on us. My mom's hand covers her mouth, and my sister's eyes are open wide as she listens to the singing little girl, who is only a year older than her daughter.

This is the first time we've had a child sing other than the children's Christmas pageant, and when we finish, the congregation gives her a standing ovation. Warmth radiates throughout my body, and I cover my mouth to hide the joyous laughter wanting to release from my lips.

For everyone else to see and recognize the talent I saw last week, it makes me just as proud as if she were my own.

Her face glows when she glances up at me, stunned at the reaction. When my eyes meet with Linda, I see the tears flowing freely just as one slips from mine as well.

We take our seat back in the pews, and multiple people turn to congratulate Cailin on how well she did.

She sits, curled up in my side for the rest of the service. Her being here feels so natural, and—I'm not going to lie—I love having her next to me.

When my dad excuses us, more people approach Cailin with praise. She modestly accepts it, making sure to thank every person and smile sweetly doing so.

Linda is holding up her phone and motioning for us to go to the side of the stage. I take Cailin's hand and head to Linda, only to see Adam staring back at me on FaceTime.

Instantly, my breath hitches.

Why am I doing this?

I should be staying away from him, yet here I am, singing with his daughter and having her curled up by my side.

Why aren't I thinking things through better? She's the one child I should be keeping my distance from, yet I keep inviting her in closer.

Way too many memories have come boiling up ever since I learned he was her dad. A trip down that lane is not one I ever want to take.

Cailin, of course, runs to him. "Daddy, did you see me?"

She yanks the phone from Linda and holds it so she can see him more clearly.

"Sugarplum, you were amazing!"

"Thank you, Daddy, and Miss Russo too!"

She points the camera my way, catching me off guard.

I wave, and Adam smirks, slightly raising his eyebrows as he says, "How could I miss Miss Russo?"

Heat creeps its way up my body, and I pray my face isn't turning bright red.

Our SONG

Linda catches my attention as a shit-eating grin covers her face that makes me flush even more.

Cailin turns the phone back to where it's facing her and begins to tell her dad every part of her performance, including the applause at the end. If Adam was on FaceTime during the song, then he already knows all of this, but he sits silently, taking in everything that Cailin says like it's the most important thing he's ever been told and he doesn't want to miss one single word.

Linda steps closer to me, whispering, "It's moments like this that make everything worth it."

I nod, tilting my head to the side in awe of the two of them. Seeing them together like this melts my heart and fades my worries away about letting her in.

Chapter 10

Sarah

Cailin and I walk to the car after school. The photographers gave up after a week of not seeing her, but we don't want to take any chances.

There's still a buzz around the town that a rock star is moving here, but since he's not arrived yet, everyone is guessing as much as I am about how this is all going to work out.

My father brought the photos up to me, saying how sad it was that I got mixed up in Adam's madness, only to be plastered on the internet like that. He didn't see how amazing it was that Adam had changed his entire schedule to dance one song with his daughter. All he saw was that Adam wasn't there to be with her every day like a parent should be.

I guess it's all about perspective, but to my father, he'll always be right.

As I try to focus on the now and what's to come, I've enjoyed my time with Cailin these past few days. Since I don't allow her to sing in class, we've made our car rides home full of singing. The funniest songs are those by Devil's Breed. She tries really hard to sing like her dad, and when there is a cuss word in the lyrics, she skips it but keeps up the tempo exactly the same as if it were still there.

When we pull up to my place, Linda's not there, so we head up to my apartment where I offer Cailin a snack.

Our SONG

As we eat our cookies dipped in milk, there's a knock on the door. I swing it open, holding up my sugary goodness to Linda, showing the milk running down it, almost to my fingers, saying, "It's cookie ti—"

My mind can't complete the rest of the sentence when I see Adam standing in front of me instead of Linda. His tall frame fills my entranceway, but his eyes feel like I can see right through them.

"Daddy!" Cailin screams, running straight for him, spilling her milk all over my counter.

"Sugarplum," he says as he swings her around in a tight embrace. His eyes close, and his face glows with pure happiness.

When they pull back, she places her hand on his face, saying, "My Chestnut." They hug again. "I thought you weren't coming home until tomorrow."

"I wanted to surprise you."

"That's not very nice, Daddy. I wanted to wear my new dress for you, so I'd look my best."

Adam and I both laugh. He runs his hand down her hair. "You're gorgeous in any outfit."

She rolls her eyes and hits him in the chest. "You have to say that; you're my dad."

He chuckles under his breath as he puts her down and notices the spilled milk. "Let me help you clean that up."

He enters my small apartment, and I finally snap out of my shock. "No worries. I can get it." I run to the kitchen and grab some paper towels.

Adam takes them from me and starts to mop up the mess. "I don't mind," he says, looking straight at me.

I rip off another paper towel and wipe the floor. When Adam leans down, placing his hand over mine, I freeze.

"Please, let me get it. You've done so much for my daughter; let me do something for you."

He's staring directly at me, and I have to think real hard to keep my body from swooning at his touch.

My mind needs to stop going there.

I can't get my mouth to function, so I slide my fingers from under his and nod before standing and getting Cailin more milk.

"Can I get you a cookie and milk too?" I ask.

I guess I'm used to offering kids stuff like this, so of course, this is my go-to.

"I'd love one." He pulls out a chair from my kitchen table as I get him a cup and pour some milk.

Cailin crawls up on his lap without a second thought.

"When did you get back?" Cailin asks through a mouthful of cookie.

He steals a bite of her cookie before answering, "A few hours ago. We left early this morning. You should have seen Max and Jack; they were not okay." Adam laughs at the memory but quiets abruptly when Cailin puts her hands on her hips.

"Daddy, did you make them get up again? You know how that went last time."

Adam sits up straight, acting just as serious. "Why, yes, I did. They knew I wanted to get home. That was their decision to stay up, partying like that."

She gives him a side-eye, and Adam engulfs her in his arms, laughing.

"I missed you, kid. It's good to be home."

She sharply turns to him, pursing her lips together.

"Oh. Sorry. I missed you, *Sugarplum*."

She sternly nods her head one time. "That's better."

I turn to start rinsing the dishes in my sink, feeling awkward, sitting in my own kitchen, watching these two interact so personally.

My dad was always around, but I never curled up in his lap or questioned something he did. I was raised that kids were seen, not heard and that there was a time and place for play, and it was not around him—ever.

Adam seems to welcome the crumbs on his lap and milk spilled on the floor.

"Hey, Sarah," Adam says, making me drop the cup I was washing in the sink.

I pick it up, trying to play it off. "Yeah?"

"You don't have to stay over there. We are in your house and all." He raises his eyebrows to me. "As long as we aren't invading your space, I'd love to hear what's going on with Cailin's schoolwork."

I wipe my hands and join them.

Cailin hands me a cookie. "Do you want another one?"

Our SONG

I swipe it from her and take a bite. "Why, thank you," I say, trying to act as normal as possible and not freak out that I'm sitting at the same table—in my house—as Adam Jacobson.

"Okay, Sugarplum, I want to hear how you're doing from you, and then I'll see if she has the same story."

I cover my mouth as a laugh escapes my lips. "I always tell my parents, I'll only believe half of what I hear about you as long as you only believe half of what you hear about me."

Adam turns to face me. "Is it that common for kids to make up tales?"

I sway my head from side to side. "Kids like to embellish a little." He pulls her closer to him. "What's your favorite part of class?"

She purses her lips together, tapping her finger to her mouth in thought. "I like cutting things, and I'm getting real good at it."

"You are?" he says, full of interest.

"She is. I used her work as the example the other day," I interject.

"Look at that, my daughter setting the bar for the rest of the class." The pride beaming from his face is palpable.

"And she's one of the best readers in the class." I can't help myself; seeing him so amazed at his little girl is beautiful to witness. If I have to tell him every little thing she's good at to have this moment continue, I will.

Cailin jumps off of Adam's lap and runs to her backpack. She pulls out a four-page printed book I sent home to practice on and holds it up for Adam.

"I'll show you!" She hops back on his lap and opens the book. With her tiny tongue peeking out of her mouth, she diligently studies the words before starting to read them.

Adam turns to me in shock and then awe. His face spreads in the biggest smile as she turns the page and continues the short story about a rabbit trying to steal a carrot.

When she closes the book and beams back at Adam, he wraps his arms around her. "That was amazing! I can't believe how smart you are."

If I'm not mistaken, he's blinking back tears but lets out a bark of a laugh when she says, "Duh, Dad. Of course I'm smart!"

"Of course you are. I never doubted it for a second." He pats her back and points his head toward the door. "You ready to get going?

I'm sure we've taken up enough of Miss Russo's"—he stops and glances at me for a brief second—"Sarah's time."

"It's no problem at all." I shrug, trying to play it off.

"Do you live here all alone?" Adam asks, doing a quick once-over of my place.

"Sure do. It's been fun, having someone here to come home with me after school."

He lifts Cailin to his side and stands up. "We can't thank you enough for your help, especially for teaching her that song. I'd love to come sometime if you guys are going to do it again."

Pure panic runs through my veins as I think of what to say. How could I not realize that he would want to see her perform in person? That will *not* work.

"Oh, um, yeah. We'll have to set up another time soon. I won't be there the next few weeks. I'm working with the teens on a special presentation they're doing," I lie and hate myself for it.

Cailin's bottom lip sticks out in a pout. "But I wanted to sing again."

I place my hand on her back. "You will. Just not right away. Let me finish this project, and we'll set up another time." More lies. *I'm going to hell for sure.*

I hurt for her. She just wants to show off to her dad, but I don't have the heart to tell her that it will never happen—at least, not there.

I'm afraid of what my dad would do if Adam were to step foot in his church. I feel bad about lying, but knowing my father, I'm saving Adam and Cailin from a disaster that is bound to happen.

I hate that my dad is so judgmental. Church should be open to every person who wants to worship, no matter how they dress or what they look like. Unfortunately, he's as old school as they come, and with what happened in the past, it's not a risk I'm willing to take.

They head toward the exit. Adam grabs Cailin's backpack as I open the door. "Will you be dropping her off tomorrow, or should I expect Linda?" I ask for more selfish reasons than not. There've been a few times I've answered the door mid-bite or while brushing my teeth, so I'll have to be prepared if Adam will be at my place early tomorrow.

Adam stops and faces me, mere inches away. His eyes sparkle brightly in the afternoon sun peeking through my doorway. I fight hard not to bite my lip or show him how his simple glance makes my heart pound and my palms sweat.

"If it's okay, I'll be dropping her off and picking her up from now on, but we'd love to keep the same arrangement, at least for a little while longer, of us meeting here still. I want people to get used to having me here before I show up at the school every day."

My stomach jumps into my throat. Every day. He'll be here every day.

How can I try to avoid him if he's here everyday?

I know my face is bright red, and the slight tug to his lips shows me he notices.

I can't get out the words, so I raise my eyebrows and nod my head, forcing a smile on my face.

"Bye, Miss Russo!" Cailin yells—*thank God!*

"Yes, bye, Sarah. See you tomorrow."

The way he says *tomorrow* offers more hope than I wish to admit. I need to remember he's from a world I don't want any part of. I cannot go back there.

Or can I?

Lord help me ...

Chapter 11

Sarah

I couldn't sleep a wink last night, and to make matters worse, I climbed down the rabbit hole again and was up at two in the morning, watching every video I could find on Adam.

I watched music videos and interviews, and I even read his own posts on social media. Now that I've seen the man in person, it's hard to imagine the lunatic jumping off the speakers into a crowd, only to be carried through the venue, is the same guy who teared up at the sound of his daughter reading.

When he shows up at my door, I'm sipping my second cup of coffee, forcing myself to stay awake.

"We brought bagels!" Cailin sings as she skips to the counter.

Adam closes the door and turns to me. "I hope that's okay."

"Yes, of course. Please, come sit down."

He takes his same seat as yesterday. He's so comfortable, sitting at my table like he's been there a thousand times, as he pulls the bagels out of the bag and places one at each place mat.

"Can I get you a cup of coffee?" I offer.

"Sure. Here, I'll help."

He steps into my small kitchen, which feels even smaller with his tall frame. I reach up to grab a mug and hand it to him. When he takes it from me, our fingers brush, and he keeps them there before pulling my hand into his.

He puts the mug into one hand and keeps mine in his other, dropping it down to hang in front of us. "I really want to thank you for all you have done for Cailin. I'd like to invite you over for dinner tonight. Are you available to join us?"

My mind goes completely blank. "Um, what? Um, I mean … dinner?"

God, I'm such an idiot! Mouth, meet words. Now, speak.

He smirks.

Of course he smirks. And, damn it, it's the sexiest thing I've ever seen.

"Yes, dinner. At my place. I just purchased the Pleasants Valley property. We're having Linda and Wayne over, and I'd like it if you could join us."

"You purchased what?"

Now, I'm more shocked than surprised by his offer. That place has been on the market for years. It's worth millions, and the people of this town always wondered who would purchase it.

The 1800s ranch-style home was fully refurbished by a builder who did it as a side project, one room at a time. Everything was brought back to its original design but with modern conveniences. The owner passed away a few years ago, and his daughter was trying to uphold her dad's dream but was barely making ends meet.

"Do you know the property?"

He lets go of my hand, and I instantly miss the tingles from his touch.

"*Everyone* knows that property. It's not very incognito if you're trying to stay low-key."

He steps to the side of me and pours his coffee, taking a sip and leaning back against the counter. He crosses his ankles, looking cool as a cucumber. "Yes, but with the gate and the land around it, I can keep people off my property to keep some kind of privacy."

The property is five acres with the house directly in the middle of tall trees and lush landscaping.

"Do people know it's you who bought it?"

"Not yet. It was purchased under my trust with my real name. I had people move us in and get everything set while I was on tour. We slept there last night for the first time."

"And it was amazing!" Cailin joins our conversation.

I step toward her, welcoming the space for a minute so I can breathe a little easier. Whenever he's close, I forget why I need to stay away from him. "What's your favorite part?"

"My room! I have a bench in my window that's covered in pillows and my bed has a sheer thingy hanging around it."

"Sheer thingy?" Adam laughs.

She shrugs. "I forget the name. I feel like a princess though."

"But will you actually sleep in there anytime soon?" he asks, setting his mug down.

She lowers her head at her father. "I will ... eventually." She takes a big bite out of her bagel like it's no big deal she didn't sleep in the bed she's excited about.

"If you didn't sleep there, then where did you sleep?" I ask before I take my own bite.

"In my daddy's bed, of course!"

Adam lets out a sharp laugh. "Yes, and this little girl can throw some massive kicks in the middle of the night." He stands up straight, placing his hand on his back like he's hurt.

"Oh, stop. You're the wild sleeper, not me. And the way your breath smells in the morning." She makes a face, and I have to cover my mouth to keep from laughing.

"Really, Cailin?" Adam lowers his head to her.

She puts her hand on her hip and gives him the same expression. "Really, *Dad*?"

The two of them together are adorable. Who would have ever thought Adam Jacobson—master of the scream, mosh pits, and wild parties—sleeps side by side with his five-year-old daughter?

I grin as I glance his direction. When our eyes meet, he winks, sending a shiver down my spine.

Damn shiver.

We pull up after school to see Adam's lifted black truck already in my parking lot. Trucks are a way of life in our small farming town, and pretty much every teenage boy drives one. Adam's is just a little newer and not covered in mud.

Our SONG

Cailin hops out of the car and into Adam's arms.

As I make my way to them, he turns to me. "Thank you again, Sarah. We'll see you in a few? Say, five?"

I inhale a sharp breath and nod. "Yes, I'll be there."

He nods back and helps Cailin get secured in the backseat.

"See you later, Miss Russo," Cailin says.

I wave at her, and as soon as I'm in my apartment, I drop my back against the door and take a deep breath. I've been a nervous wreck all day. Fighting an internal battle. My mind is screaming stay away, but two seconds later, it's dying to go tonight. I've never felt so torn.

I call Maggie. She denies my FaceTime call but calls right back as a normal phone call, so I bring the phone up to my ear.

"What's up, girl?" she says after I answer

"He invited me over for dinner tonight."

"Who's he?" She snaps her gum in my ear, and I wish I could see her face for what I'm about to say.

"Adam Jacobson." I pull the phone away from my ear, awaiting the impending scream.

"What?"

Yep, there it is.

I laugh, knowing she'd have this reaction.

"Are you going to his house? Will his daughter be there too?"

I breathe in, thankful for the reminder. I'm going because of Cailin, my student. Nothing else. "Yes. He's having a barbeque with Linda, the woman who has been taking care of Cailin, and he invited me."

"Holy shit, girl. What are you going to wear?"

I scrunch my eyebrows. "He's already seen me today. Wouldn't it be weird if I changed?"

"OMG, have I not taught you anything? And let me guess; you have on skinny jeans, ballet flats, and a tank top with a cardigan over it?"

I glance down at my outfit that she pretty much nailed. "How do you know that when you can't even see me? Where are you anyway?"

She pauses as the click of her high-heel shoes stops. Instantly, I can guess where she is. Bleecker Street. The place my life changed forever. That's why she didn't answer my FaceTime.

My stomach turns, but I push it aside and forget I asked the question. "Never mind. Okay, is that bad if I don't change?"

Thankfully, she rolls with the punches like that didn't just happen and groans into the phone instead. "Let me repeat this slowly. You are going to Adam Jacobson's house. Do you want him to notice you as Sarah or Miss Russo?"

Memories of the way he said my name makes my heart flutter. *I think he already sees me as Sarah.* I close my eyes, my internal battle having an all-out brawl.

"Now, you have my nerves pinging," I say, looking up to the sky for any guidance.

"Why do I live so far away? Why is it you and not me getting this opportunity? God, what I would do to climb on the man of my dreams."

"Did you forget that I'm going to be there with his daughter?"

"Have you learned anything more about that? Where's her mom?"

I bite my inner lip. Even though Maggie's my best friend, I still feel weird about sharing anything about Cailin. Adam obviously kept her hidden from the world for a reason.

"I don't know much. I've never asked about her mom, and all I know is that Linda's a family friend."

"I've tried to follow the news apps and blogs, but since no one could find anything out, the story has kind of fizzled. You've done a good job, helping to hide her. I'm hoping, now that his tour is over, it picks back up. I'm dying to know the scoop."

My stomach knots for other reasons. I don't want Cailin to be forced into the media. No little girl should have to endure that.

"Okay, I'm walking into a meeting, and I've got to go. Text me photos of outfits if you want my opinion, and I expect a *full* report when you get home!"

We say good-bye, and I head to my room. If I'm going to change, I have a lot of work to do.

Every time I thought about it today, one thing came to mind: he's probably the only person I can be myself around here. I've tried for so long to force that person away, yet here he is.

I put my faith in the hands of the Lord years ago, asking him to guide me. If this is his guidance, he's either brilliant or he has a horrible sense of humor.

I inhale a deep breath, ready to give my life to my faith and see what happens. I figure, why not see if the woman I used to be still exists under this coat of armor I've been living under?

Chapter 12

Sarah

I take apart my entire closet, trying to decide what to wear. I still have most of my clothes from when I lived in New York, but I haven't worn them in years. When I moved back home, I went back to dressing the part of the pastor's daughter, and when I started teaching, I completely gave up on any style I'd once had.

I don't wear skirts or dresses like most women do here, but I don't wear my short shorts or tank tops either.

I want to come off cute but not seem like I am trying too hard. This is just a dinner at his house with the other people who have been helping him with Cailin, so I don't want to go overdressed.

I decide on a pair of ripped shorter shorts to show off my legs. It's been years since I've let these puppies out, and I'm ready to rock them. For my top, I choose a muted fuchsia color sweater that's a V-neck and tapered yet on the baggy side, so I can bunch up the arms and look more casual. I slide on some cute sandals and am out the door.

When I pull up to the Pleasants Valley estate, the gate is closed. I hit the intercom button, and Adam's voice comes over the loudspeaker. "Come on in."

The gate opens just as fast as my nerves turn my stomach upside down. I can't believe I'm here, at Adam Jacobson's house. My entire

74

life, I've wanted this—to meet a man who is just as into music as I am—yet I gave up on that dream years ago.

How is it all coming back now?

It makes me want that dream again. I feel like I'm an alcoholic walking into a bar, not sure if I should take that sip and fall down that hole again. Those feelings I felt back then, they're resurfacing, and I can't help it.

I'm sick of being so afraid of them.

I try to rid my thoughts as I glance down at my outfit, hoping I made the right choice. I inhale deeply through my nose and drive onto the property.

Cailin runs down the stairs of the two-story home with a wraparound porch. The house is painted white with dark steps leading down to a circular driveway. Flowers and trees line the concrete driveway that leads to a massive play structure where Cailin has her bike, scooter, and mini basketball hoop sitting next to an adult-sized one.

"Miss Russo." Cailin gives me a hug.

Being in such a personal setting, I feel kind of odd, having her still call me that, but I don't want things to change at school, so I disregard it and wrap my arms around her instead.

She grabs my hand and pulls me toward the house. Adam is casually leaning against the entrance.

Our eyes meet, and his lips slightly tilt up. "Hi, Sarah."

"Hi, Adam." I realize this is the first time I've said his name to him. It feels … intimate. And *right*. "Thank you for inviting me," I say.

He places his hand on my back, sending warmth up my body as I enter the house. "Glad you could make it."

I head toward the kitchen where Linda is at the sink. After drying her hands, she opens her arms to give me a hug. "So glad you could join us, dear. Can I get you anything to drink?"

"Sure. I'll take whatever you have."

Linda pours me an iced tea as Cailin opens the sliding glass door to the back patio where Adam stands over the grill.

His jeans are loose on his hips, and the metal-looped belt that holds his pants up is sticking out from his fitted black T-shirt. His lean body is hard in all the right places yet skinny in other spots.

I stare for a second too long, and Linda smiles a knowing smile when she hands me my iced tea.

Embarrassment heats my face. Thankfully, she doesn't say anything and turns to head back to the sink where she washes lettuce.

Needing to keep busy so I don't ogle the homeowner, I say, "How can I help?"

Linda glances around. "I think everything's set. Adam made the potato salad and got everything ready for the grill before I even got here."

"He cooks?" I say, a little too surprised, which I know I shouldn't be. How come we never assume famous people actually live normal, everyday lives outside of their jobs?

"Yes, he's a pretty amazing guy."

I fidget with my fingers, drifting my eyes around the room until I see place mats along with table settings sitting out, ready to go, so I jump on the opportunity. "Here, I'll help set the table," I say, picking the items up.

"Oh, yes, please do. I think Adam wanted to sit outside."

Cailin left the sliding glass door open, so I step through, and Adam places the tongs down and heads my way.

"Here, let me help you." He takes the silverware off the plates as I place everything else on a picnic table on the wraparound porch.

My eyes glance to a swing that looks so enticing to waste a day away on. This place is so homey and not what I would expect a rock star of Adam's stature to purchase or call home.

"Thank you," I say.

As I set each place mat down, Adam follows closely behind, placing napkins and the utensils on the correct sides. Every time I step to the next setting, his scent disappears, only to reappear when he comes closer.

I'm not a fan of a man who wears so much cologne that you know his presence five seconds before he even enters a room. Adam isn't this way. His scent is subtle and intoxicating as it plays with my senses. It's woodsy, it's spicy, and it's all man.

I tilt my head to get a look at him and see he's doing the same to me. Once the last seat is set, I rub my hands together, thinking of what to say or do.

"Glasses," I say too loud and want to roll my own eyes.

I'm acting so strangely, and I know he notices. How could he not?

"It's okay. Everyone has their drinks already. Maybe see if they need refills before we sit down?" Adam says as he heads back to the grill.

"Oh, yes, right. Can I get yours? What did you have? A beer?"

He shakes his head. "Nah, I have my iced tea right there. Cailin will take milk or water. You can get that for her, if you want."

I move quickly to the refrigerator, pausing for a second so I can breathe behind the open door before I grab the milk when Linda comes to my side.

"Don't be so nervous. He gets that from everyone everywhere he goes. He invited you here to get to know you, so try to get to know him as a person, not as what everyone else knows him as."

I sigh, dropping my shoulders as I set the milk on the counter. "I'm sorry. I'm really trying. It's just … it's Adam Jacobson."

I want to tell her it's so much more than just him. It's everything. My life. His life. I was trying to be him, yet here I am, years later, standing in his house. Everything that was thrown away in the blink of an eye, that I tried to bury years ago, is rising up, deep in my soul. All of what could have been flashes through my mind.

Add in how attracted I am to him, and I'm a jumbled mess.

She lets out a bark of a laugh. "I know. And you should treat him like just Adam and nothing more."

"How long have you known him?" I feel brave enough to ask as I pour the milk.

She pats my arm. "Long enough, dear. Long enough."

"Chow's on!" Adam yells, and we head outside after I place the carton back in the fridge.

Cailin comes running up from the swing set with Wayne and climbs up to the seat next to Adam. He dishes her some potato salad while she whines about not liking it. Watching the interaction between them brings my nerves down a notch.

I hold up my plate, hoping if Cailin sees me wanting some that it will help. "Potato salad is my favorite. Have you tried it, Cailin?"

She crosses her arms in protest. "No, but I was there when he made it today, and it smelled awful!"

"That's just the egg. You like eggs, right?"

She glares at me. "Eggs do *not* smell like that."

"When you dye Easter eggs, they do. Will you not dye Easter eggs because of the smell?"

Our SONG

She turns to her dad. "I don't remember them smelling when we dyed them last time."

He taps her nose with his finger. "That's because I cooled them down, getting rid of the smell before we did."

She purses her little lips together in thought. "Fine. I'll eat it, but next time you make this, I get to dye the eggs first. Deal?"

We all chuckle at her offer.

"Deal," Adam says with a nod to his head and a scoop on her plate before placing some on mine.

Our eyes meet, and I don't see the rock star anymore. I see normal. I see the man, the dad he's trying to be.

By the end of our dinner, I feel even more comfortable, sitting here with them. Linda shares stories of Cailin that have me laughing so hard that my sides hurt.

"You know I love the way you guys make up lyrics, but this new one had other moms glaring at me at the park the other day." Linda eyes Adam, and he laughs out loud, clapping his hands together.

"Oh, come on. That's the best one," he says, still laughing.

"I haven't heard this one," I say, wanting in on the little joke they have going on.

"Ready, Cailin?" Adam asks.

Adam stands, and Cailin's quick to join him. He holds out his hands in front of him and pretends to play the saxophone, even making the noises with his mouth to a tune I recognize but can't quite put my finger on until they both sing, "Now, I can see your butt crack!"

They high-five, and Cailin's giggle brings a huge smile to my face as they rejoin us at the table.

"The lyrics talk about making your hands clap, not seeing your butt crack," Linda deadpans as she raises her eyebrows to me.

I almost spit out my drink and cover my mouth to make sure nothing flies out.

These two really are something special together.

Adam talks about how Cailin's kept him on his toes all these years, and I think back to the time I first started following him. I had already liked their music for a while when I first saw the bad-boy rock star on the front of a tabloid magazine.

His eyes caught my attention first. I'm not one to long after famous people or even lust after hot guys, but there was something about him that made my heart pound and my stomach flip. I used to imagine what his life was like, and knowing now that he was home with a baby—and actually being a dad to that baby—blows my mind. It's making me even more curious how there's no mention of her mom. I've heard stories of nannies, maids, and even Linda helping out, but nothing about the woman who gave birth to her.

Linda places her napkin on her plate. "Well, this has been fun, but it's getting to be my bedtime. Why don't I help you clean up before we head home?"

Adam stands and grabs her plate from her. "It's no big deal. You've already done so much for me. I've got this."

He grabs Wayne's plate and then his own.

I reach for the others and stand. "Here, I can help."

"Come with me. Let's get you ready for bed before I take off." Linda holds out her hand, and Cailin grabs it, skipping into the house.

Adam and I meet at the sink, and he takes the plates from me.

"What can I do?" I ask.

He gives me a quick peek. "I've got it, but you can stay here and keep me company."

I lean up against the counter, keeping my hands behind me on the granite. "You've done an amazing job with her. I'm impressed."

"Coming from a teacher, that means a lot. Thank you."

I chuckle under my breath. "Just because I'm a teacher doesn't mean I know how to raise a child. I only get them for a few hours a day. You've had her for years."

He grabs a cup while glancing my way. "You do better than you know. Cailin tells me all about her day, and every sentence has something to do with you."

I've gotten compliments from other parents, but hearing it come from him means something different, something more. It makes me proud of what I've become, knowing I've made a difference in his life similar to the way he's made a difference in mine through his music.

"She's a joy to have," I say, putting the salad dressing in the fridge.

"The potato salad was good. Did you really make it?" I say, covering it with the tinfoil that was sitting next to it.

"Does that surprise you?" he asks with a smirk on his face.

I shrug. "A little. I guess I never pictured you as a cook."

Our SONG

He places the last plate in the dishwasher, closes it, and grabs a towel. As he dries his hands, he leans against the counter. "So, you've pictured me then?"

My face instantly flushes. "I mean, by the pictures I've seen online, you don't look like you'd be at home, dicing eggs."

He laughs and places the towel on the handle of the dishwasher. "There's a lot about me that people don't see."

I tilt my head as I ask, "Why not?"

He pauses. Our eyes meet, and I see so much more than a rock star, a father, and a cook. I see a man who hides a lot from the public. I see a man who has a private persona that he keeps guarded closely. *But why does he hide?*

"She's all ready for bed, but she wants a bedtime story," Linda says as she enters the kitchen.

Adam turns away, not answering my question. "I'll be right up."

"Actually, she wants Miss Russo to read to her." She glances my direction. "If that's okay with you."

I jump at the chance. "I'd love to."

As I climb the stairs, I look down the long hallway, wondering what else is up here. An open door on the left catches my attention. My chest tightens at the thought of Adam's bed only a few feet away from me, and I have to stop myself from exploring more.

Instead, I step into her room to see the pink sheer net she explained hanging from the ceiling. White dressers line the right side, and straight back, I see the window she loves.

"Come sit next to me." Cailin holds up a book.

I curl up alongside her. "What do we have here?" I ask.

"It's my favorite book, *I Knew You Could*. My daddy reads it to me a lot, but I want to see what it sounds like with your voice."

I glance down at her. "You think it will sound different?"

"I know it will. It's just like a song. If someone else sings the lyrics, it sounds totally different."

I laugh more to myself than to her. This little girl is wise beyond her years.

I read the book all about the trials and tribulations of life and how, through it all, they knew the little train could do it. With every page, I love the book more and more, which I surprisingly have never read.

The book is so motivating, so uplifting, and by the end, I have to inhale to stop my quivering lip as I read because I'm so moved by it.

As I close the book, I turn back to the cover to make a mental note of the author and title. I flip the page to the front to see when it first came out, and that's when I notice a handwritten dedication I didn't see before.

Adam,
I knew you could do it! I've never been so proud in all my life.
Love,
Linda

I run my fingers over the handwritten note.

"Linda got this for my daddy years ago," Cailin says.

I see the book came out in 2003. I think I was around fourteen years old in 2003, and I thought Adam was around my age. This seems like an odd book to give a fourteen-year-old boy.

"And he's kept it all this time?" I ask as I close the pages.

"Yeah, he said it was the first gift he ever got. You didn't sound that different from when he reads it though." She shrugs like she's surprised.

"What do you mean?" I ask.

"Linda has read it to me a hundred times, but only my dad's voice cracks as he reads the end, and yours did, too."

The smile that graces my face is nothing like the one forming in my heart. "Must be an age thing. He's around my age, right?"

"Ohhh, don't tell Linda she's getting old. Wayne says she's sensitive about that."

A sharp laugh escapes my lips. "I didn't mean it like that. Here, let's get you tucked in."

I stand and pull the covers up around her. "Good night, Cailin."

Adam enters the room. "Good night, Sugarplum."

She raises her arms up high, waiting for Adam to lean down so she can wrap her arms around his neck. "Night, Chestnut."

"I'll be downstairs if you need anything, but how about you try to sleep in your own bed tonight, okay?" Adam says.

I step toward the door, giving them their moment, until Cailin

Our SONG

yells out, "I really liked having you here tonight, Miss Russo. Can you come over again soon?"

Adam answers for me, "I'm sure we can set up another time for her to come over again."

I grin and nod, not able to get any words out as we both exit her room.

Chapter 13

Sarah

I walk down the stairs, hyperaware of Adam directly behind me. Linda and Wayne left, so I head toward my purse in the kitchen.

"Thank you for inviting me tonight. I had a great time," I say as I pick it up.

He places his arm on my elbow, and I'm instantly warmed by his touch.

"I thought you might stay awhile." He shrugs. "Hang out a little. We can sit out on the back deck."

I inhale a quick breath, letting my mind enjoy the thought. "Sure, I can do that."

His smile makes my body warm, and the slight tug it causes on my lips feels pretty good from it.

"Do you drink coffee or tea?"

"Coffee, please," I respond.

He pulls out the coffee. "So, tell me how you got into teaching," he says.

I place my fingers under the counter and pull the front of my body into it. For a quick second, I want to tell him the truth but decide against it. I don't want him to think I'm a freak stalker person who wants to use him to get back into the music scene. My time has sailed. Instead, I go with what everyone else in this town thinks they know.

"My mom was a kindergarten teacher. I moved to New York for college, thinking I wanted more, but ended up right back here, following in her footsteps, at the same school even."

"That's cool you had her to guide you. What did you originally want to do?"

I fidget with my sweater. *I wanted to be you. I wanted to help people through music. I wanted to hear fans screaming out my lyrics while they danced with joy.*

I try to hide the sadness ripping through me that I haven't felt this strongly in years. "Oh, you know, I was a small-town girl living it up in the big city. Things didn't work out."

He starts the coffeemaker and leans back against the counter, crossing his arms. "Why not?"

The way he asks so nonchalantly makes me want to laugh. It's such a loaded question that I still don't understand. I've asked myself *why* more times than I can remember. My father was quick to point out why, but I don't want to believe him. When I'm really down on myself though, I can't see any other reason.

"It wasn't in the cards, let's just say." I inhale, ready to change the subject back to him. "What about you? Did you always want to be a singer?"

His eyes narrow slightly as he places his hands behind him. He's reading me like a book, and I get the feeling he knows something's about to be unveiled.

He purses his lips together with a slight shrug. "I guess it *was* in the cards."

His short, pointed comment hangs in the air. I want to ask him so much more, but how can I when I am being so elusive myself? We stare at each other, almost in a dare to share what the other is truly hiding, until the coffee dings, and he grabs a cup, pouring us each some of the dark liquid.

"Shall we head outside?" He motions for me to go in front of him, completely dropping the subject.

I pick up my cup and slide the glass door open, feeling the slight breeze rush across my skin.

I head toward the swing, and to my surprise, Adam sits on it as well. His legs are long enough to touch the ground, but mine hang freely, so I tuck them up under me and face him more.

His jaw is lined in dark stubble, and with the one light shining brightly by the door, his features are more on display than I've ever seen before. His nose to his cheekbones and even his lips are so defined. Almost perfect.

He drops his head on the back of the swing, and his Adam's apple protrudes, casting a shadow. Barely turning his head, he lets out a deep breath.

"I bought the house because of this swing," he says before turning his gaze up at the stars that peek through the overhang.

"Couldn't you have added a swing to your last place?"

He shakes his head. "This is the first place I've bought. I've been living out of hotels and high-rise apartments until now. It was easier to hide Cailin that way. We knew the secret would come out with her enrolling in school, so I decided to finally get a place and settle down."

"I'm impressed you were able to keep her a secret for that long."

His head turns toward me again, but he keeps it resting down on the bench. It's not in an exhausted way or lazy way. He just looks content, and it's helping me to feel the same way.

"I'd do anything for that little girl," he says almost breathlessly.

"I can tell." I take a sip of my coffee, and he sits up to do the same.

I have so many questions I want to ask but know I shouldn't—at least, not yet. Linda's words of getting to know him as Adam and nothing else ring through my head. But every question I can think of comes back to his career.

He licks his lips before taking another sip, and my mind goes right in the gutter, not helping my current predicament.

"So, you grew up here?" he asks, thankfully, taking me out of my lust-filled thoughts.

I take a sip and nod. "Yep. Born and raised. Swore I'd leave and never come back, yet here I am." I hold out my arm to my side with a sigh.

"Doesn't seem to be a bad place. Linda likes it here."

"I'm surprised I don't know her better, she's lived here for a while though, right?"

He nods, keeping quiet for a few seconds before saying, "As long as I've known her."

"Did you grow up around here?" I ask, hoping I'm not digging too far.

He sighs and shrugs his shoulders. "A few towns over." He's quick to change the subject. "So, tell me more about Cailin. Do all kids read as good as she does?"

"She's one of my top students. Except for her little singing habit." I playfully eye him.

He lets out a throaty laugh, hitting me deeply into my soul. "What can I say?" He grins from ear to ear like the proud father he is.

"It's pretty cute how you guys make up lyrics together."

He perks up, excited to share his story. "It was hard, connecting with a little girl, you know? I didn't know much about kids, and even with the help of nannies, I wanted to be as hands-on as possible. I did *not* do dolls"—his eyes lower, making me laugh—"and we could only be together inside, so music was my go-to."

"Music is a great way to connect with anyone."

He tilts his head and tries to hide the tug on his lips. "You mean, you like more than just religious songs?"

I teasingly slap his shoulder. "Yes. Just because I sang *Jesus Loves Me* with your daughter doesn't mean that's all I know. I enjoy church, but it's not my entire life."

"What is?"

I eye him, not sure what he means.

"What's the best part of your life?" he asks.

I glance over my shoulder at the playground he installed for Cailin and then back at him. "Not sure yet."

His hand reaches out to touch mine. "I think you found it already."

My heart pounds at the way his fingers rub across my skin.

"Do I make you nervous?" he asks.

I shake my head, my eyes wide open, staring at where our bodies are together, even in this little way.

"Then, why aren't you breathing?" He smirks, and I laugh, breathing out.

"Okay, maybe a little." I slowly raise my eyes to meet his.

"Here, let's start this over." He sits up straight and holds out his hand to me. "I'm Adam. I hear my daughter, Cailin, is in your class."

I can't help the nervous giggle escaping me as I shake his hand. He doesn't let go and drops it between us.

"See? All is good now."

"Except you're still holding my hand."

He slightly raises his eyebrows. "That I am. Good observation, Sid."

"Oh my God, did you just quote a kids cartoon to me?"

"*Sid the Science Kid* is our favorite show." He turns his large frame, so he's facing me, his knee bent to one side. "I don't get to know many people. I invited you here for more reasons than to just thank you for giving Cailin rides to school. She speaks very highly of you. Linda does, too. I wanted to see what they saw."

I swallow hard. "And?" I say barely above a whisper.

"And I see what they see. But I see more. I wanted to see if I felt more, too."

My heart stops, and when my phone rings from inside the door, I jump to my feet to get it. After I realize how silly my reaction was, I turn back to him to apologize, but he's chuckling to himself.

"It's okay. Get the phone."

I step inside to see it's Maggie calling. I swipe it on. "I'm still here. Can't talk, but I'll call you back."

"You're still there?" Her voice is loud and clear. "It's what, past nine?"

"Yes," I speak quietly into the phone.

"Why are you whispering all of a sudden?" she mimics my tone.

"Because Cailin is asleep upstairs, and I don't want to wake her."

"Wait." She pauses, and I can only imagine her holding up her hand out in front of her. "You're there *after* he put her to bed?"

"Yes. We're sitting outside, talking. You interrupted us."

"I hate you, you know that, right?"

I laugh through my breath. "Yes. Now, good-bye."

I hang up and turn to see him standing behind me.

He takes my hand in his. "I'm sorry if I was too forward before. I'd like to get to know you better. If that's okay with you."

I tightly close my lips, trying to hold in my emotion, and nod. "I'd like that."

He lowers his head to catch my eyes better. "I'm just Adam Tyler. Nothing else. Especially when we're here." His eyebrows rise slightly. "Do you think you can see me that way?"

I stand up taller, exhaling before letting it all out. "I'm sorry. It's just … there's a lot going on in my head, and I've been following you for years. It's just weird how I'm here all of a sudden."

Our SONG

He stands back a tiny bit with a shit-eating grin on his face. "Following me?" He smirks, and I want to smack him.

"You know what I mean."

He grips my hand again. "Come on, I'll walk you out."

I grab my purse and follow him out to my car.

He opens the door and pauses with it between us. "This is new to me too, you know. I've never really gotten to know anyone outside of Linda and the guys in my band. I haven't met anyone I cared to actually get to know."

I smile as I take in a deep breath. He talks so nonchalantly, like him wanting to spend time with me isn't a big deal. To me, it's astronomical, yet to him, it's just getting to know someone. I need to remember that.

I place my hand over his that's holding the door open. "I'd be honored to get to know you, Adam, just by what I've learned from Linda and your daughter and nothing more."

His expression softens, and I see it—the man who just wants someone by his side. A friend, a confidant, maybe even a lover. He's ready to let someone else in. I just hope I'm strong enough to be that person.

Chapter 14

Adam

I'm asleep on my stomach with my pillow curled under my arms when Cailin comes running into my room.

"Did Miss Russo stay the night?"

"Excuse me?" I ask, trying to hide my surprise while being half-asleep.

"I thought she was going to have a sleepover." Her little lip pouts out, so I reach out to her, pulling her into my bed to cuddle with me.

"No, sweetie. Adults don't have sleepovers like that." I close my eyes while kissing the back of her head.

"Why not? It'd be fun to wake up and have breakfast together, and then we could hang out."

"Maybe we can call her later." I sigh, closing my eyes, hoping for a few more minutes of sleep.

Last night was the first night—without Cailin hitting me—in my bed in months, and I don't want to get up yet.

Cailin sits up and turns to me. "Oh, please, Daddy, can we?"

I open one eye to see her pleading with her hands curled up under her chin. I fall to my back and push out my arms to stretch my body awake.

I didn't think about how wanting to get to know Sarah better could affect her. Cailin knew her first, and she's her teacher. Is there some line I shouldn't be crossing when it comes to Sarah? Linda was quick to point out how she thought Sarah would be good for me. If it's wrong, I don't think she would have suggested such a thing.

Is this all moving too fast though? I don't even know the woman, and Cailin's begging for her to come over when she barely left a few hours ago. I don't want Cailin to get attached and then have something happen, putting Cailin through unnecessary sadness.

I cross my arm over my eyes. So, this is why I haven't dated all this time. Why am I putting my feelings over wanting to get to know a woman better in front of hers? But she likes her too. I guess that's better than bringing a stranger around, right?

I tell my brain to shut up and sigh, giving in to both of our desires.

"We'll give her a call, but I don't know if she already has plans, so I don't want you to be upset if she can't."

She climbs off my bed. "I'm going to go get dressed. Get up, so we can call her."

I glance at the clock to see it's seven twenty—otherwise known as too early. It will take some getting used to, being on a more normal schedule. While on tour, we'd stay up late and crash on the bus until we arrived at the next venue.

I should have gone to bed last night after Sarah left, but being around her made my mind buzz with lyrics. I stayed up until two in the morning, jotting everything down.

It's been a while since I had inspiration like that, and I didn't want to stop until I got it all out.

Devil's Breed's lyrics are raw and gritty, but everything coming out of me last night was anything but. It wasn't sweet and lovey-dovey, but it had meaning. I use a lot of my past to fuel my songs. I like to give people something to believe in through my music. I want them to know they aren't alone in their anger, their anxiety, and the fucked up lives they were born into.

The lyrics I wrote last night were hopeful. They were looking toward the future instead of dwelling on the past.

I slip on a T-shirt and head downstairs, walking straight to the coffeepot and pouring the morning goodness.

"What are these?" Cailin asks as she climbs onto the barstools next to the kitchen counter where I was sitting last night, multiple pages of my lyrics strewn about. She picks one up and reads the title, "*Hear Me Now*? What's that?"

I take a sip of my coffee before setting it down and reading over the pages she has in her hand, impressed she can read it at all. "It's the title of the song I was working on last night."

"Is it finished?"

"Not yet, but I got a start on a few different ones too."

She picks up the other sheets and tries to read my handwriting, but as the night went on, my writing got messier and messier. "Daddy, you have bad handwriting. Miss Russo can help you too. She has these sheets that I trace, so you can learn to write the letters better."

I'm lucky I already swallowed my coffee, or I would've spit it out in laughter. I love Cailin's innocence and how she's always looking for ways to help.

"I know. It's pretty messy. When I'm on a roll, I'm more focused on getting the words out instead of my handwriting, but I'll try next time."

We head to the living room to curl up and watch cartoons for a little while.

Once we've watched a few, she hops off the couch and heads toward the kitchen. "Can I have cereal for breakfast?"

"Sure." I head to the pantry and grab the box as she takes the milk out of the fridge. After I pour it and grab a spoon, she asks, "Did you call her yet?"

I put the milk away and grab a few eggs to make my own breakfast. "It's still early. Let's give her some time. Besides, I don't have her number."

She grabs my phone and reaches across the counter to hold it up to my face to unlock the screen as I crack the eggs.

"Did you just unlock my phone?"

"Yep! I like this one so much better than having to get your thumbprint." As her tiny tongue sticks out, she opens my phone app and dials Linda.

"Morning," Linda answers happily.

"Hi, Linda," Cailin says with it on speakerphone while lying the phone on the counter between us. "Can you give us Miss Russo's number? I want to call her to see if she can come over to play today."

"Morning, sweetheart. I can give it to you, but make sure it's okay with your dad before you call her. He might not want her to come over to play today."

Our SONG

"Yeah, I want to play with Miss Russo," I shout toward the phone. Linda chuckles under her breath. "Adam ..." she says teasingly.

"What? You asked; I answered."

I hear giggles again as she says, "I'll text it to you. You guys have fun today."

We both thank her as Cailin ends the call and goes back to eating her breakfast.

"What should we do today with Miss Russo?" I ask. "When you call someone, you should have a plan in mind. Our cover has already been blown, so no having to hide out at home. Where should we go?"

"How about the zoo?"

"Isn't that a little far?"

Her tiny shoulders pop up to her ears while she holds her hands out to the sides. "I don't know where it is. I just want to see the giraffes. I heard they had some here."

I pick up my phone and search for the closest zoo. It shows one about forty minutes away, and yes, they have giraffes, so I guess that works.

Since we have a plan that we should get on the road sooner than later, I decide now is as good a time as ever to call Sarah. I click the number and step into the hallway as the line rings.

"Hello?" Sarah says, and my lips instantly tug into a smile.

"Good morning," I say, seeing if she'll know who I am.

The audible gasp into the phone says she does. "Adam?"

"Yes. Sorry, I hope it's not too early."

"Oh no, it's fine. I'm used to getting up early."

I step further into the family room, wanting that little bit of privacy with her. "Cailin wanted to invite you to join us at the zoo today. Are you available?"

"The zoo?"

"Yes. I know it might not be the most enjoyable thing, but Cailin wants to see—"

"No, I'm sorry. I didn't mean it like that," she says, cutting me off. "I'd love to go with you guys."

Cailin comes running around the corner. "Can she come?"

I nod as I say, "Great. We'll pick you up in, say, an hour?"

"Sounds good. See you then."

"Yep. Oh, and, Sarah?"

"Yeah?"

"Make sure to save my number, okay?"

I hear her breathy laugh through the receiver. "I will. Don't you worry," she teases, and it feels real.

I like that she's able to play with me like this. Maybe, today, she'll finally get past *what* I am and start to see *who* I am.

We pull up to Sarah's apartment, and she's already outside, waiting, since I texted we were on our way.

She looks a little more casual today in jeans that are ripped in a few places and a black top with a long necklace. There's no cleavage showing, and her jeans aren't super tight, but goddamn, she looks sexier now than any woman I've ever seen.

I love that she's not flaunting her body or going over the top. She seems comfortable in her own skin, and that is damn hot to me.

I jump out of the truck to greet her before she makes it to us. "I think I'm supposed to come get you, aren't I?" I tease.

She blushes. "I didn't want you to have to get Cailin out of the truck."

I pause and look into her eyes. "You look good." I scan her body up and down just because I want to see her face become even redder. I don't know why that turns me on as much as it does.

She tucks her long, wavy hair behind her ear. "Thank you. So do you."

A tattoo that seemingly wraps around her entire shoulder, which I didn't know was there, shows from under her top. "Nice," I say, rubbing my finger over the ink of flowers mixed with music notes.

"I figured it was okay to show it off while I'm with you."

"Hell yeah, it is. I can't wait to see the rest of it." That flush reappears, and I have to stop before my cock wants to come out and join in on the conversation.

I open the door and assist her into to the tall truck. Cailin's excited voice as she greets her makes me so fucking happy to hear.

When I sit back in the driver's seat, I hear Cailin talking about the giraffes she's dying to see. Sarah not only engages in conversation with her, but she's also actually teaching her about the giraffes.

"Did you know a baby giraffe is six feet tall when it's born?"

Cailin's eyes go wide. "That's bigger than my daddy!"

"Um, not quite. I'm six-four, but that's pretty damn close." I hold up my finger to make my point before putting the truck in gear. "What should we listen to, little girl?"

Cailin taps her finger to her lips as she thinks. "Has Miss Russo heard your new album?"

I let out a hard laugh. "She doesn't have to listen to that."

"It's okay. I really like your new stuff," she says, surprising me.

"You do?" My eyebrows rise in question.

She grins as she tilts her head at me. "Yes, I do. *Tears Don't Fall* is my favorite so far."

I nod slowly, impressed she even knows the name of one of the songs. "So, you're okay with our harder stuff?"

Tears Don't Fall is a more personal song I wrote about my past with my mother as well as Cailin's mom. No matter what happened, it's time I've dealt with it all, especially for Cailin. I've always done what I wanted, but now, I owe it to her to not mess things up.

She shrugs, faking nonchalance. "I like them all. The harder stuff gets me going more." She gives me a grin, mischievously narrowing her eyes, and I have to stop myself from leaning over to kiss her.

The urge is real and strong. And it's not even truly sexual. It's happiness. She makes me fucking happy, and I'm taking it in like a drug, wanting more every time I'm around her.

The drive to the zoo is relaxed and comfortable. Sarah keeps up in conversation with Cailin while I fall for her even more. Gone is the nervous girl I thought would never see me as a normal person, and in her place is the woman Linda and Cailin raved about.

I park the truck when we pull up to the zoo and hop out to help Cailin with her booster seat. When Sarah meets us from the opposite end of the truck, her expression makes me question what's going on as she searches around us.

I drop my head to hers and whisper in her ear, "What are you searching for?"

Her wary eyes meet mine. "Aren't you afraid people will recognize you?"

I reach in, grabbing my black hat and pulling it down low. "This will help a little. It's going to happen though. Just get ready. I try not to allow it to slow me down, so I can live my life."

I throw Cailin's backpack we grabbed with our water bottles and snacks over my shoulder and shut the door.

"But what about Cailin?" Her sincerity is admirable.

"She's my daughter. That's a fact that I only hid for her sake, not mine. It's time the world knew she existed. She's old enough to handle it now, and I'm sick of having to try and hide. Right now, I'm more interested in showing my daughter these giraffes she's dying to see."

I wink as I grab Cailin's hand and nod my head to Sarah, motioning for us to head toward the entrance.

I pay our admission, and we enter through the gates as I open the map to see everything the place has to offer.

"Should we see the lions, snakes, or monkeys first?" I ask, faking nonchalance.

"Daddy!" Cailin yells. "Which way are they?"

"Hmm ..." I search the map. "Giraffes, giraffes... where are they?"

I glance up to see Sarah's lips trying to hide her grin. I match her expression as I announce, "Found them!" I point my finger to the right. "This way, my dear."

Cailin takes off running, and we jog behind her. Once they're in sight, Sarah and I slow down and stroll the rest of the way with our eyes glued to Cailin.

"You like to play with her, don't you?" Sarah asks.

"It's my absolute favorite thing on earth. She's so easy to mess with, and seeing her face light up is the best thing ever."

"Daddy, hurry, hurry. Look how tall they are," Cailin yells, calling us over to her.

"See what I mean? How can anyone not love that?" I run over to Cailin and pick her up, so she's closer to where the giraffe is feeding off a tree.

"His tongue is crazy!" she says in amazement.

Sarah joins us on my side. "Their tongues are almost a foot and a half long."

I turn to her in shock. "Seriously?"

She slightly drops her head back. "Yes, seriously. That's how they get the leaves off of tall trees."

"How do you know this stuff?" I ask.

Her eyes crinkle at the sides. "I teach kindergarten, remember?"

Our SONG

Cailin wiggles her way out of my arms and runs to where a baby giraffe is walking toward us. "Daddy, come here. Is he taller than you?"

I head to where she is and stand up tall to the animal that seems to be my same height.

Sarah takes out her phone. "Here, let me take a picture of you two."

I make a silly face at the giraffe, hoping she'll get the shot. Laughter from both her and Cailin make me turn to face them.

"She meant me and you, not you and the giraffe, Dad," Cailin says through a fit of giggles.

"Oh, sorry." I fake ignorance while I pick her up, and we pose with the baby animal.

"Perfect," Sarah says.

Cailin runs toward her. "I want to see!" Her face lights up at the vision on the screen. "Now, one with me and you, Miss Russo."

I pull my phone out from my back pocket and click on the Camera app. "Yes, let me take it."

Sarah leans down to pose with Cailin. As I stare at the vision of the two of them through my screen, something hits me in the chest. I've never wanted Cailin to go without, and I've tried to give her the best life I could, but I've never seen her radiate happiness the way she is now.

Peacefulness I didn't even know existed flushes through my body. I thought Cailin was the ultimate high, but seeing her with Sarah has just taken that up a notch. I never thought that Cailin needed anyone else besides me and maybe Linda, but have I been wrong—for both of our needs?

"Thank you for going with us today," I say after getting settled on the freeway, heading back home after having dinner together.

Cailin didn't even make it this far before passing out.

I sneak a quick glance at Sarah and feel a pain in my chest when I meet her eyes. There's something about her that makes my heart pound for seemingly no reason at all.

"I had so much fun. I've never been with just one child who's old enough to walk on their own and actually be interested in the animals. I brought my niece a few years ago, but she was a little too young. It's fun to be able to relax more and enjoy the animals without stressing over where everyone is or if they are taken care of."

"Do you enjoy teaching?"

She lets out an uneasy breath, and I turn to see her expression. She's staring out the window like she's thinking. I touch her hand. I can feel that whatever she is thinking isn't good. I felt it last time we had this conversation too. There's something she's not letting me in on.

When our fingers first meet, she flinches ever so slightly. When she doesn't turn, I grip her harder, opening her palm and entangling my fingers with hers.

I feel the tension slowly leave her body as I run my thumb over hers.

Finally, she speaks, "It's not like I don't like teaching. I love it actually. It just wasn't my first choice."

I decide not to push her and ask what that first choice was. Obviously, it's something she still struggles with, and who am I to bring up sore subjects from the past?

We drive in silence, hands intertwined. *Like a Nightmare* by Deadset Society comes on the radio, and I turn it up slightly, using the control on the steering wheel.

Out of the corner of my eye, I catch Sarah singing. "You know this song?"

"Yeah. I used to listen to My Darkest Days, so I followed them when they started the new band after Matt Walst left."

I'm stunned to silence. I expect people to know band names and even song titles, but I don't know many people who care enough to actually know the intricacies of band members and following those members when bands breaks up, only to create new ones.

I try to keep my eyes on the road as I also stare at her in shock.

She drops her shoulder, giving me a deadpan expression. "Why are you so surprised I know that?" My eyebrows rise, and a genuine, deep belly laugh escapes her sexy lips. "I'm not everything you see."

A grin spreads across my face. "I can tell, and believe me, it makes me want to see more."

Her cheeks flush, and I squeeze her hand tighter.

Our SONG

As we get off the freeway, Cailin wakes up, yawning as she asks, "Are we home yet?"

"Almost," I say. "We have to take Sarah home first."

"How come she can't just stay with us? Have a sleepover?" Cailin whines as I hear Sarah choke on the water she was drinking.

I wink in her direction while responding. "Maybe another time, but not tonight."

Sarah covers her mouth as she coughs harder.

When I pull into her complex, she says goodbye to Cailin as I open the door. "Stay right here, okay, sweetheart? I'm just going to make sure Sarah makes it up to her apartment." I put on a song Cailin likes and close the door before rushing to Sarah's side.

Sarah drops her water bottle when she sees me appear on the opposite side of the truck. After leaning down to pick it up, she fidgets with her hair, making sure it's smooth and in place.

"You don't have to walk me up. I'll be fine," she says, looking everywhere but at me.

I reach for her fingers, lacing them with mine. "I want to."

Her eyes meet mine, and I nod my head toward her door.

"Thank you again for inviting me," she says as we stroll in the direction of her place.

"We'll have to plan something again soon."

Her lips tug up to a smile. "I'd like that."

We reach her door, and she takes out her keys, unlocking it but not pushing it open. Instead, she pauses and glances up at me, waiting for what I'm going to say.

I step closer, so our bodies are inches apart. "I'm not going to rush this."

Her eyes widen, but she doesn't say anything.

"I've been with girls I never wanted, but I've never been with anyone I actually wanted a future with, especially this bad. I don't want to screw this up. I'm going to kiss you though."

I run my fingers across the nape of her neck. Her pulse is thumping out of control. Mine feels the same way.

I slowly lean in. "Is that okay with you?"

Her lids close as she nods ever so slightly. Her scent is the first thing I notice as I take her in—cherries, vanilla, and so fucking mine.

Our mouths brush against each other as I hold her in place. Her lips parting slightly, I lick them, seeing if she'll invite me in. When she does, I have to hold my breath and make myself not take more than she's willing to give me right now as our first kiss.

I wasn't kidding. I want to take this slow. I want to do this right.

It takes everything I have to pull back as I place my forehead to hers. "Slowly," I whisper more to myself than anything else.

She nods, and I can't help myself when I lean in again, entangling my tongue with hers and pushing her against the wall, wanting just a little more.

I pause our kiss, keeping her pressed to my body as I breathe her in one more time.

When I step back, everything I'm feeling reflects back at me, written all over her face. I take my thumb and wipe her bottom lip, needing one last touch from her.

"I'll see you soon," I say as I step back.

She waves goodbye as she picks up everything that she was holding that's now on the floor. I try not to laugh that she dropped them, knowing, with a kiss like that, I might have done the same thing if something were in my hand.

Chapter 15

Sarah

I close my door and instantly fall against it. This cannot be happening. Adam Jacobson just kissed me. And holy hell, did he kiss me.

I touch my lips, still wet from his. Chills run down my spine and pool in my belly. I've never been kissed like that. With so much want and need that I could feel it in my toes.

My entire body is shaking. I need to do something. A cold shower maybe? I don't even know what I need as every nerve in my body is on fire.

I look out the window to see Adam jumping back in his truck. His movements are so smooth, and seeing him lights me on fire even more. I want to run out, ask him to stay, but I know he can't.

He shouldn't. He has Cailin. This is not a normal dating situation, and I need to remember that, especially since she's my student.

I grab my phone and call Maggie, not caring that it's later there and she's probably asleep.

"This'd better be good ..." she mumbles into the phone.

"He kissed me," I blurt out.

"And I'm up," she replies, more aware. "Who kissed you?"

"Adam." My ear stings from the scream escaping her mouth. "Yep. That was pretty much my reaction too, internally at least."

"I want details. Is he a good kisser? What happened?"

"God, Maggie. He was *amazing*. He walked me to the door and kissed me good night."

"Why didn't you invite him in?"

"Because his daughter was still in the car. We'd spent the day at the zoo and then had dinner."

"Wait. Are you, like, dating him now?"

I bite my lip as his words ring in my head. I can't believe I'm going to say this. "I think so?"

"You fucking *think* so? Sarah, this is Adam Jacobson we're talking about."

I plop down on my couch and drop my head back. "I know. He's so much more though. He's actually really funny, and he's a *great* dad."

"Oh my God, you're falling for a rock star. Isn't this the most crazy turn of events in your life?"

I inhale deeply, remembering everything I went through. Of course Maggie would remind me of that. She was right there through the entire thing—the highs and the lowest of lows.

"Don't remind me of that part. I'm trying not to think about it."

It actually scares me to death. I've tried so hard to forget that part of my life, pretend it never happened. My dad definitely makes sure I'll never forget. I thought he was going to disown me at one point. He even said I was an embarrassment to him. If I thought my injury was my low, it was nothing compared to the way my father shamed me for it.

I should have learned my lesson then, yet here I am, falling down that same path.

What the hell am I doing?

"Stop getting inside your head," Maggie interrupts the thoughts she knows are running through my mind.

We sit in silence for a few beats.

"Don't let the past prevent you from being happy. I knew you had a thing for him when you first started talking about Devil's Breed years ago. You never talked about any famous person—ever. I don't think this is a coincidence that he just happened to show up at your doorstep—or literally, your classroom step. You always say you're leaving your life in the hands of your faith. Well, *fate* brought him to you. Don't forget that."

I stay silent for a few more breaths before she yells, "You did not

Our SONG

wake my ass up to have a pity party. Now, quit it and tell me more about this kiss."

I fill her in on the day. Once we say good-bye, I scroll on my phone, looking at our pictures from today.

It's mind-blowing to have photos that I took of a man who I'd admired for so long, yet now, I'm getting to know him personally. Each one makes my body yearn to get to know him more.

It's not just physical attraction. At first, I felt this magnetic attraction to him. I'd see his photos, and something inside me would sing, but I never understood it.

Now, it's so much more. The person he is makes my insides jumble with nerves, butterflies, and leaps of joy, all at the same time. He has an old soul and isn't afraid to show it when we're together.

He's nothing like what he portrays to the world, and that thought makes me wonder.

Cailin I get, but it's more than that. Yes, I've never personally known true rock stars—only people like me, who were trying to become them—but he is nothing like what I imagined.

I think we put these people up on pedestals, but really, we need to realize they are human beings, just like us. It would be silly if every day of his life was like what he portrayed onstage.

I'm starting to see him more like Adam Tyler and less like Adam Jacobson. With this breakthrough, I don't question when I pull up my phone and text him a few pictures from today along with another thank-you for inviting me.

To my surprise, his reply pops up right away.

I was just looking at the pictures I took as well. I think this one is my favorite.

I wait as the image comes across my screen and close my eyes in complete bliss when I see the selfie he took of the two of us.

I'm not sure what to say, so I send the red-heart emoji and then instantly regret it, afraid he'll read more into my intentions than I planned. He texts back.

My exact thoughts.

My eyes widen at the sight, and I blink a few times at the message on the screen.

Cailin was asking if we could see you again tomorrow after church. Are you finished the same time or later since you have this other thing going on?

Reality smacks me across the face, and she's a cruel bitch to bring down my high this fast. I felt bad about lying before, but now, I feel even worse since I'm getting to know them like this.

I should stop this. I already went down this road with my father, and it took me years to gain his trust back.

I hate feeling like the bad seed in a family who is looked upon in this city as royalty. I want to be close to my mom, and with my nephew coming, I can't leave now, but that's exactly what will happen if my dad finds out I'm seeing Adam.

Where will I go? What will I do? Will my mom and Emily be on his side, or will they fight for me?

I scroll through the pictures again, each one putting an even bigger smile on my face. *How can I not want this?* I was happy today. Truly happy. I haven't felt that way in a very long time.

Maggie's words ring in my head.

Fate.

I've left my life up to fate for years. My beliefs are what have helped me through those dark years where everything I ever wanted was completely gone. I didn't know what I was doing, where I was going. I prayed every day for an answer or some kind of guidance to lead me down a new path.

Even though my dad said the accident was God's way of getting back at me, I didn't believe him. I didn't want to. The God I know and love wouldn't do that.

Faith. I just have to have faith that I'm doing the right thing by following the path that's been laid out in front of me. I didn't search him out. I haven't been going out of my way to make this happen. Faith is making it happen, and I need to trust it.

I close my eyes to take that leap and text back.

I'll be finished a little later.

Our SONG

How's dinner at my place sound?

Sounds perfect.

I respond, feeling slightly guilty but trying to move past it. I'll have to figure something out—and quick.

He texts back the rock-star-hands emoji as his thumbs-up, I presume, making me laugh out loud as I set my phone down and get ready for bed.

As I'm dozing off a few hours later, I hear my phone ding.

Are you awake?

Yes.

I just wanted to say thank you.

For what?

For opening my eyes.

My heart pounds as I read the words over and over again. If he only knew how much he was opening my eyes as well.

When I don't respond, he texts:

Good night, Sarah.

Through my ridiculously large smile, I send him the heart emoji, and he sends it right back to me.

This is *really* happening. Fate has brought me the kind of man I've dreamed of. A man who loves life, music, and wants to be a father.

I close my eyes and pray.

I've asked you over and over again to show me the way and to guide me through my days of darkness. I see now that you've heard my prayers. Please, Lord, give me the strength to fight for what I want. I ask that you guide my father in your same light of forgiveness and acceptance. Amen.

Chapter 16

Sarah

I wake up the next morning to multiple messages from Maggie pointing out that my picture is all over entertainment news sites. I guess I should have expected it since we were out in public together, but I'm still surprised news of us at a zoo would spread so fast.

I can't imagine living this way day in and day out. Everyone wanting to take a picture of you must get old real quick.

After scrolling through multiple sites, all questioning if we're a couple, I drop my phone and get ready for church.

When I arrive, I feel a buzz that seems to be circling around me. My father is in a meeting in his office, and Emily is busy with Emma on the playground, so I walk around, greeting people as they enter, but something just feels off.

The way a few people look at me from afar or seem to be whispering about me makes me pause.

They've seen the photos.

My eyes meet Cindy's, and her expression tells me she's the one showing everyone they exist.

Why does she care? Why is my life anyone else's to judge?

I know Cindy wouldn't go straight to my father, so I walk out to my sister to get a feel of what she knows and how far the word has spread.

"Hey, Sarah. Want to get Emma for me, so I can run to the bathroom real quick?" Emily says as I approach.

She must not have seen them because that would have been the first thing out of her mouth.

"Sure," I reply and head toward my niece, cleaning her off before I go back inside before the service begins.

When I enter, I get a better feeling for who's churning the gossip mill and can tell it's staying to just a small group. I sit a little taller in front of them, hoping if they see I'm not affected by their antics, they'll drop it altogether.

As I sit in the pews at church, another uneasy feeling washes over me. I'm set to sing in just a few minutes, and knowing I lied to them about not singing today isn't sitting well with me.

When my time comes, I change the song last minute, going for a shorter ballad so I can get it over with. Once I finish, I'm quick to sit down and remind myself that lying to them is worth it and a good thing.

At least for now.

Once I get home, I change and try to rid the feelings running through me.

I FaceTime Maggie for moral support. "I'm such a shit," I say when she answers.

"Oh jeez, what now?" she responds, rolling her eyes and then grinning.

I plop down on my couch and sigh. "I lied to Adam and Cailin, saying I wasn't singing at church today."

"Um, don't you sing every Sunday?"

"Yes, and Adam wanted to come watch me and maybe see Cailin sing again."

The hard laugh that escapes her lips makes me drop my head back in frustration. "Yeah, that won't work."

She came to my hometown once. That was all it took. She had planned on attending church with me but backed out last minute. Growing up in New York, she had seen all walks of life. That is, all walks, except those of a small country town and an old-school church.

Knowing she wouldn't fit in with her short skirts and even shorter hair, she gracefully bowed out and drove to San Francisco for the day where she felt she could be more herself. I didn't blame her. I love the message and the feelings I get when I'm here. I just wish all the guilt and judgment didn't go along with it.

"That's why I lied." I sigh, staring into the phone and giving her my *duh* expression. "But you know that shit nags on me."

"Yes, your soul is just too pure." She places her hand over her chest, giving me a peaceful tilt to her head and smile.

"I'm serious!"

"Girl, I know you are but stop it. You lied because you had to. Get over it. Now, tell me when you'll see him again."

"I'm supposed to go over there in a little while." I bite my lower lip.

"Did you seriously just say that like you're dreading it? What's wrong with you?"

"You're right."

"Damn straight I'm right. Now, go for a run or shower, get rid of that angst you have going on, and go get you some Adam Jacobson."

I grin as I drop my head to my chest. "Yes, Mom."

"And call me to tell me all about it when you get home, but I have to run now, so peace out."

This is why I called her. She always reminds me of the person I want to be, not the person I turned out to be.

I take her up on the run idea and quickly change, grabbing my headphones before I head out. Of course, the first song that comes on my playlist just happens to be a Devil's Breed song.

As I run, I listen to Adam's voice and his lyrics as they touch me deeper than ever before. Knowing him now brings many more questions about the words he chose in these songs.

The man I met has shown nothing but love and happiness for his daughter, yet his songs are full of pain and anguish.

The more I pay attention, the more it makes me want to know his truth. I want to know the man who worked through this kind of pain to build the amazing life he has now. He must have amazing faith to never give up.

After hopping out of the shower, I notice a text from Adam.

Cailin and I are going to go to the park. Want to join us?

Sure. I just got out of the shower. Give me a half hour, and then I'll leave here and head your way.

Our SONG

Shower ... tell me more ...

I freeze, instantly turned on but at a complete loss of what to text back. I decide words can be overrated and just send him a winky-face emoji. When he replies back with the heart-eyes one, I put my hand over my mouth to hide my smile but feel my grin against my palm anyway.

This feeling right here is what I need to remember. This is what it's all about.

Even more now that I genuinely like the guy. I'm really starting to fall for him, and I just have to have faith that I'm going down the right path.

I arrive at his place forty-five minutes later, and to my surprise, the gate opens before I even press the button. Cailin comes running down the steps and meets me at my car.

"Miss Russo!" she says as she wraps her arms around my legs.

"Hi, sweetheart. Is your daddy in the house?"

I hear his footsteps and glance up to see him in the doorway. This angle makes him look even taller how he takes up the entire frame. His hands are in his pockets as he nonchalantly stands there, though his face says anything but.

His eyes are smoldering with the way they're taking me in, and when his mouth parts slightly to let out the breath he's holding, my heart begins to pound out of my chest.

Our kiss replays in my head as we stare at each other. The way his mouth felt against mine, the heat radiating from his body as he pushed me against the door. When my lips part, I watch his tug into a slight grin.

"Hi, Sarah," he says, and I want to melt from the sound of my name on his tongue.

Cailin grabs my arm and pulls me toward him. I'm thankful when my feet don't give out on me, and I make it up the stairs.

She lets go of my hand and runs into the house. "I'll get my shoes on, and then we can go!" she yells, but neither one of us seems to care.

I stare into his eyes, stuck in his trance. When his hands wrap on either side of the nape of my neck and pull me in for a kiss, I melt into him.

The sweetest, most innocent touch filters through me as he

presses his lips to mine, breathing me in and holding me there as his grip gets a little firmer.

When he pulls back, he kisses my forehead, keeping me close to him before saying, "I'm glad you're here."

I glance up to his piercing blues when I say, "Me too."

Cailin runs past us and toward his truck. "Let's blow this popsicle stand!"

A laugh escapes my lips. "Does she get these sayings from you?" I place my hand on his chest, feeling his heart thump.

He grins, knowing I feel how I affect him, before he kisses my head and locks the door.

He picks Cailin up and places her in the seat behind mine. When it's my turn, he places his hands on my hips, lifting me before running them down my sides. His touch lights my insides on fire.

While at the park, I watch as he swings on the swings and even goes down the slide with her. Their game of tag turns epic, and when he comes around the corner, tagging me and then running away, I join in on their fun, chasing Cailin around the play structure and into the toddler area.

She's hiding behind a giant turtle, not knowing I can see over the top of it, so I climb over it, tagging her before tickling her into a giggling fit.

Adam comes running from the other side of the park. "Oh no, she got you! I'm coming to save the princess from the tickle monster."

We both laugh as Adam wraps his arms around me, swooping me up into him and swinging me around to the other side of the turtle. My cheeks start to ache from the laughter, and I can barely catch my breath.

Adam places me down, making sure I'm secure on the ground before entangling his hand with mine. "Okay, us old people need a break. Go play while we sit on the bench over there."

Cailin jumps up and runs to where another kid has entered the playground.

"You guys are so cute together," I say.

"So are you."

He walks us to a bench where he sits with his knee crossed over his leg and his arm draped across the back of the wood structure.

We sit in silence until he inhales and turns to me. "I take it, you

Our SONG

saw the news stories about you." He exhales as he looks off in the distance. "I'm sorry you have to deal with that."

I turn to face him, not really sure what to say. I guess if I'm going to hang out with him, this is going to happen. I need him to know it's okay, but I'm still not sure if it is. I don't want my dad to find out this way, but I might not have a choice.

He places his foot on the ground, resting his elbows on his thighs as he lets out a deep breath. "Just get ready for it, okay?"

I place my hand on his arm, scooting closer to him. "For what?"

"The haters."

I sigh, looking off into the distance, knowing they've already come out.

"Believe me, people can be ruthless, and mean things are said about me every day. Now, their attention will be on you." He turns his head slightly my way and glances at me through his lashes. "It's hard when everywhere you look, people are talking about you. I just want to make sure you're prepared."

I want to let out a nervous laugh but bite it back. After today, I know exactly what that feels like.

I take a second, searching for Cailin. A group of moms who arrived just a few minutes ago are now gathering their kids to leave. I notice the glares we're getting from a few of them over their shoulders.

I see one mom yanking her daughter away from Cailin, saying they have to go even though that child is whining, saying they just got there.

My vision goes to Adam's, wondering if he's seeing what I am. He doesn't look my way, but when his eyes close and his head drops, it's all the conformation I need. He saw it, too. They're leaving because of him.

The stupidity of people makes my blood boil. I place my hand in his, showing him I'm here and not going anywhere.

There's no doubt in my mind that both of them are worth it.

I wrap my other hand around his arm, pulling myself even closer to him and leaning in to softly kiss him before whispering, "I can take it."

He moves his lips to touch mine again, and we hold it there for a few seconds, enjoying the feel of each other.

Chapter 17

Sarah

As I walk up to my classroom, Ashley's mom is waiting for me. "Good morning, Mrs. Everson. How was your weekend?" I smile as I unlock the door.

"Can I have a word with you?" Her expression is one that says I'm about to get an earful, but I'm not sure why. Her daughter is one of my better students.

"Sure," I respond, trying to stay positive as I swing open the door. "Come on in."

She steps in front of me and makes her way to my desk where she sets down her purse with a little more force than necessary.

"What can I help you with?" I ask.

If my mom taught me anything about how to deal with parents, it's to keep calm, no matter how absurd they can be. And believe me, they can be absurd on *so* many levels.

"I'm not comfortable with you being my daughter's teacher anymore. So, I am removing her from your class. I wanted to make sure you knew exactly why."

Whoa, is she serious right now?

I step up to my desk and see the way her jaw is locked and her fists are clamped together. She's being very serious.

I know this has to do with Adam, but against my better judgment,

Our SONG

I ask, "Is there a problem? Did I do something wrong?"

A smug, mean-girl look crosses her face, making me slightly step back. Her eyes narrow as she reaches into her purse and grabs a tabloid magazine, holding it out to me. "Do I really need to explain more?" she spits out.

I grab the magazine that shows Adam, Cailin, and me at the zoo together. I flip through the pages, thinking they dug into my past and found nothing but lies that cover over the spreads, yet I find nothing. Only innocent, wholesome pictures of us spending the day at the zoo.

I glance up as I hand it back. "I'm sorry. I don't see what you mean."

"Are you dating this drug-infused, crazy madman?"

I have to stop myself from laughing out loud. "Did you really just refer to him as a drug-infused, crazy madman?"

She places her hands on her hips and quirks her head as she sneers, "Well, he is."

"Really? Says who?"

Her eyes roll back, and my blood begins to boil.

"Says everyone. The man is an out-of-control disgrace, and I don't want my child anywhere around that."

"You do realize he is Cailin's father, right?"

"God, that poor girl. I doubt he's had anything to do with her life. That's the real reason he kept her a secret—because she was basically a secret to him too. I can only imagine how she's being raised without a stable parent. Someone should be calling child protective services instead of being all infatuated with the two of you."

My chest pounds, and I have to take a deep breath before I truly give this parent a reason to remove her daughter from my class. I'm a very nonconfrontational person, but this woman is about to push me over the edge.

I stand up straighter to make sure she knows I mean business. "You don't know what you're talking about. How would you feel if someone assumed things about you that weren't true?"

"But they *are* true. I can show you news story after news story to prove it. The man's a menace, and he shouldn't be allowed on school grounds. His songs are not appropriate, and don't even get me started on his attire."

She shakes as if she's disgusted, and I want to slap the smug look off her face.

Instead, I stop and inhale a deep breath. The nerve of this woman. This is what Adam was talking about last night. I've experienced one side of the industry, but I never imagined how this side would be. Haters do come in all shapes and forms, and seeing this woman stand in my classroom makes me cringe for humanity even more.

Her phone rings, making my eyes open wide in shock at her choice of songs for her ringtone. The song "I Don't Mind" by Usher sings out as her ring tone. The irony is both humbling and sickening with the song lyrics referencing that just because she dances on a pole doesn't mean she's a ho.

She reaches into her purse and silences the phone before turning back to me, completely unfazed at what just transpired.

"Mrs. Everson, can I ask you a question?" I nonchalantly lean back on one of the desks.

She eyes me. "What?" she asks nastily.

"Are you a stripper for a living?"

She looks appalled, and I have to bite my lip to hide the smile I want so bad to spread across my face, knowing I hit my target.

"Are you against the dancing profession? I mean, you wouldn't want your daughter to become a stripper, would you?"

"I am disgusted you would talk about my daughter and even suggest her becoming an exotic dancer one day." She grabs her purse and flings it over her back. "I will have your job. I'm going straight to the principal, to the school board if I have to. You're finished."

I nod slowly, letting her think she's got me. Once she gets to the door, I stop her. "You know, for someone who is so quick to judge who a person is by the way they act or are portrayed, maybe you should look at yourself and the ways *you* are influencing your daughter."

She spins with her lip turned up, just dying to bury me. "What are you talking about?"

I stand and stroll toward her. "You came in here, assuming just because Adam Jacobson portrays a certain image to his fans that he's not fit to be a dad. But I can tell you from firsthand experience that he is one of the best dads I've ever met, and Cailin is lucky to have him. His music has meaning. Have you ever actually listened to his songs? He talks about hardships and overcoming them to be a stronger person."

"What are you babbling about? You're only trying to save his ass because my next call is to child services."

"So, you can truly stand there and say he's not fit to be a dad? What if I said that about you solely based on your ringtone there?"

She tilts her head and steps closer to me. "Seriously? My ringtone?"

A small grin forms on my lips. "Yes, your ringtone that teaches your daughter it's okay to be a stripper. What does he say? *Go make that money*? Now tell me, what kind of message is that teaching your daughter?"

"Oh come on, it's just a song, don't be ridiculous." She shakes her head, trying to blow me off.

"How is that fair? You came in here, saying the same kind of things about Adam without knowing one bit about the person he actually is."

Her eyes narrow. I know she's trying to find something to say but falling short.

I purse my lips and nod my head as I talk down to her. "I'll tell you what. You go *actually* listen to his lyrics and come back to me when you find something that's degrading to women or involves sex or drinking, and then we can talk. Just because popular music glorifies partying and sex, it doesn't make it right. Devil's Breed might have a harsh approach, but their music helps heal people. You might actually find some happiness through their songs, so you don't have to come in here, making unfounded claims against him as a person and a father."

Mrs. Everson swings around and yanks open the door with sheer force and storms out. At this point, I hope she does go to Principal McAllister because I got her so worked up that she'll make a fool of herself.

Once I'm alone, I inhale deeply, loving the rush pushing through my veins. I've never stood up to anyone like that. It feels amazing to actually say what I feel and fight for what I want.

I've had conversations where, for days after, I go over every word said in my head, thinking about all the things I wish I'd said, but never once have I actually said it. There was no stopping me though.

If anyone deserves to have someone fight for him, it's Adam, especially when it comes to him being a father. I've totally fallen for him because of the man he is, not because of who he is in this world.

More people need to see that man.

Chapter 18

Adam

"How was your day, Miss Russo?" I ask as I reach for her hand and place a kiss on her cheek when I arrive at her place to pick up Cailin from school. I love that I get to see her every day before and after school like this.

Her head tilts to the side, giving me the cutest grin. "It was good. How about you?"

I rub my thumb over her hand that's still in mine. "Better now. I was hoping you'd come shopping with us tonight to pick up a costume for Halloween. Cailin wants to be Cinderella. Sounds like she has another idol to look up to."

Her expression as she glances over to Cailin is priceless. I know I've just met this woman, but knowing my daughter loves her only makes me fall harder.

"Are you saying you're her first idol?" she teases.

"I'm her dad. Fuck yes, I'm her idol. I'm the man she's going to judge every man against for the rest of her life."

Her eyes narrow. "Oh, really?"

"Yes, really. I set the bar pretty high too." I move closer, bringing her body into mine. *Goddamn, she feels fucking good.* "So, you'll come?"

She grins. "Yeah, I can come."

"Good. Then, dinner at my place too." I leave her side before I have to adjust myself. "Ready, Cai?"

She pops up from the puzzle she's doing on the coffee table. "Are you coming shopping with us, Miss Russo?"

"Sure am, sweetie. I'll see you soon, okay?"

Cailin runs over, wrapping her arms around Sarah to give her a hug. When she's back standing next to me, I wink my good-bye.

"See you in a few, Sarah."

I love the way her face flushes when I say her name. *I can only imagine what that might look like when she's under me.*

I force myself to leave before I do something very inappropriate.

We arrive at the Halloween store with my ball cap pulled low over my brow. Word's obviously out that I live in town now, and people stare as we walk by. Thankfully, it's a small town that's off the beaten path, so the paparazzi isn't as bad as it would be in a big city, but there are still people who break out their phones to take pics as we walk by.

Cailin runs toward the kids section and searches for her costume. "What size am I, Daddy?" she asks as she picks up a Cinderella dress.

I take it and hold it up to her body. "That looks about right."

Sarah laughs as she steps toward the rack. "That's a large. She's definitely a small." She grabs a small one and holds it up to Cailin, proving I'm wrong.

"See, that's why we needed you to come with us." I smirk, and she shakes her head in a chuckle.

"Come on. They have a dressing room back here. We can try it on to make sure." She leads Cailin toward the back where she gets her set up. "When you're finished, just come out to show us. We'll be right outside."

I place my arm around Sarah's shoulders from behind when she joins me, and I love the way she leans against my chest, like it's something she's done a hundred times.

When Cailin comes out, my heart stops at the precious blue dress that falls down to her ankles.

How is that my little girl?

The costume makes her look like more than a made-up princess. She's my princess.

She turns to Sarah, who finishes buttoning her up.

"You look gorgeous," Sarah says as Cailin twirls around to show off the outfit.

"Will you help me with my hair?" Cailin asks as she attempts to pull her hair off her shoulders and place it on top of her head.

"Sure, we can do that."

"Will you have your hair up too?" Cailin asks.

I see the hesitation flash across Sarah's face as her body stiffens. She tries to recover, but when she glances my direction, it makes me wonder even more why she would react that way over a question about hair.

"We'll let you be the true Cinderella on Halloween. If I wore my hair up too, no one would be able to tell us apart," she says as she places a crown on her head.

Cailin giggles as she turns to view herself in the mirror. When Sarah stands up straight and heads back to me, I can sense that something's different with her. An uneasy feeling touches me from the inside.

I wrap my arm around her shoulders, bringing back to our same position as before, and whisper into her ear when I pull her into me again, "Everything okay?"

She nods as she inhales a shaky breath. I know it's a lie, but I let it go for now, hoping she'll open up to me soon if something is bothering her.

"My gloves!" Cailin yells as she turns around.

Sarah pulls away from me again, all too eager to help Cailin with her costume accessories.

I try to ignore the voices telling me something's wrong and place my focus back on my daughter, who holds out her hands to me once they are donned in long white gloves. I take them and swing her around before placing one hand out to dance like they do in the movies.

Cailin steps on my feet, and we take a few turns, causing a bit of a spectacle before I place her back on the storeroom floor and tell her to go get changed.

Sarah's face is covered in a smile, but I can tell it's not as genuine as it normally is. Whatever just went through her mind is big, and I need to figure out what it was.

Chapter 19

Sarah

Today is the first day I haven't seen Adam. Even if we don't hang out, we see each other when he drops and picks up Cailin every day for school. Now that it's Saturday, I realize just how nice those opportune meetings are. We haven't had to plan anything or had those awkward moments of calling each other. It's been natural since we're already together.

Now, I've spent all day wanting to call him, see what they're doing, and I'm noticing just how bad I have it for the guy.

I busied myself with home chores, cleaning my kitchen and bathrooms, and then going grocery shopping. I noticed the few glances I got as I walked by, which only made me think of him more.

My sister asked if I could help her with Emma, and I jumped at the chance to hang out with my niece, who I hadn't seen as much of lately. We went to the park, and I hoped Adam would show up the entire time.

It's pathetic, I know.

I should have called him, but since we'd been seeing so much of each other and it'd only been a few weeks, I decided I could wait until Monday and go about my life.

I just finished dinner and am curled up on my couch, deciding to

Our SONG

read the book I started over a month ago and have neglected since I started hanging out with Adam.

I start to doze off when my phone dings with a text message.

Are you busy?

My tiredness fades quickly as adrenaline takes its place just from seeing his name. Man, I do have it bad.

I laugh at myself as I text back.

I was just reading. What are you doing?

Standing outside your place.

I jump off my couch and run to the window to see his truck parked. I can't fight the grin plastered on my face as I type back.

Do you want to come up?

Come for a drive with me.

I glance down at my outfit—leggings and an oversize sweatshirt.

Let me change. I'm in my cozies. I'll be right out.

Don't change. We're just going for a drive. You'll only see me, and I'd love to see what you have on.

I bring my hand to my lips, thinking about his words and checking out my outfit one more time. The leggings show off my legs, and I'm comfortable, which is what he's making me when we're together. I smile as I stand up and text back before I grab my shoes.

Be right out.

When I approach his truck, he's standing by the passenger side, waiting for me. His hand reaches out to grab mine, and he pulls me in for a quick kiss.

"Thanks for coming out," he says as he helps me into his truck. When he hops in on his side, I ask, "How was your day?"

He shrugs. "I had to go help put everything in storage and figure out what we needed to keep and what we could get rid of from the tour. Linda is watching Cailin, so since she's staying the night with her, I thought I'd take advantage and come see you." He grins in my direction, and my heart flutters. "How about you?"

"Nothing big. Just did some chores and got to see my niece for a little while. Where are we driving to?"

His eyes turn to me, and he shrugs. "No clue. I just didn't trust myself in your apartment, alone."

A sharp laugh escapes my mouth, and I cover it, trying to hide my reaction.

He chuckles under his breath. "Just being honest." His hand reaches out to grab mine as he winks at me before turning his attention back to the road. "You grew up here. Where can we go? Is there a lookout maybe? A place where people go to make out?"

I laugh out loud again. "I thought you didn't trust yourself to be alone with me?"

"Oh, don't you worry. There's no way I'm fucking you for the first time in the back of a truck. A bed, on the other hand …"

The way he said *fucking* and left his statement hanging there for my imagination to fill in the blanks flames my desire past a bright red stage and straight to blue, the most intense a fire can be.

His thumb rubs mine, sending tingles up my arm. I close my legs to try to ease the ache and love when his lips tilt the slightest amount.

Once I can breathe without gasping for air, I say, "I know where we can go."

I give him directions up the side of a canyon. I've actually never been there at night, but I can only imagine the view of the lights below us. I direct him to the country and turn when we hit Mix Canyon Road.

The street is void of any streetlights and crowded in darkness from the large trees that block the moonlight. A few houses come into view when we turn the dark corners as we climb up the hill.

After we make it to the top, I point to where to park, and he turns the engine off, killing the lights at the same time. Up here, the trees are sparse, and the moonlight beams brightly above us.

Our SONG

His hand grips mine, and the electricity in the air gets so thick, I can barely breathe. We've never been this alone, and if he's thinking anything like I am, we're in trouble.

The sparks are starting to ignite as my body temperature rises. My breath hitches as his eyes bore into mine.

I turn to him, bringing my knee up so I can face him more. "So, tell me something, something I don't know yet," I say, trying to break the buzz around us.

The chuckle that escapes his mouth makes my chest tighten. He's so gorgeous. I haven't been able to ogle him this way, and I'm not trying to hide that I'm checking him out in every way right now.

"What, like a truth or dare?" He raises his eyebrows in a seductive question.

I playfully slap his arm, and he grabs my hand, holding it there.

"No, more like get to know some secrets about you."

"Secrets can ruin moods. How about something lighter?"

My own secrets come to mind, and I can't agree more. "Okay, good point. What's your guilty pleasure?"

"Besides daydreaming about what you'd feel like underneath me?" My breathing stops completely, and he smirks, continuing so I can recover. "I'm a sucker for sweets."

"Sweets, huh? What kind?"

"Chocolate, ice cream, whipped cream." His eyes blaze into mine, and all I can envision is him licking said whipped cream off my body.

I reposition myself in the seat to ease the sudden ache, and he grips my hand tighter.

"What about you? What's your favorite thing to do?"

Besides think about you? I try to hide the flush creeping up my face by glancing down.

"What just went through your head?"

I look up to him too quickly. "Nothing. Why?"

He reaches his hand out to touch my cheek. "Your face is telling a different story."

I lean into him, and he leaves it there, our eyes locked on each other.

"What is it saying?" I whisper.

I watch his chest move up and down as his vision bounces back and forth from my lips back to my eyes. The pause in his answer is building so much electricity in the air that I feel like a match would ignite us to flames.

"How about we check out this view?" he says. He sighs and opens his door before I can say anything.

I take a minute to gather my wits before I step out of the truck. He's leaning against the front, one foot resting up on the bumper, staring off in the distance.

Lights flicker from the city below us as we sit in silence, taking it all in.

He pulls me close to him, my back to his front, and wraps his arm around my shoulders. The sigh he releases is full of content, and my entire body reacts the same way.

Being in his arms makes me feel so free, so protected, as pure elation floats through me whenever he's near.

His breath tickles my ear, and I lean further back into him, rubbing my hands down his thighs.

"I'm trying to be a good boy here, Sarah. It's getting hard though."

I laugh at his choice of words. "See, you're just as dirty as I am."

He kisses my neck, causing chills to run through me. "I can't get you out of my mind," he says barely above a whisper.

I lean my head back, slightly turning it, giving him more access to explore my body. My fingers interlace with his as I say, "Feeling's mutual. I had to stop myself multiple times from calling you today."

"Why didn't you?" he asks as he holds me closer against him.

I bite my inner lip, trying not to sigh when I feel him push his cock up against my back. His spicy smell washes over me, and I have to inhale to calm the lust racing through me.

He's barely touching me, and we're sitting in the wide open, yet I've never been so turned on, so needy for a man's touch, as I am right now. I try to breathe to bring my focus back to him and not the urgency racing through me.

"I wasn't sure if you were busy. I didn't want to bother you," I say as I lift my arm behind me and run my fingers through his hair.

He flips me around to face him. "You'll never be a bother to me."

Our eyes meet, and in the moonlight, his normally crystal blues darken as his gaze drops to my lips and then back to my eyes.

"I don't know how long I can be good for," he says, licking his lips.

Our SONG

"I'm sick of being good," I say without any hesitation.

The growl that escapes his mouth shoots right to my core as he yanks me to him, kissing me with pure abandon, throwing out everything holding us back as we both completely forget where we are.

My want goes directly to need as I rub my hands up his back. He reaches under my sweatshirt, dancing around my skin, leaving a path of heat every place he touches.

He stops himself, placing his forehead to mine.

Why did he stop? Please, for the love of God, don't stop.

My heart is pounding out of control. I feel like I've taken my first hit of drugs, and I'm addicted—addicted so bad that I might not be able to breathe if I don't get more.

"I'm sorry," he says after taking a deep breath.

He might be sorry, but I'm not. This is what I want. Every single part of him, and I'll be damned if he doesn't fuck me right now, bed or not—a truck will work just fine.

I interlace my fingers with his, pulling him to the passenger side. Our eyes stay locked on one another, his expression stoic.

I open the door and slide into the seat, gripping his shirt and pulling him into me. I go straight for his lips, making sure he knows exactly what I want and not holding back one bit.

His hands wrap around my head, holding me steady as he explores my mouth. Every swipe of his tongue fuels my desire, and every exhale I feel against my skin makes me want to have him inside of me.

I wrap my legs around his waist, yanking him in, grinding into him, loving the friction it's inducing. His labored breaths only fuel me more. He might want to go slow, but I want this man so bad right now, and I need to show him, so he has no doubts.

I reach under his shirt, running my hands up his bare back, feeling his soft skin and lines of other tattoos I haven't seen. I move his shirt up higher and remove it completely, taking in the man of my dreams, who is staring back at me with so much lust in his eyes that I almost come undone completely.

I lift my own shirt, doing a slow striptease for him, keeping my eyes glued to his. When he licks his lips, my chest tightens in anticipation for this man—this gorgeous man that I want to give my entire body to. I want him to show me exactly what he's feeling, thinking, dying to do to me.

He crashes into me, pushing me further into the truck and down to the seat. After climbing on top of me, his fingers make their way up my body, exploring my curves, feeling my breasts. When he pulls my bra down and wraps his lips around my nipple, my lower back instantly lifts off the seat, pushing harder against him.

He moves to my mouth when bright lights break our trance, pulling our attention to the police car parking behind his truck. He grabs his shirt, slipping it over his head and placing his feet on the dirt road.

I take a deep breath while I put my sweatshirt on, making sure my outfit is lying flat and doesn't look like I was just being mauled.

Adam stands up straight and steps toward the officer, who I see exiting his car from the back window. "Can we help you, Officer?" Adam asks.

"Stay right there," he demands, shining his flashlight on Adam.

"Are we doing anything wrong?" Adam says, standing still.

"A thug like you? I can only imagine. You know your kind isn't welcome in our town," the officer spits out.

"My kind?" Adam says in disbelief.

I exit the truck, but Adam reaches out his hand, keeping me behind him, protecting me.

"I don't know who you have behind you there, but she's not welcome either. Now, pack up whatever drinks or drugs you guys have and get out of here."

"Excuse me? Are we on private property or something?"

"As I already stated, your kind isn't welcome here. Go back to the city or wherever you came from. We don't allow riffraff like you here."

Adam tenses, and I feel his hand turn to a fist against me. "How am I riffraff? We've done nothing wrong here. You can't just come and harass us like this."

The cop steps closer. "I've asked you nicely to leave. If you'd rather me force you to leave, we can make that happen."

"Force me?" Adam stands taller, not backing down.

The cop reaches out to grab Adam, but he yanks out of his grasp. "Don't you dare touch me," he growls.

The guy gets in Adam's face, and I jump in between the two of them.

Our SONG

"Stop. Just stop. There's no reason for this to escalate like this. Officer, it's okay. We weren't doing anything."

"Sarah?" the officer asks in disbelief.

I turn to get a closer look and recognize who he is instantly. "Yes, Officer Kelly. It's me. Now, can I ask what's going on here?"

He glares over my shoulder at Adam. "I should ask you the same thing. What are you doing out here with this trash?"

"Trash?" Adam asks in shock.

I place my hand on Adam's chest, trying to calm him down. "Officer Kelly, I'd like to introduce you to Adam Jacobson, the owner of the Pleasants Valley property and my friend."

I watch as his jaw twitches. I left out who he is, knowing when I mentioned the Pleasants Valley property, all would click into place.

His eyes flick from me to Adam and back to me. "Does your father know you're out here?"

My chest tightens, but I try not to back down. If I do, I know he'll go straight to my father, filling him in on my evening before I even wake up tomorrow.

"No, I haven't lived with him in years, and I'm not in the habit of telling him of my every move. I was showing Adam around his new town. His daughter is in my class, and we were just looking out at the view."

His eyes narrow as he takes me in. He purses his lips and shakes his head. "Well, we don't allow people to come out here. We've had some problems with drinking and leaving a mess, and the homeowners have been complaining. So, why don't you guys pack up and head back down the hill?"

Relief floods through me, glad that the situation is ending there. "We will."

I reach behind me, grasping Adam's hand, making sure he's calming down as well and praying he doesn't say anything to ignite another fire. He has every right to with the way he was just verbally attacked, but I hope he knows that some fights aren't worth it.

He grips my hand tighter, letting me know he's okay, and when Officer Kelly leaves to get back in his car, I turn and meet Adam's eyes. The fury is evident as his jaw is still clenched shut, his vision glued to the police car.

I place my hand on his cheek, trying to bring him back to me.

126

"Don't let him bother you. You heard him; there've been problems with teenagers. That's all that was."

He tilts his head, giving me an exasperated expression. I have no doubt that he's not buying my excuse for the way he was just treated. I at least hope he's not too offended by it.

We stand in silence as, through my eyes, I try to apologize to him for the stupidity of other people.

He lets out a sigh and slightly shakes his head. "Come on. Let's get out of here."

Once we're back in the truck, I reach for his hand, and thankfully, he lets me hold it as we make our way back down the hill and to my apartment.

Chapter 20

Adam

Since last night was ruined, I invited Sarah to my house tonight for dinner to try to forget about how frustrating that cop had been. After we eat, Sarah helps me in the kitchen, and when it's Cailin's bedtime, she comes with me to tuck her in and read her a bedtime story.

Having her as part of our routine feels good. Being able to share these precious moments with someone else makes me almost whole again.

As we exit the room, I run my fingers through hers and nod toward the backyard. Fall is definitely in the air, so I set up the firepit before she arrived.

"Hang with me out back? I have stuff to make s'mores."

"S'mores?" She giggles in question. "And you're keeping them from Cailin?"

"She's had plenty. Tonight, it's just us. Let me grab the stuff." I head toward the kitchen, getting what's needed before opening up the sliding glass door.

A breeze comes over us, making Sarah wrap her arms around her body.

"Don't worry; I got us blankets too." I kiss her head and show her the way to the firepit.

After placing the items down, I light the papers I have stuffed between logs to get the fire started. "How do you take your marshmallows? Do you like them burned or just lightly toasted?"

She curls her feet up underneath her while unwrapping the blanket. "I'm not picky."

Once the fire gets going, I take the graham crackers and place pieces of chocolate on top, setting them next to the fire, and then make my way to where she's sitting.

"The trick to a good s'more is to get the chocolate melted first," I say as I motion for her to lean forward, so I can sit behind her and have her cuddle against me.

"Are you a s'mores pro or something?" she teases.

"One of the best. Just wait and see." I wrap my arm around her front, running my fingers down her arm.

"Did you go camping a lot when you were little?"

A hard laugh escapes my lips before I can stop it. "Yeah, that's a no."

She turns slightly to look at me. "Why'd you laugh?"

I pause, remembering the horror that was my childhood and questioning if I should go there.

She takes my silence as my answer. "It's okay. We don't have to talk about it." She cuddles more into my side.

Hearing her say it's okay makes me want to talk about it, to finally open up to someone else.

It's been years since I've been down that road, but I also haven't had a reason to. I don't share anything of my life with anyone but Linda and Cailin.

Linda was there, so I haven't had to tell her anything, and they're things I never want Cailin to hear. Besides Max, the rest of my bandmates only know what they need to know—it was shitty. Period. A lot of my lyrics are built on my past, so either they don't ask or they don't care as long as our success continues as it is now.

I notice the chocolate starting to melt, so I lightly pat her arm, motioning for her to get up so I can start to load the marshmallows on our roasting sticks.

After I have the perfect toast coating each side of the sugary goodness, I place them on the semi-melted chocolate, cover it with another square, and hand one to Sarah.

She takes a bite, and the moan escaping her lips makes my dick stir instantly. I try to ignore it while I take my place back, seated behind her.

"This is amazing," she says as she licks chocolate off her fingers.

When I see a tiny bit of chocolate on her mouth, I lean in to kiss it off, holding it there to enjoy her for a brief moment.

The slight breeze mixed with the crackle of the fire and Sarah in my arms warms my body in a peace I haven't felt in a while. Being on the road is hard, especially since I'm away from Cailin. I've never felt more at home than I do now.

I inhale a deep breath and begin, "Did Linda ever tell you how I know her?"

She takes another bite before she shakes her head. Covering her mouth, she says, "She just said she's a family friend."

I take my own bite of the s'more and love it when Sarah wipes a little bit from my mouth with her finger before sticking it in her mouth with a grin covering her beautiful face.

"I wouldn't say she was a family friend. You'd have to have a family to be considered that."

She stops mid-chew as she takes in what I just said.

I glance to the fire before continuing to say things I've never really said out loud, "Have you ever heard of CASA?"

"Isn't that *house* in Spanish?"

I can't help but chuckle at her confused expression. "Yes, but it's also an acronym. It means Court Appointed Special Advocate."

She covers her mouth to hide the next bite she took while she says, "Court Appointed? Why?"

"When you're in the foster system, they assign you a CASA, and Linda was mine."

My eyes meet hers, and I feel the pain radiating back at me.

"You were in the foster system? For how long?"

I inhale a deep breath before taking a trip down memory lane.

"One night, I walked out of my room in search of food. I just remember being really hungry. It was getting dark, and I'd only had crackers to eat. My mom was either passed out, on drugs, or coming down and itching for her next fix every moment of the day, so I never knew what I was going to get and tried to hide in my room most days. When she saw me, she asked me to curl up with her, so I guessed she was flying high."

I shake my head, letting out a sad chuckle. "Sad to think that the only time she wanted me near her was when she was on drugs."

Sarah reaches her hand out to me, and I willingly take it as I spill my innermost demons.

"At eight years old, I shouldn't have known any of that, but when you're pushed into that world at a young age, you learn about a lot of things, survival being one of them. I knew when to talk to my mom and when to hide under my bed, praying she and whatever guy she had around forgot I existed."

Her eyes boring into me get to be too much, so I lean back, wrapping my arm around her and pulling her back into my side.

"The house was freezing, so I had a blanket wrapped around me, and I crawled up on the couch with her. She squeezed me tightly, and silly me took it in like the air I breathed. I remember being so desperate for her affection."

Sarah hugs my arm against her body, intertwining our fingers. It's the exact interaction I need to continue.

"I asked her for food, and when her lips pursed together, I knew my answer."

Sarah turns to meet my eyes, waiting for what I meant.

"She'd already eaten and spent the rest on whatever she was on." We stare into each other's eyes for a moment before I turn back to the fire.

"She tried to play it off, asking if there was anything in the fridge but she already knew the answer, or maybe she was too gone to remember. The fridge had stopped working a few weeks earlier, and I'd finally thrown everything out due to the smell. When you're hungry, the awful smell only makes your stomach turn even more."

Sarah flinches under me, and when I try to move to give her space, she holds me tighter, making sure I don't go anywhere.

I think back to those days and how miserable I was. I can't imagine Cailin ever having to live through that. No kid should.

I close my eyes, inhaling deeply before I continue, "I hadn't had a real meal since school went on winter break. While at school, I at least got breakfast and lunch. I should have been smart and saved my chips and fruit then, knowing I wouldn't have anything during the break, but I wasn't thinking."

"No kid should have to think about where their next meal is

coming from," Sarah says, leaning her head into me for support.

"It's sad how many kids do." I sigh before continuing, "When I turned back to my mom, she was passed out, so I hopped off the couch. Funny how I still remember how freezing my toes were through the holes in my socks on the cold floor."

"Your memory associates physical feelings of things to help you remember," Sarah says as she starts to play with my fingertips like she's associating physical touch with this moment right now.

"As I made my way through the living room, the front door was kicked in. I remember standing there in shock as a man towered over our entryway. I'd been in some sticky situations, but standing there by myself with my mom passed out was the most terrified I'd ever been."

She curls into my side, her strength wrapping around me like a glove.

"He asked me where she was, and I just screamed and ran to my room to hide under my bed. Thankfully, he didn't follow, but the screams and the sound of my mom's body being flung around was almost worse than if he had. When it got silent, I held my breath, praying whatever had just happened was over and whoever it was would leave. The sound of his footsteps were beyond terrifying. I remember not feeling like I could breathe; my heart was pounding so fast. When he pulled me out from under the bed, I thought I was going to pass out; I was so scared."

Sarah sits up in a rush and turns to face me, placing her hand on my cheek. "Oh, Adam."

My eyes meet hers, and I have to blink away tears I feel forming, which frustrates me even more. That woman doesn't deserve my emotions; they died with her years ago.

I try to push Sarah away, but she doesn't budge. Instead, she gets closer. Making me look her in the eyes.

I lean my head back against the rest as I stare at her.

"I'm so sorry to hear this. I don't care what age you were, you shouldn't have had to go through that."

I bite my inner lip, needing to finish my story and hoping I can make it through.

"He dragged me out of my room and down to the living room. Visions of my mom covered in blood made me want to throw up, so

I covered my mouth, afraid even more of what this man would do if I threw up on him."

I break our line of vision and stare up at the sky. "He dropped me on the ground and leaned down to my level. The smell of cigarettes and BO made me feel even sicker to my stomach. He told me to keep my mouth shut or that he'd be back for me."

"Adam," Sarah says, trying to get me to look at her again.

I pull away, not wanting anyone's pity, instantly going back to the defenses I've put up for years, but her other hand comes up and stops me, forcing me to look at her. We lock eyes, and I'm done for.

This girl can forever do no wrong in my eyes from this moment on.

The strength she's giving me just through her touch affects me to the core. I know Linda cares for me, and my bandmates are like family, but I've never had the voluntarily true care of a woman like the way she's showing me right now.

I allow her to catch me as I fall for her even more. I pause, breathing in this newfound feeling running through me.

She takes me in, running her finger down my face before asking me to continue. "Is that when Linda came into the picture?"

"Not for a few years. It was two days until I was able to get help. We lived in a run-down shack behind some guy's property, and he was gone for Christmas. It wasn't until he got back that I got some help."

My stomach turns at the thought of those days that I've pushed aside for years now.

"He called the police, and I thought everything would be better, but it wasn't. I was tossed from foster home to foster home. I was afraid to speak for years after that. Foster parents got fed up with me either not communicating the way they wanted or storing food in my room just in case it was the last time I got a meal."

Her gasps remind me of just how sad that is. At the time, I was still in survival mode. I'd get picked up and left at a new house with nothing but a garbage bag of the clothes that were either too big or too small.

"Not every kid is assigned a CASA, only the truly troubled ones. I guess I was lucky."

She pulls her leg under her, so she's more comfortable, facing me. I tuck a lock of hair that fell in front of her face behind her ear. When she leans into my touch, I can't help but take in the moment and realize how happy I am to be here with her.

"So, how old were you when you met Linda?"

I think about that time and allow myself to poke at the boy I was. "Thirteen. Man, I was such an ass."

"You had the right to be," she says.

I sigh. "Linda didn't think so. She was the first person to truly take an interest in me."

Her head tilts to the side. "How?"

"By this time, I'd been kicked out of every foster home in the area. The little boy thrown into the system turned into a very pissed off teenager. I still didn't talk much, so people who were in it just for the money were quick to toss me to the curb. I was sick of people coming into my life, only to leave a short time later."

"So, I take it, she stayed," she teases, and I love that she can help make light of this heavy topic.

My body relaxes as I say, "Yeah, she stayed. It took her a while to get through my thick skull, but she never gave up on me."

"She really cares for you and Cailin."

"Yeah, we became her family just as much as she became ours. She was never able to have kids. She was looking to adopt through the foster system when she found out about CASA. She thought she would be needed more there, and damn, was she right."

"Did you move in with her?"

"Nah, it's not like that with a CASA. They're just there to be support. She was able to break down my walls. It took months of her picking me up and taking me places before I even said one word to her." I shake my head in embarrassment as I remember how mean I was to her at first. "I'm lucky she stuck with me."

"How'd she pick you up?"

"Part of the CASA program is, you have to spend time with the kids. Get to know them and show them you're there to fight for them. They attend scheduled court dates and work as the liaison between the courts and the foster system. No matter how much of an ass I was, she'd still show up at every scheduled meeting to take me places. I guess you could say she was the first person to semi-restore my faith in humanity."

She grips my hand. "Adam, wow. And look at what you've become after all you went through. God has been great to you in so many ways."

I try not to flinch at her statement that makes no sense to me whatsoever. Thankfully, the grin that covers her face makes the same one appear on mine even though my mind is saying there's no way in hell what's she's saying is true.

She continues, and I try not to let her thoughts change our mood. "I can see that in Linda. She's so great with Cailin."

I nod. "She is. I don't know what I'd do without her—then and now. She's the one who introduced me to music."

Her eyes widen. "Really?"

"Yep. That's why I took her last name for my stage name. She'd take me to the park and set up a CD player on a picnic table, and we'd listen to an entire CD in silence. I still can't believe she'd sit there for an hour in total peace as we did nothing but take in the music. She'd say the music would heal me eventually, and it did."

"That's so cool."

I inhale a deep breath. "It is. I owe her everything. I didn't want anyone to know about my past. I wanted a fresh start. Even before I started the band, I went by Adam Jacobson, so it's been easy to hide Tyler."

A rush of emotions floods through me again at the memories of how Linda made me who I am today.

"Before then, I knew nothing about music or how lyrics could change so much in someone's life. She was smart in choosing what artist we'd listen to. There was a lot of classical rock 'n' roll. Once I started to show interest, she'd talk to me about the songs and their meaning. Learning about history of the Vietnam War or the death of Buddy Holly through music opened my eyes."

"I couldn't agree more. Music's always been my escape too."

A shit-eating grin covers my face. *How did this seemingly perfect girl come into my life so easily and so fully?* "I knew I liked you for a reason," I tease, hoping I'll get to see the flush rise up her face—and I do.

I reach out, motioning for her to lie back against me. She does, and I wrap my arm around her. I play with her fingers, enjoying the simplicity of the moment. It's rare that I get times like this, just kicking back and relaxing where no one wants anything from me or is expecting anything from me.

"I like this. Just being with you," I whisper, almost to myself more than her.

She leans down toward my lap, turning just enough to look me in the eye.

I can't help myself when I take in a deep breath and lean in to kiss her. Not because I just poured my heart out to her, but because the way her blue eyes feel like they see past all the bullshit and really see me.

Me.

The true Adam. Not who everyone sees or who every woman tries to get with.

Right now, I'm not thinking about anything but how at peace I am, sitting out here, and it's all because of her.

Our lips touch softly as we breathe each other in. I open my mouth to caress hers again, and when I slip my tongue out for a taste, jolts of electricity fly through my spine.

I lift my hand up to her head, running my fingers through her hair and holding her closer to me. When her arm wraps around my head, I pick her up and swing her onto my lap.

She meets my lips again, leaving both hands on either side of my face. I've never had a woman touch me this way. I've never kissed a woman who affected me this way either.

I deepen our movements, not able to get enough. I only get this rush when I'm onstage, but right now, I have nothing on my mind but the way her body feels against mine.

I fucking love it.

The cold air brushes against us, but it does nothing to stop the fire blazing deep within.

My heart pounds as I caress her back and push my hard cock up against her. When she moans into my mouth, it makes what I'm doing snap into my mind.

I promised myself I wouldn't do this. I promised I would take it slow with her, yet here I am, ready to fuck her on this outdoor furniture like she's any other girl I've been with.

Not with her. Not like this.

I slightly pull back, slowing our kisses until I break free and place my forehead to hers. "I wasn't lying when I said we should take this slow. I really don't want to screw this up."

I watch as she mulls over my words. She sits in silence as her breaths roll over my lips. The slight roll to her hips causes a friction that I feel down to my toes, and it says more than any words. She wants this just as bad as I do. I have to bite my tongue to stop myself from following through with every urge rushing through me right now.

Slowly, she rolls off my body, and my dick wants to slap me for her loss. I close my eyes and drop my head back as the pain of my erection fights through my pants.

Her fingers wrap around mine. "Walk me out?"

When I open my lids, I'm greeted by the angel herself, surrounded by the glow of the fire all around her. We lock eyes and stare for a second as the hunger we both feel radiates through our touch.

Once I feel like I can move and not break my cock in half, I stand and wrap my arm around her.

"I don't want you to leave, but I'm not sure I can handle being around you and not doing every little thing I want to do to you right now," I whisper into her head as I kiss the top of it.

I feel the shivers run down her body as goose bumps cover her arms.

A half-laugh escapes me as I urge her forward, knowing if she doesn't leave soon, I won't be able to stop myself.

At her car, she opens the door and pauses to turn to me, keeping the door firmly positioned between the two of us.

Smart girl.

"Thanks for dinner," she says.

I run my finger over her jaw, inhaling a deep breath, nodding while not saying a word. My tongue is tied, and my vision is glued to her lips. I love the way the bottom one is just slightly bigger than the top, and she has this cute freckle on the right side of her top lip.

I brush my finger over the freckle, and she moves her lips to match my motion.

How can a simple touch make me so fucking hard again?

The pain radiating from my zipper makes me look up and into her eyes. "I'll see you tomorrow?" I ask, almost out of desperation.

She leans more into my touch and nods.

Our SONG

"Why don't you just come over after school? I'll plan something for the three of us to do."

"Okay," she whispers, making it even harder to say good-bye.

"Night, Sarah."

I know I shouldn't, but I can't help myself when I lean in for one last kiss.

When I pull back, she says, "Night, Adam," before leaning down and getting into her car.

Pushing it shut physically hurts my soul, but I do and step away, almost thankful so I can get my wits about me. Every emotion running through me right now is new, and I need to take things slow for my sake and hers.

She waves as she drives away, leaving me standing helplessly in my driveway with the biggest fucking hard-on of my life.

Chapter 21

Sarah

When we pull into Adam's driveway, Cailin yells out, "Uncle Max is here!"

Uncle Max?

I park as she jumps out and runs to the door. I hop out and make my way up the stairs. When I hear yelling, I hurry my footing.

Cailin is frozen in the doorway as whom I'm assuming is Max stands with his back to us in the kitchen, obviously not okay. His shirt is half-tucked in and wet with sweat marks. If I'm correct, I see blood covering his knuckles. The way his body is hunched over and swaying as he reaches for something on the table makes me rush to her.

I don't know what's going on, but I know for a fact that this is not a scene Cailin should be around.

"She was my sister." Max picks up a glass and throws it across the room before stumbling to the ground.

Adam storms out of the kitchen, picking Cailin up and escorting us both outside.

"What's going on?" I ask as I try to cover her eyes from seeing anything else.

"He's whacked out of his mind. I've been trying to calm him down, but you guys shouldn't be here."

Our SONG

Adam places her back in my car as tears fall down her face. "It's all right, baby. Everything's going to be fine. Just go with Sarah back to her place, and I'll be there soon, okay?"

She mumbles an okay as her lower lip trembles. He kisses her forehead and closes the door before turning his attention back to me. "I'm so sorry. I haven't seen him get this bad."

"Is that Max from your band?" I ask, jumping when I hear another thing break inside.

Is this something Cailin has seen before? Is this a normal part of his life?

"Yes. I'll handle everything. Please, just get Cailin out of here." His stern face makes my body quake.

I nod, wanting to know more but wanting even more to get her out of here. There are certain adult situations kids should never witness, and that is definitely one of them.

He's quick to head back toward his house, so I get in the car, starting it before she has to witness anything else.

"Why was he acting like that?" Cailin asks through her tears.

"Oh, sweetheart," I say, turning to touch her knee. "I'm not sure, but I know your daddy can handle it, so try not to think about it, okay?"

She nods as she wipes the wetness from her eyes.

"Do you want to get a treat before we go back to my place?"

She nods her head again but keeps it tucked down low to her chest, not saying anything.

"Do you want ice cream or frozen yogurt?"

Her head tilts up, eyes red from crying. "If I get frozen yogurt, can I get toppings, too?" she asks so sweetly that it pulls on my heartstrings even more.

"Yes, sweetie. You can get toppings."

A few hours later, Adam pulls up to my apartment. I kept Cailin busy with some puzzles, but now, we're curled up on my couch, watching *The Little Mermaid*.

I run my hand down her arm. "Here, let me up for a second. I'm going to go outside real quick."

"Is my daddy here?" She perks up.

"Yes, he is. Is it okay if I talk to him alone first?"

She hesitates but then sits back down to continue watching the movie.

"We'll be right back."

I make my way down the stairs and meet Adam right outside his truck. "Is everything okay?"

His eyes tell me the pain he's seen tonight. I place my hand on his cheek as his crystal blues bore into my soul.

"Is Cailin all right?" he asks, motioning up to my place.

"She's fine. I took her for frozen yogurt, and now we're watching a movie."

He holds out his hand to take mine, pulling it into him. "Thank you for taking her. I didn't want her to see that."

His hands are fixated on mine, and I lean down to try to break the spell he's under.

"Where did he go?"

"I finally got him to calm down and pass out. He was on some heavy shit."

I nod slowly, biting my inner lip. *Is his life always like this?*

We sit in silence as he runs his fingers over mine.

"Did Cailin tell you who he was?" he asks after a few minutes.

"She said he's her uncle." I step toward him, trying to give him the courage to speak. "I didn't know you had a brother."

His head tilts back as he lets out a deep breath before meeting my eyes again. "He's her mom's brother."

"Oh ..." I say, as my mind goes blank. I'm not sure how to respond. "Is that how you met him?"

He lets go of my hand, and I feel the instant loss.

"I met them both at the same time. We were all in the foster system together. I always said it was better that he had a sister at least to be with, and he always said that was what made it harder for him, feeling like he had to watch over Michelle just as much as himself."

His hands dig deep into his pockets as he looks around us. I can tell he's uncomfortable with this subject, so I don't want to push him.

"He blames himself for what happened."

His head drops to his chest, and I step closer, placing my hand on his stomach.

Our SONG

"Why? What happened?"

The exhale he releases tells me everything I need to know. She's gone.

"How did it happen?"

His weight shifts back as he leans against the truck. The gap that forms between us is quickly erased when he pulls me into him. I place my head on his chest as his arm wraps around my shoulders.

"It's awful, being in the foster system. She was a year older than him, though you'd never know it. She aged out and was having a hard time, making ends meet. She always suffered with depression, and pills and drinking were what she used to get by. When we formed the band, things took off kind of fast. We were able to book gigs, make a little money. Michelle started hanging out with us more and more, though I don't think it did her any good."

He pauses, and I let him have his moment with memories that are obviously hard to take.

"Instead of keeping her away from drugs, Max was feeding them to her. They thought things were better just because we had money, but money doesn't solve old problems."

"So, what happened?"

"I feel kind of weird, talking about another girl to you."

I laugh and hit his chest. "It's okay. I know you've had sex with this woman. It's kind of obvious," I tease.

He chuckles under his breath. "Well, we were never a couple, but she ended up in my bed probably more times than she should have. On one hand, I feel like I was helping Max. At least if she was with me, we knew where she was."

His hand roams down my back as I feel his shaky words leaving his body. I wrap my arms around him more.

"When she got pregnant, things were pretty bad. She wanted an abortion, but I begged her to keep it. I wanted Cailin more than anything in the entire world. So, I paid her."

"You what?" I ask, making sure I heard that right.

He bows his head. "I paid her to have Cailin. I said I'd set her up for life if she stayed sober, gave me my child, and then walked away."

I glance up, and our eyes meet. I know I should be surprised, but after seeing him with Cailin, I'm not. He was made to be a dad. Knowing he did everything in his power to keep his little girl, the life

God had created, just solidifies my feelings for him more.

"I can't believe she didn't want to be a part of her life at all."

"Not everyone should be a mom. Michelle had a horrible upbringing, and the thought of being a mom scared the shit out of her."

The wind picks up, and I shiver, both from the cold and the harshness of this conversation.

"She took my offer, and from that moment on, she was in rehab and had someone by her side every minute until she gave birth. When Cailin was born, she wouldn't even look at her. I was on tour, but we had Linda step in to help with Cailin and make sure Michelle was okay."

He pauses, and I give him a moment to work through whatever is going on in his head.

"I'll never forgive myself for missing her birth." His voice cracks, so I wrap my arms around him tighter, letting him know it's okay to have these emotions, no matter how tough he is.

"In the end though, it was a blessing I did. Michelle gave my real name on the birth certificate, and no one questioned a thing. We knew she was due around that time, so I was at my last show and able to come back right as they brought her home. I gave her a week to see if she would change her mind, but she was eager to sign over her rights and get the money."

I can't imagine a mom walking away from her own daughter. God knew what he was doing when he gave her to Adam. He knew Adam would protect her from everything, including her mom if he had to.

"So, what did Max say about all of this?"

He sighs. "He wasn't too happy about the entire situation, but he thought getting Michelle clean and making sure she was taken care of would be a good thing."

"Then, what happened?"

"A month after Cailin was born, he found her with a needle in her arm, dead from an overdose."

"Oh my God ..." I cover my mouth, feeling the pain they must have felt. Even though she didn't want anything to do with Cailin, she was still her mother.

"Today is her birthday ..." Adam says, rubbing his eyes. "That's why Max was having a shit fit. He still struggles with the loss. She was his only family."

"So, Cailin knows this?"

"She knows her mom passed away, and Max is her uncle; that's about it. She's too young to know the rest."

I place my head back on his chest, digesting everything.

He rubs his hand through my hair. "I need to get Max help. His addiction is out of control."

"Is he like this a lot?"

"It's getting to be more and more."

"Well, um … I mean, is this …" I pause, having no clue how to ask this, so I just come out and say it, "Is this something I have to worry about with you too? I mean, when you're out on tour?"

He places his hand on my arm. "No. I don't do anything like that."

"You don't? You mean, like, ever?"

"People think just because I'm a rock star, I party heavy, but no, I'm not like Mötley Crüe was in the eighties. Believe me. I'm straight edge."

"Straight what?"

He laughs. "Straight edge. I don't do drugs or alcohol. Never have. I watched what it did to my mom, and that was enough for me."

"Seriously?" I nod in surprise but also appreciation for the way he goes against the grain in every aspect of his life.

He chuckles under his breath. "Why are you so surprised?"

I want to tell him everything I personally know about his rock-star lifestyle but not right now. We've already had a heavy enough conversation, and I don't want to put the focus on me.

I shrug. "I just figured it went with the territory."

"Yeah, I've seen a lot of bands break up due to it too. I learned early on that I don't need it. The music is enough for me. It gives me the high I crave. Last time I felt I needed more in my life, I had Cailin. And now …"

He pauses, and I glance up into his eyes. The moment stands still as he takes me in. His gorgeous blues so full of hope.

His finger touches my cheek. "And, now, I have you."

When his mouth presses to mine, I have to hold on to him, so I don't lose my balance. His lips are so soft, this kiss so meaningful. I feel it. I feel what he's saying, and he shows me with every breath and every motion. He needs me, and I'm starting to believe I need him too.

Chapter 22

Sarah

Adam's been staying close to Max the last few days, so I've offered to pick Cailin up before school and bring her back to his place afterword. As we pull up to the house, I see Max outside on the porch swing. Cailin runs in, eager to play with the new doll set Adam got her.

Adam strolls out, his hat pulled low and his jeans sitting perfectly on his hips. The man can wear anything. I swear, it only takes one glance, and I'm panting with need to be next to him.

I make my way up the steps, and he leans down to kiss me hello. Funny how that simple act can send jolts of pure happiness through my entire body.

"How's he doing?" I ask, placing my hand on his chest.

"It's been a rough day. I think he needs to go into a treatment center, but he's not interested."

"What do the other guys say?"

We've only briefly talked about his other bandmates, and I have no clue where they all stand on this issue.

"You'll find out tonight. Everyone's coming over."

"Here?" I ask, nerves jumping through me.

He laughs at my reaction. "Yes, here. They all want to meet you too."

"Oh jeez, what have you told them?"

Our SONG

"Just that I'm falling for a teacher." His lips meet mine again, and I inhale every inch I can before he pulls away. "Come on. You can help me cook."

We prep the meal while Max stays outside. My heart breaks for the guy. He's obviously hurting, both emotionally and physically.

When the doorbell rings, my stomach turns over in knots. I'm nervous to meet the rest of the band. I mean, they *are* Devil's Breed, for goodness' sake! But knowing that I'm meeting him as … *what, Adam's girlfriend? Is that what I am?*

I don't know how they'll react to me. It doesn't seem like he's ever really had a girlfriend.

Will they think I might cause some Yoko Ono–type drama with the band? Should I even be here?

The past few hours, this has been the quagmire swimming around in my head.

Cailin runs to the door, and Adam's quick on her heels.

"You can't just open the door, Cailin, no matter who we're expecting."

It still brings a smile to my face to hear how much of a dad he is.

I dry off my hands on a towel and hang it on the oven handle, inhaling a deep breath before making my way toward the door.

"What up, bro?" I hear one say right before the slapping of two hands connects.

"Hey, glad you guys could make it," Adam says, opening the door wider.

"How's Max doing?" someone else asks.

"He's in the backyard, probably still passed out from the last time I checked. He's okay for now, but it hasn't been too long, so withdrawals haven't set in yet. Come in."

Adam steps back, and two guys walk toward me, their presence engulfing the space, dressed casually in tight jeans, dark T-shirts, and boots.

Noah, the drummer, has a shit-eating grin on his face, and I can see why he's such a lady killer. I've heard stories of this guy and his … let's just call them *ways*. He's not as handsome as Adam, but you can tell he thinks he's God's gift to women with the way he struts, his hair perfectly spiked and his shirt showing off muscular arms and abs.

Jack, the bassist, is more laid-back, and it's obvious, just looking

146

at the two, that he's more into hitting the drugs and alcohol than the women, like Adam mentioned before they arrived. He looks like he's been ridden hard, and it's starting to take a toll on his skin. His clothes show off nothing, and if I'm not mistaken, I see a tiny forming of a beer gut.

"So, this is her," Noah yells, eyeing me up and down. "The girl who finally caught the uncatchable."

A surprised laugh escapes my lips. "Excuse me?"

"He's lucky too. If he were anyone else, I'd steal your ass." He wraps his arms around me in a hug as Adam slaps him on his back.

"Back off, asshole," Adam says.

Noah leans back to spy on him and then winks playfully at me. "This is going to be fun. These two"—he motions to Jack and Max, who's still outside—"only take my leftovers. I've always gotten first pick of the litter. Too bad Adam got to you first."

I eye him up and down. "Don't you worry your sweet little heart there. I wouldn't have wanted you anyway. Have you not seen this man?" I dramatically point to Adam, playing it up for him as he was for me.

Everyone laughs, and Adam leans over to kiss me, right here in front of everyone, including Cailin.

"Yeah, you're definitely mine," he whispers to me before turning to the guys. "Noah here thinks he has a chance with every lady he meets—"

"I don't think. I know." Noah leans in, smirking.

"Oh God, go away." Adam slaps him across the side of his head. "And this is Jack. Guys, this is my girl, Sarah."

"And she's my teacher too!" Cailin is quick to add in with the most excited voice I've ever heard from her.

"Yep, *hot for teacher* fits it perfectly." Noah bites his knuckle before Adam tucks one hand around my waist and hits him in the stomach with the other.

Jack has stayed pretty quiet, and when I glance behind me to see if he's coming, I catch him staring at me. It's not creepy or sexual; it's like he's thinking about something, but when he sees me, he snaps out of it and follow us into the kitchen.

"Man, I almost forgot about your cooking," Noah says as he inhales the spicy aroma of enchiladas. "We need to add a better kitchen to the tour bus next time, so you can cook for us."

Adam huffs. "Fat chance. You're lucky I'm feeding your ass tonight."

Noah turns to Cailin. "I didn't get my hug yet, baby girl." She jumps into his arms. "How are you liking school?"

Cailin beams from ear to ear. "I love it! Miss Russo taught me how to read, and I can write the entire alphabet!" The excitement on her face brightens everyone.

Jack turns to me, his lips pressed in question as his eyes narrow. "Your last name is Russo?"

I nod. "Sure is. She's doing so good in class. She's one of my best students."

Cailin's face lights up, and when I glance to Adam, he's wearing the same expression. These two constantly light up my life with nothing more than a simple smile of joy.

The additional noise must have woken up Max, and the sliding glass door opens. "Not going to say hello, fuckers?" His skin is pale, and his eyes are red.

"No, we weren't. If it's your dumb ass or this hot chick I get to talk to, you know which one I'll pick," Noah teases, faking nonchalance before chuckling and going over to slap his hand. "How's it going, man?"

His head gives a quick nod. "Seen better days. How about you?"

"Same old shit, different day, different pus—"

"Noah," Adam scolds.

Noah glances around, remembering Cailin is in the room. "Pus-shhes to mow. Man, the bushes in my yard really need a good mowing. A hard, firm mowing."

Adam slaps his head again, and I get a feeling this is common between the two of them. Noah just rubs his head, laughing.

The timer on the oven beeps. I grab the oven mitts and remove our food to put on the stovetop.

"Max? Are you up to eating something?" Adam asks.

"Yeah, dish me up some. I'll try to get it down."

I grab the plates, handing them out one by one before I plate some for Cailin on her My Little Pony special set.

We gather around the dining room table. I sit and take in the dynamics of the group. Noah is obviously the friendly, outgoing one while Max and Jack are more laid-back, quiet in their own subtle way.

There's no mention of why everyone is here, and they keep the conversation light while we eat. I'm sure it's for Cailin's sake, but I also notice Max's shoulders loosen as the night goes on.

Stories of the tour and new music get tossed around, and they crack me up with how easygoing they are together. They really are a family of sorts.

"So, tell me how you all met," I say once our meals are finished and we're just hanging out.

Cailin has moved into the living room to play with her dolls again, and just us adults are hanging out in the kitchen.

Adam nods to Max. "Well, you already know Max and I go way back. Noah we've known since our senior year in high school, but unlike us, he had a loving family to go back to when all the shit was ending for the night."

"I just didn't want to go back to them." Noah laughs. "They're all goody-two-shoes types, and I tried like hell to make them sick of my crazy ass."

"Seriously?" I ask.

Noah nods, leaning back while he rubs his hands up his shirt, showing off his stomach. "Yep, I'm the baby of the family. I have a brother who is a fucking insurance salesman now. We literally had the white picket fence and dog to match their perfect lifestyle. I couldn't stand that shit."

His face gives away that he's obviously kidding, and I shake my head at his notions.

"No matter how much I tried to piss them off, they would kill me with their 'love.' " He air quotes. "Can't blame Mom and Dad though. At least they had the money to buy me a drum set when these two poor asses couldn't afford one. That's why they forced me to be the drummer. I could have been our front man." He pauses, standing up straight, trying to act sexy with a nod to his head and rise to his eyebrows.

Adam throws his napkin at him. "Bullshit. That's my job." He turns to Jack. "Then, this guy actually came to us from a Craigslist ad. He's been all over but landed here in Nor Cal to be with us."

"Oh, yeah? Where's all over?" I ask Jack.

He's been fairly quiet through all of this, and I jump at the chance to engage him.

Our SONG

He shrugs. "I did the Austin scene, then New York, and then moved out here after some shady shit went down there in the underground music scene."

My stomach tightens, and my heart stops. Cailin comes running in, taking all focus off what Jack just said.

"Daddy, can I put on a movie?"

Adam scoots back from his chair. "Sure, let me help you."

I let the other guys talk and start cleaning up the kitchen.

Adam comes up behind me, wrapping his arms around my stomach and leaning his chin on my shoulder. "You don't have to do this," he says.

"It's okay. I don't mind. Why don't you guys go outside and I'll finish up in here and get Cailin ready for bed?"

He kisses my cheek. "Thank you."

I smile, my nerves still reeling from Jack's mention of New York. I'm thankful I am alone for the moment to gather myself.

The guys are outside for a while, but I don't mind. After getting Cailin tucked into bed, I question if I should just leave when my phone dings with a text message from Adam.

Please don't leave yet. It won't be much longer.

My heart swells with happiness. He shouldn't be thinking about me right now, but seeing this text selfishly makes my night. I text back.

Okay. Take your time.

I click the television to the Reelz network. Ever since I found the station, it's been my go-to channel. I love watching the true stories of famous people and real-life situations. *Breaking the Band: Fleetwood Mac* is on, and suddenly, it hits me as a weird feeling surrounds me.

For years, I've loved these shows, but now that I know Adam and am in this situation with Max, I see just how invasive these shows are. They take private moments like this and put it out there for the world to know.

I try to imagine what they would say years from now about Devil's Breed, if it'd be good or bad and how honest they would be.

The thought makes me mad. It's no one's business.

I quickly grab the remote, change it to a movie on HBO, and curl up under a blanket, vowing not to watch the show anymore.

150

I awaken when soft lips press against mine, holding me there as two hands wrap around my face. I lean into the kiss, loving the tingles spreading through my body.

"Wake up, sleepyhead," Adam whispers when he pulls back.

I open my eyes to see the most gorgeous man I've ever seen. A grin covers my face. "Hi."

His forehead pushes to mine as I close my eyes again.

"Goddamn, he's whipped," I hear Noah yell.

Adam picks the pillow up that I had on my lap and throws it at him.

Laughter erupts as Noah says, "Good night, Sarah. It was nice to meet you."

Adam stands up, and I glance at the guys. "It was nice to meet you too."

I notice all three of them are by the door, even Max. I look up at Adam, asking him with my expression how everything went.

He nods his head with a small smile on his face. "Do you mind staying here tonight with Cailin? We found a place to take him, and we're heading there now."

I pull the blanket off of me and stand. "Don't worry about Cailin. I can watch her for as long as you need."

He leans in to kiss me again. "Thank you."

I place my hand on his chest. "I'm happy to help. Call me if you need anything." I wave goodbye to the guys as we both walk toward the front door.

Before he leaves, he stops and turns to me, leaning in to whisper, "I never thought the first time you slept in my bed would be without me." He softly kisses me. "Have a good night, Sarah."

"You too."

I close the door, locking it behind me, and take in my surroundings. Everything feels different now.

I'm going to sleep here, alone, in his house. I inhale a deep breath and head upstairs to his room.

It's down the hall from Cailin's, so I peek in to check on her. The sweet little girl is on her side, and her shoulders are bare, so I step into her room and pull the covers over her to make sure she's tucked in.

I make my way to his room and push open the door. It feels almost as if I'm invading his privacy. If he hadn't mentioned sleeping in his bed, I probably would've stayed on the couch.

I like the fact that his king-size bed isn't made, and the shirt he wore yesterday is strewed across the chair in the corner. He's a normal guy, and seeing this drives that home even more.

Atop his dresser are a few pictures of him and Cailin, and the only thing that says I'm in a rock star's room are the gold records he's earned over the years displayed on the walls in the corner, not even as a central focus.

After getting ready for bed and swishing with his mouthwash, I take off my jeans and T-shirt. The urge is too great to not take advantage of his shirt lying there to sleep in, so I grab it, slip it over my head, and instantly feel him with me. His scent engulfs me, filling me with tingles of happiness and need.

Biting back any more urges, I slip under the covers, pull them tightly over me, and try to sleep in a bed I never thought I'd be in, in a million years.

Chapter 23

Adam

I've never been so thankful for having met Sarah as I was last night. I know I could have brought Cailin to Linda, but being able to have her tucked safe into her own bed made what we were doing that much easier and took away any guilt I had for leaving her to be with my band.

The rehab center we took Max to was a few hours away. I love that we all went with him. We're his family, and he needed us tonight.

Walking in my door a little past six in the morning, I'm absolutely exhausted. I check on Cailin first. Curled up tight with her pink blanket, my sweet angel is thankfully still asleep.

I head toward my room, and when I see Sarah fast asleep in my bed, I have to pause before I rush toward her. Every part of my body is screaming to rip the covers off and take her like I've wanted, but if history proves anything, Cailin will be up shortly. The last thing I want is her walking in on me making her teacher scream to the gods.

I quietly toe off my shoes and make my way to the opposite side of the room. After removing my shirt—keeping my jeans on to provide the barrier I need to keep from doing something I shouldn't—I pull back the covers and slide into bed.

My arm reaches around her waist, and she stirs, momentarily frightened until she registers that it's me. Her sleepy smile fills my

Our SONG

heart. When she turns back over, scooting her tight ass next to me and holding my arm firmly against her body, another part of me fills. I take full advantage and press it into her.

I hear a giggle release from her mouth at the same time I hear a little girl not quite tiptoeing.

Just as I predicted.

"Daddy, is it too early, or can I get up?" Cailin says from the hallway.

"It's too early." I hold Sarah tighter, grinding into her one more time. "Go back to bed," I yell over Sarah's shoulder.

"I saw the sun in my room. It can't be *that* early …" Cailin drawls out as she opens my bedroom door. "Then, can I get in bed with you?"

Sarah's body tenses as Cailin comes into view, and I can't help the chuckle escaping my mouth as I hide it in her hair.

"It's occupied already," I say.

"Miss Russo!" Cailin whispers. "No fair. That's my spot."

I hide my laughter again as Sarah sits up.

"Good morning, sweetheart. Actually, your daddy just got home a few minutes ago. I've been here the entire night by myself."

Seeing Sarah squirm while trying to explain why she's in my bed is so cute. Cailin's innocence on the matter plays in my favor—at least for a few more years. I have to save her though.

I sigh and sit up. "She's right. We took Uncle Max to a treatment center, and I just got home a few minutes ago. How'd you sleep?" I rub my eyes while I yawn.

Cailin jumps up on the bed, sitting cross-legged at the end. "I slept great!" she says with the cutest sleepy smile. "What are we doing today?"

Sarah turns to me, placing her hand on my shoulder. "Go ahead and get some sleep. I'll take Cailin downstairs and get some breakfast. I have no plans, so don't worry about us."

"Yay! Breakfast with Miss Russo!" Cailin jumps off the bed and runs toward the door.

I lean over and kiss her on the cheek. "Thank you."

I lie back down but only after sneaking a peek of her getting out of my bed in nothing but my shirt and heading toward my bathroom. Those legs leave nothing to the imagination, and it takes all I have not

154

to grab her and bring her back to bed with me.

When she exits, she turns and catches me checking her out. Her flush face makes my dick even harder as she pulls on her jeans.

To my surprise, instead of walking out of the room, she comes over to me and softly kisses me. I wrap my arms around her waist and pull her onto the bed over me.

Our lips intertwine as I tuck my fingers through her belt loops and pull her down against me more. I want this chick so fucking bad.

She pulls back before I lose control and slips off my bed. "Get some rest," she whispers.

I adjust myself in my pants. "Yeah, that's not happening now."

She giggles as she steps out of my room, leaving me with nothing more than my hand and a memory.

Sarah

Once I'm in the hallway, I fall against the wall, needing a second to catch my breath. I hear Cailin in the kitchen and make my way to her, hoping my face isn't flush and she can't just tell what I was doing with her dad.

"I want cereal," Cailin says when I turn the corner. "Do you want some too, Miss Russo?"

Hearing her say Miss Russo after I exited her dad's bedroom in the morning makes me feel very wrong. I lean down to her level. "You know, if you want, you can call me Sarah when we're outside of school."

Her eyes widen with excitement. "Really?" she asks.

My shoulders bounce with how sweet this little girl is. "Yes, really. Just make sure you stick to Miss Russo in the classroom. You don't want the other kids to start calling me that. Just you, okay?"

"Deal."

She holds her hand out to shake on it. I do before I stand and start searching the cabinets for bowls.

We sit at the breakfast bar, both eating our cereal and mapping out our day.

Our SONG

"Your dad had a long night, so why don't we go to a movie or something?"

Cailin jumps up. "Can we?"

I love how simple things like going to a movie makes kids so happy. "Sure, we can. But it's still early, so how about we finish up our breakfast and watch some cartoons first?"

As we enter the house after I took Cailin to lunch and a movie, I call out for Adam but don't hear anything back in return. We've been texting, so I know he's awake.

I move to the back of the house and see Adam sitting at a piano. It wasn't here when we left, so I wonder where it came from, but when I hear Adam start a song, I pause, not wanting to interrupt as I slowly make our way toward him.

I've always thought he has an amazing voice, and as I listen to him sing with no other instruments or loud stage performance, I'm blown away.

The talent this guy has is nothing short of spectacular.

The slow song he's singing surprises me as I recognize the lyrics of *Turn the Page* by Bob Seger. The classic rock tune is different than Adam's normal hard stuff and shows off the talent of his voice like nothing I've ever heard.

It's obvious the lyrics are meaningful to him. His body moves with the words, and his voice gets a little deeper with certain spots. All of his emotions are pouring out onto the keys, sending chills down my arms.

I lean back against the wall to enjoy the show when Cailin comes up behind me, trying to peek through to see what I'm staring at.

"This is one of my favorites that he sings," she says.

"You know this one?" I whisper, not wanting him to stop.

She nods. "He sings it to me whenever we're playing on the piano."

"It's always been one of my favorites too," I say more to myself than Cailin as I place my head on the wall and take in the man I'm falling head over heels for.

With every key he presses and every dip of his shoulder, my heart feels like it's going to burst with emotions.

To witness the magic of this moment is almost too much, and I close my eyes as I mouth the words along with him, letting every note take over my body as I wrap my arms around my body.

When he sings the last lyrics, "*There I go*," I imagine the sound of the saxophone playing the iconic notes from the song as a huge smile graces my face.

Perfection. Absolute perfection.

Cailin breaks the moment as she pushes past me, asking, "When did the piano arrive?"

Adam turns suddenly, like we surprised him. Our eyes meet, and I inhale, remembering that I need to breathe, his performance moving me so much. Cailin jumps up next to him, and he wraps his arm around her.

"Just a few minutes ago," he responds after he kisses the top of her head.

She places her hands on the keys and practices a song.

The grin that covers Adam's face is adorable as he pats her back and climbs over the seat to greet me. "How was the movie?"

He kisses me hello, and I have to try hard not to melt at his feet after what I just witnessed.

"It was fun. I'm amazed at what I just heard." I point toward the piano. "I wouldn't have pegged you for a Bob Seger fan."

"It's Linda's fault." He grins, and I know that's not meant to be completely honest. "This is one of her favorites. So, when she started teaching me piano, I promised I'd learn it." He shrugs like it's no big deal as he turns his attention back to Cailin.

I grab his hand, making him look back at me. "That's always been one of my favorite songs too." Our eyes meet, and I know there's something more to this story, so I wait to see if he'll continue.

He motions for us to go back to the piano and join Cailin. I stand, placing my elbows on the back of the baby grand.

He rubs his hand down Cailin's hair before meeting my eyes again. "It's funny how the song means so much more now."

"Do you feel like you're *playin' star* sometimes?" I ask, using the lyrics of the song as my motivation.

The song's like a journal entry from the singer living on the road. He doesn't feel like he's any different, yet everywhere he goes, people treat him like he's someone big.

He chuckles under his breath while nodding and slightly raising his brow. "Sometimes."

"I think that's what the song is supposed to mean. He wrote it well into his career, just like you are. It's okay to feel like that, but it's also okay to celebrate your success too."

He inhales deeply as he slowly nods his head, looking down at the keys and playing a few notes as he exhales.

I wonder how much living in this town has brought out a different meaning as well. There's a moment in the song where the singer is being judged by his looks as people glare at him. I've seen the stares as well as people pointing, and the incident with the cop has to still bug him. He acts unfazed, but no matter how much he says it doesn't bother him, deep down, it has to get old.

Something's weighing on his mind, and if we were alone, I would ask him what, but before I can do anything, he perks up and says, "Why don't you guys perform your song you did the other day?"

Cailin jumps up in excitement, clapping her hands together, and I can't help but smile at her enthusiasm.

"Move it, Dad. This is Sarah's spot."

His eyebrows rise to me again as he tilts his head and stands up for me to take his spot. "Sarah, huh?"

"Yeah, you know, after waking up in her house, I figured she could call me Sarah when we're out of school." I wave my hand like it's nothing.

He kisses my forehead and whispers, "I like it."

I take my seat and place my hands on the keys. "Do you want to go over the words, or do you remember them?"

She waves her hand in front of her. "I remember. Let's do this!"

I glance up to see if Adam thought that was just as cute as I thought, and the glimmer in his eye proves he did without any words said.

We start our song, and just like before, she hits every note on cue.

Adam's lip trembles as we finish, and I celebrate by wrapping my arm around her shoulders and bringing her to me.

"Great job, sweetheart."

Adam claps his hands together. "Beautiful. Absolutely beautiful. Both of you."

I grin shyly his way before I stand up to give him his spot back.

"Can we sing it tomorrow again at church?" Cailin asks.

I stumble on my words, remembering the lies I told. "We'd have to learn a new song first. Maybe we can find time to work on a new one since the piano is here. When I'm done with the other things I have going on, I'll see what I can do."

Her bottom lip sticking out guts me. I've gotten to know them both better, and I feel even more horrible for lying. Now, I've created this lie that I have to figure out.

"It's okay." Adam's arm goes around my waist. "We have all the time in the world."

The words weigh heavy on my shoulders.

"What should we plan for dinner?"

I fidget with my hands, biting the inside of my lip. I don't deserve to be here after lying to them like that. "You know what? I actually have to get going."

Adam's eyes narrow, but he doesn't question as I slide out of his hold. I lean in to softly kiss him, begging for forgiveness through my lips.

"Sorry," I whisper.

He tilts his head in question. "About what?"

I glance to Cailin, who's playing away on the keys. I chicken out by saying, "That I can't stay."

"It's okay. I'll walk you out." His hand grips mine as I say goodbye to Cailin, and he follows me to my car.

Once there, he opens the door, standing behind it like he does every time we say good-bye. The stance is starting to make me laugh, as I'm pretty sure he does it to keep the distance between us so we don't devour each other.

"Thank you for everything these past few days." He leans in to kiss me, and I'm thankful the door is there, so I don't jump him right here in the driveway with the way his tongue is working the fire in my body to a raging inferno.

He pulls back, and I lean in, wanting just a little more and kicking myself for already saying I had to go.

"I'll call you tomorrow," he says as he positions his arm on the handle, getting ready to close it.

I slip in and start the car. "Bye, Adam."

He closes the door and waves his goodbye before backing away and heading back to his daughter, where I'd be if I wasn't a big, fat liar.

Chapter 24

Sarah

I'm the biggest piece of shit ever. Lying to Adam again about church broke my heart. I must find a solution to this before I really cause a kink in our relationship. I can't imagine what he'd do if he found out I was lying. *Would he forgive me? Would he understand? Oh God, would he hate me?*

The thought makes me ill, and I stop to take deep breaths, promising I'll figure this out today.

I just wish my father weren't so close-minded. I've stayed here because it's all I know. I tried to live my life outside of his grasp, and look what happened.

At the same time, I can't help but think what's been happening since I've been back. Each day, a part of me is lost. My happiness, my soul is dying here. I've been scared to try again, to put myself out there, but that fear is floating away.

What happened in the past is totally different, and if I can move on, then so can my father. Isn't that the Christian way anyway?

Lumping Adam in that category just because of his looks and career is not fair. I need my dad to see who Adam is—as a man, a father, and a boyfriend.

I stare in the mirror, trying to see if the person I once was is still there. Lately, I've felt that rush, that happiness that I thought I'd never feel again. I've been lost for so long, and being with Adam is finally bringing me back. I don't want to lose that.

All the memories flash through me, and I close my eyes, ridding them from my head and focusing on Adam instead. When I reopen them, I see her. The girl I thought had died years ago. The girl with drive, passion, and a dream.

Adam is giving me her. I won't let my dad or anybody take her again.

I reach in my drawer to pull out the dark lipstick I threw in years ago. I don't want just a portion of me back. I want it all. Damn what anyone says. Just like Adam mentioned, there's always going to be haters.

I swipe the dark rouge across my lips, loving the way it brings out my eyes and plush bottom lip. With a renewed sense on life, I pull my hair up, put on a top where my tattoo shows the slightest bit, put on a little more blush, and lift my chin to the mirror.

Bring it.

At church, a few of the older woman seem caught off guard, but I also get a few compliments from the younger ones. I smile sweetly at them all, trying to prove that it doesn't matter what I choose to look like. I'm the same person on the inside, and I'm ready to let everyone else here meet the real me.

When my father sees me, he's quick to request I walk with him to his office.

"Is there something I need to know about?" he questions, giving me that expression I feared as a little girl. "Why did Officer Kelly tell me he ran into you up on Mix Canyon? Who were you with? And what's with the makeup?"

I stand tall, not willing to back down. "I was with a friend. We weren't doing anything wrong, and once he saw it was me, he backed off."

He places his hands on his desk, leaning forward. "Who's this friend?"

My heart rate spikes, and I inhale a breath, feeling more ready than ever to tell him exactly who he is. "He's—"

"Pastor Russo, we have a visitor who wants to meet you before you start the service," the church secretary says as she walks into the room.

Our SONG

Dad takes a breath and straightens his tie. "I'll be right there." He turns back to me. "This conversation isn't over, young lady."

I turn on my heel and exit his office, more determined than ever to bring *me* back.

I was set to sing another song, but after I greet everyone, I make my way to the stage where the band members are sitting and ask for a song change. It's one I've done many times, but today, it's feeding my soul with the strength I need to get myself back.

When it's my turn to sing, I get up, belting out the words to one of my favorite songs, "Power," feeling every word, every note rip through my body, changing me even more.

There was a time I questioned if I'd get back to her, get back to having my faith fully in God the way I'm putting myself in his hands right at this moment. I'm depending on him, feeling his strength, just as the lyrics suggest.

I've sung many times in this church, in class, and just on my own but not the way I am now. There's a difference between letting the lyrics fall from my lips and actually feeling the song deep down in my soul.

As I sing the last note, applause breaks out, reminding me that I'm here, in front of everyone, and not lost in my own world that I escaped to momentarily. And by their reaction, they noticed it too.

I inhale slowly, taking it all in and breathing out the old Sarah completely.

After making my way to my seat, my mom comes over, wraps her arm around me, and cries into my shoulder. I know she saw it too. From that moment on, I let the tears fall, enjoying the feeling of relief each one gives me.

The rest of the service flew by. I couldn't wait for it to end.

I want to call Adam. I want to be by his side and feel this free in his arms. It's because of him that I'm able to be this way, and I want to share it.

People approach me, saying how amazing my performance was. I take it all in, letting the happiness wash over me.

Once I'm ready to leave, I step outside and see Linda with a puzzled expression on her face. All the glee I was feeling washes away as I search around for sights of either Cailin or Adam nearby.

I approach with caution, having no clue if she's even talked to Adam about me at all, especially when it comes to church. "Hi, Linda."

Her sigh tells me instantly that she knows. "Miss Russo. Sarah. I … I just don't know what's going on, and I've tried very hard to stay out of Adam's personal affairs because, honestly, they are none of my business, but …"

She lets out a long sigh, and my heart breaks in two.

Please don't let her think badly of me.

"I asked Cailin if she wanted to come with me this morning because I actually enjoyed the sermons, and I thought it would be good for her to continue to hear things like that. But they said—"

I place my hand on her arm. "Please, I can explain."

She holds up both of her hands in front of her face in surrender with her eyes turned down to the street. "No, you don't owe me any explanation. As I said, it's none of my business." She looks back at me. "Just please don't string them along. I get the feeling he really likes you. He's had a hard life, and there are not many people he trusts."

My eyes well with tears as she places her hands over mine.

"Just be careful with his heart. Whatever reason you didn't want them here with you is yours, but please don't lie to him. Tell him the truth. Believe me, he'll thank you for it."

I nod as I inhale a shaky breath. "I didn't mean to lie. I promise there's a good reason."

She nods. "And I believe you. Just"—she pauses, glancing around at the people leaving the parking lot—"be honest, okay?"

"I will. I promise."

She wraps her arms around me. "He's an amazing man. Don't let him slip by, you hear me?"

I nod, sniffing and wiping my eyes. She gets in her car, and I slowly make my way to mine.

My father's glare is seen from the front door of the church, but without a second thought, I head straight to Adam's house. His chipper voice at the call box gives me the strength I need. I know he'll understand. I just hope I have the strength to tell him about my past.

Chapter 25

Sarah

To my surprise, Linda is there when I pull into the long driveway. I meet her at the front steps.

"I thought you'd be coming here." She smiles, and I feel the weight lifted just a little. "I'm grabbing Cailin, so you guys can talk."

I whisper, "Thank you," just as Cailin comes running out of the house.

"I'm ready!" she yells, holding her small purse over her shoulder. "Miss Russo! I didn't know you were coming over."

"She surprised us," Adam says as he steps through the front door, dressed in dark jeans and a long-sleeved Henley scrunched up to his elbows.

Cailin's puzzled expression makes me laugh, as she glances between the two of us, not sure who she should hang out with.

"It's okay. Go with Linda. I'll be here when you get back, and we'll play a board game."

"Candy Land?" she asks with excitement beaming from her pores.

"Yes, we'll play Candy Land."

She holds out her hand to shake mine. "You got yourself a deal." We shake one solid shake before she jumps off the rest of the stairs and into Linda's car.

As they drive off, I nod my head toward the swing that's around the back of the house. "Shall we?"

Adam suspiciously eyes me. "Everything okay?"

I wrap my fingers around his. "Actually, it's more than okay. I just need to fill you in on something."

We make our way to the swing and position ourselves side by side as I nuzzle up close to him.

"Do you remember when you asked me if I always wanted to be a teacher?"

He rubs his thumb over my shoulder, leaning down to kiss the top of my head. He feels I need the strength from him right now, and knowing he's here to catch me if I fall helps guide me forward even more.

"Yeah," he whispers.

"Meeting you was bigger to me than just meeting *the* Adam Jacobson." He laughs out loud before I continue, "I moved to New York when I was eighteen. I had a dream."

"What was that?"

I turn slightly to face him. "I wanted to be a singer."

His eyes sparkle. "Everyone says you're an amazing singer. Both Cailin and Linda rave about your voice, and I love what I've heard so far, even if it was a children's religious song."

I inhale a breath and lean back against him. "They've heard me sing gospel, which I like, but I wanted to be a rock singer, like Jen Ledger from Skillet or Hayley Williams from Paramore."

He sits up, shocked. "Shut up! Seriously?"

I cover my eyes. "I told you I listen to rock music. Don't seem so surprised."

He tilts his head and grins at me. "I can see it."

I hit his chest with the back of my hand and curl back into him. "Seeing Diamante making it has been hard and brought back a ton of memories. That should have been me. Though I couldn't have pulled off the blue hair like she is." I try to bring light to our conversation before the bomb I'm about to drop.

"I chose New York because I knew it was big enough that I could try to make a name for myself, and my parents wouldn't catch on because I was there to attend Columbia in their eyes."

"Why would they be against you wanting to sing? They obviously enjoy your voice if you sing at your father's church."

Our SONG

I inhale and slowly let it out, picking up his hand and toying with his fingers. "I lied about having something to do at church."

He stiffens. "Why?"

I rest my head against his shoulder. "It's my father. I'm afraid he won't accept you."

His laughter bellows out from his chest. "Yeah, I'm a dad too, remember? No one will ever come near Cailin. Nope. Over my dead body."

His carelessness over the mater makes me smile. "It's more than that. When I was in New York, I was making a name for myself, booking shows and really starting to see progress. I felt like I was going to make it."

He runs his other fingers over my hair, tucking it behind my ear. "Then, what happened?"

I reposition myself to bring my legs up on the swing. "There was a band that was going head-to-head with me. We were booking the same gigs, and I was getting more attention due to being the female lead. The other group was all guys, and they didn't like me taking the spotlight away from them."

I pause, and he eggs me on, "So, what happened?"

I turn my head to show him the scar that runs up the back of my head. Before this morning, I wouldn't have dared to show anyone this scar, and I wear my hair down to cover it at all times.

He runs his fingers across the deep line in silence as I let him take it in.

"One night, I was walking down Bleecker Street with my guitar player, Tony, and drummer, Donnie, after a gig. All I remember is people screaming around me and being thrown out of the way by Donnie before everything went black."

His arms grip around me tighter as tears start to fall, and I wait until I am composed enough to continue.

"They both died that night."

"Oh, Sarah." He pulls me into his lap, and I go willingly.

"I haven't spoken about that night in years. My best friend, Maggie, is the only person who knows besides my family. I was keeping my singing a secret from everyone back home. I even used a different last name, like you do."

His grin shows me he understands our connection even more now.

166

"The lead singer from the other band tried to run us over. He's in jail for murder now. I couldn't believe someone could have so much hatred for someone else just because they were more successful."

"Is that why you moved back? Gave up on your dreams?"

I nod as I wipe a tear. "My dad was furious with me when he found out what I'd really been up to and why he'd attacked us. He's an old-school pastor and very set in his ways."

I take a deep breath, ready to fill him in on what's really been bothering me. "He calls rock music *devil music* and said it was God's way of getting back at me."

"Are you shitting me?"

I tilt my head down. "I wish I were."

He picks me up and sits me next to him, so I'm looking straight at him. "You can't honestly think that. This is why I hate religion. Making someone feel guilty for their misfortune because some asshole was jealous is just flat-out wrong."

"I didn't want to think the God I love would do this. But I questioned why something like that happened to me all the time." I reach my hand up to his face, feeling his stubble under my palm. "That is, until I met you. I had my faith that God had a plan for me. And look, he brought me you. You've shown me the good in people again. You've shown me the truth that's out there, and it doesn't matter what you listen to or who you want to be in life"—I place my hand on his chest—"it's what's in here that counts more."

He leans in, meeting his lips to mine in a move so loving and soft that I lose my breath. I reach up to place my hands on either side of his face, and his instantly go on my head, holding me there as he intensifies the kiss.

His touch is soothing me, and his lips are healing me. Being able to open up to anyone about this is like breathing a breath of fresh air, and knowing that he not only understands my pain, but also wants to hold me through it means so much to me.

I love this man. I love the person he is, the dad he is, and I love the way he lights my soul on fire. He's everything I thought I'd never have. Him being in the industry I've been running from for years is no coincidence. We were meant for each other, and without Cailin here, I'm ready to show him just how much he means to me.

He stands and leans down, picking me up and taking my body

with him as he walks into the house. I go as easily as possible, making sure he feels no hesitation. I've never wanted anything as bad as I want him right now.

Our breaths intertwine as our tongues dance in perfect rhythm. I never take them from his as he makes his way to his bedroom, kicking the door shut and laying me down on the bed. My heart pounds as he slowly lowers his large frame over mine.

I move my hands to the bottom of his shirt, pulling it up and over his head. His smile meets mine, and I wrap my legs around his waist, wanting to feel his body pressed against me.

His hands repeat my movement and slip my shirt over my head. Our bodies pressed against each other builds a hunger deep within me as I kick off my shoes and reach for his pants.

His smirk could melt my panties right off of me as he places his hand over mine, stopping my movement.

"I don't want to rush this. Cailin will be gone for hours. We have time." He leans down and kisses up my neck as he takes his hand into mine, bringing it above my head.

After bringing my other hand to the top, he motions for me to leave them there as he runs his finger down my face, my neck, and to my cleavage where he swirls his fingers up and down the valleys before pulling the straps of my bra down and engulfing my breast with his palm.

I lift my back off the bed, wanting more of his touch as he pulls my other strap down. When his lips wrap around my taut nipple, a zing of electricity jolts through my body and lands down low.

My legs tighten around him, pulling him right into where I need the pressure. The chuckle that escapes his lips is not lost, but I don't care how greedy I am being right now.

I've never been so turned on in my life, and having to keep my hands above my head is both torture and delicious pleasure. It's almost too much, watching him take his time as he roams my body.

When his mouth finds my other nipple, the same effect ripples through me, and I bring him even tighter to me, rubbing against him, trying to build the friction I so desperately need right now.

I lower my hands, and he's quick to put them back.

"Don't ruin it," he whispers. "You're so fucking hot right now, and I want to cherish this moment."

I drop my head back in pleasure and frustration. I do love this, but my heart is starting to pound so hard that I can feel it right in my pussy that is dying to be touched.

He moves his fingers behind me to unclasp my bra. After he pulls it free, he lowers himself completely on top of me as he loses himself in a kiss so passionate that I can't help but lower my hands and hold him against me.

Feeling the warmth of his skin on mine, him pressing against me, is pure magic. I've never wanted to feel another man the way I want to feel him right now. I want it all—his heat, his heartbeat, and his love that's overflowing onto me.

I whimper when he breaks our kiss and runs down my neck to my chest, belly, and then the button on my jeans. My breath hitches when he runs his lips on my lower stomach as he unbuttons the top one, slowly moving the zipper down afterward.

He shimmies them down my legs, leaving a path of kisses in its wake. After he pulls them off completely, his mouth lands on my mound, and I jump from the jolt of excitement it leaves.

His heat and wetness breathe against my pussy, making me shiver. His chuckle turns me on even more as I run my fingers through his hair, holding them there for a second longer.

I feel his fingers wrap around the sides of my panties, and he slides them down my waist. Once they're pulled from my toes, he pauses and takes me in.

The stare he's boring into me has never given me more confidence than I feel right now as I lie, completely naked, in front of the man of my dreams. His eyes are dark, and his mouth is parted.

I watch as his chest rises and falls. He fists the bulge in his pants, dropping his head back when he gets the slight relief he needs.

My eyes stay glued to his hand as he reaches in his back pocket and pulls a condom from his wallet. One button at a time, he pops his fly free until the last one is open.

His cock lies thick behind the black cotton of his boxer briefs, and I sit up to assist him in removing the remainder of his clothing. When he stands back up after stepping out from his pants, I wrap my hand around his cock while he opens the condom.

I love the softness of his shaft, and I have to lick my lips as I swirl my finger around the tip that's coated with pre-cum.

Our SONG

A moan escapes his mouth, giving me motivation to lean in and lick it off. His eyes close for a moment before he opens them and places his hands on the nape of my neck as he pushes me back while kissing my lips.

He covers himself with one hand while trying to keep his tongue in pace with mine. Once he's ready, he pulls back and places his forehead on mine, making sure I'm ready.

I nod ever so slightly as I place my hands on his back and urge him closer.

Slowly, he pushes himself inside me, enjoying every centimeter without moving his vision from mine.

The emotions of the moment mixed with the beautiful way his body is stretching mine become too much, and I close my eyes, arching my back off the bed as he fills me to the brim.

He pauses, dropping down to softly kiss me before he picks up his rhythm. I can't help the deep moan escaping my lips as I welcome every movement he does to my body.

With each thrust, I take him in more. With each pull back, I instantly miss him. I let him fully own my body as he plays it just like an instrument, bringing me to the cusp of greatness with every chord played.

His arms tightly grip my shoulders as he holds me, sliding in and out with ease.

My toes curl, and my breath hitches, as a feeling I've never experienced starts to build low in my core. I grind against him, chasing an internal orgasm I've never felt before.

He moves his hands to mine, gripping each one in his fingers and pulling them above my head. Losing all control to him only turns me on more and intensifies the sensations that are now pulsing lower and starting to tingle deep inside.

"I feel you, Sarah," he says as he slows down, pausing at each thrust and pushing deeper inside me. "God, you feel so fucking good."

I start to pant uncontrollably as he takes my body to heights I didn't even know existed.

"Let go, baby," he whispers, and it's my complete undoing.

My body goes rigid as my insides clench against him. He pauses his movements while I ride my wave, wrapped around him.

His head falls to my forehead again. "So beautiful," he says before closing his eyes and releasing his own orgasm inside me as he presses his lips to mine.

I take in every grunt that escapes him as my own body relaxes against his. I wrap my arms around him, holding him to me, as we kiss until our bodies are limp and we're fully sated with each other.

Chapter 26

Sarah

I take one more glance at my costume before running to get the door. Adam is bringing Cailin over before school, so I can help with her hair. I want to make sure I don't look silly with something out of place.

I open the door, and Cailin's eyes light up.

"You *are* Cinderella," she says in awe.

I pick her up and twirl her around. "So are you. Let's hurry up and get your hair done, so we can take pictures together."

After placing her down, I turn to Adam, who's wearing a cheesy grin.

"Don't laugh." I point to him.

He leans in, giving me a kiss. "I'd never laugh. You look amazing. I've never had a thing for the Disney princesses, but you might just change my mind."

I eye him as Cailin yanks me toward the bathroom, so we can do her hair.

As I pull it up into a tight bun, she glances at me through the mirror. "My daddy said you're his girlfriend now."

A smile big enough to hurt my cheeks grows on my face. "Did he now? How do you feel about that?"

"I love it! I'm super excited to tell everyone you're gonna get married."

I choke on my breath and cough. "Whoa, um … let's not jump to that yet." I pause, not wanting to confuse her. "I'm not saying I don't want to marry your daddy. There's just a long process to get to that step."

Her tiny lip pushes out in a pout. "Then, can I tell them you're his girlfriend?"

I purse my lips together in thought. I don't want people knowing my personal business, yet with the tabloids, I'm sure people already suspect it, so what's the harm in making it official?

"Sure, sweetheart. You can tell them I'm dating your daddy."

I finish the bun, and she jumps up to celebrate.

"Yay! Okay, let's go take a picture and blow this popsicle stand."

She runs out of the bathroom, and I notice the flush my cheeks have taken. I close my eyes, enjoying the happiness rushing through me.

I'm his girlfriend.

I head toward the living room where Cailin calls me over.

"Here, let's stand right here and take the photo."

Adam holds up the camera as I wrap my arms around her little shoulders, and we take a picture, both dressed up as Cinderella for Halloween.

Cailin runs up to see the photo, and I grab my purse from the counter.

"Everyone ready?" I ask.

"Let's go!" Cailin opens the door and runs toward my car.

"You're welcome to come and watch the parade that starts at nine," I say to Adam.

"Wouldn't miss it." He quickly kisses me before placing his hand on my lower back to usher me out the door.

"She also told me she's going to tell everyone I'm your girlfriend." I grin at him, and he laughs.

"Well, good. I told her you are, so everyone else should know too."

I turn to wrap my arms around his neck, kissing him longer than I should but I can't help myself. My heart is so full right now. It's solely because of him, and I want him to know exactly how happy I am.

"You'd better watch it, or I might have you wear this costume some other time when it's just the two of us. A Disney fantasy is starting to come to mind," he teases.

A hard laugh escapes my lips as I slap his chest and turn back toward my entryway.

Cailin and I make our way into the school. A few people comment on how cute it is that we match, and we even take a photo for the yearbook.

After our morning routine of the pledge and going over the calendar, I have everyone line up to get ready for our Halloween parade where every kid walks around the playground while we invite parents to come out and watch.

When we get to the door, I open it up and am surprised to see my mom.

"Oh, look at how cute you all are!" she says with her hands on her face.

She's volunteered a few times in my class, so all the kids know who she is, and a few of them even run up to give her a hug, including Cailin.

"Did Sa—" She stops and smiles my way. "I mean, Miss Russo tell you that she and my daddy are boyfriend/girlfriend?"

My breath hitches, and my eyes open wide.

"Are they now?" Mom tilts her head toward me as a grin covers her face. "No, I didn't know that."

My mom knows nothing. Not that I've been hanging out with a student's father and definitely not who Adam is.

"She's going to have to fill me in." Mom rubs her hand down Cailin's back. "I see you're happy about that though."

Cailin nods her head over dramatically. "Totally!"

"Okay, everyone, line up. We have to walk in a straight line around the playground. Does everyone understand?" I say toward the class, purposely not looking my mom's way.

The students all nod their response, and we head out the door.

It's no surprise that Mom's on my heel. "You have a boyfriend?" she whispers toward me. "When were you going to tell me? Isn't she the daughter of the rock—"

Of course, Adam approaches me just as my mom stops in her tracks. I'm relieved when he respects the facts that I'm with my class and that other parents are around, and he just lightly touches my hand in hello instead of kissing me like he normally would.

Mom's eyes open wide as she takes him in.

I stand tall and take the plunge. "Adam, I'd like you to meet my mom, Sandra."

Adam's lips turn to a gorgeous smile as he reaches out his hand. "It's an honor to meet you."

To my surprise, my mom covers his hand with her other hand as they shake. "Same here. I noticed something was different with my daughter these last few weeks. Now, I know I have you to thank." I turn to her in surprise, and she nudges my shoulder. "Don't think I didn't notice. I felt like I finally had my daughter back."

Adam turns his expression to me, making my heart flutter.

"Daddy." Cailin comes running up and into his arms.

"Hey there, Sugarplum," he says as they rub noses before putting her down. "Go get back in line with your class."

She waves her goodbye and joins her other classmates.

My happiness halts when my eyes meet with Mrs. Everson's, Ashley's mom. She glares at me and then Adam before flipping her hair and storming off.

I try not to let her ruin my joy, and instead, I turn my smile back to Adam before saying good-bye. Heading back to my class, I guide them the rest of the way for the parade.

My mom stays until the first recess and is quick to get back to the topic of the day. "So, how long have you known Adam?"

I take a deep breath, not sure where she's going with this. "A few weeks," I say as I lean down to pick up some papers on a student's desk.

She stops me by putting her hand on my arm. "Sarah."

I meet her eyes, and I can read them like a book. "Don't say it, Mom."

"I'm not saying anything." She feigns innocence.

"Yeah, but I know what you're thinking. He's a great guy, and I'm really falling for him."

"I wasn't lying when I said I noticed there'd been a change in you."

She sighs as she looks around the room where she practically lived for thirty years. "I know you don't love it here. I didn't realize how unhappy you'd been until these past weeks. I see that shine in your eyes again, and your smile is genuine now. I just worry about you. I want to make sure you're stable enough to go back to that world."

I crumble the piece of paper I was holding and toss it into the trash. "Don't worry. I'm not. He lives here now, remember? Far away from other people in the industry."

I step away, and she reaches out for me.

"That's not what I mean. We just worry about you."

"We or you?"

"You know your father worries just as much."

"Enough to let me live my life and not judge Adam before he even gives him a chance?" Her head drops, and I have my answer. "That's not fair, and you know it."

"Just come clean with him. Talk to him, so he can understand."

"Understand what? That I'm finally happy? That the man of my dreams is saying I'm his girlfriend? This has nothing to do with what he does for a living when it comes to how I feel about him. He's an amazing man and father and shouldn't be judged as anything but."

I head out the door, and am surprised when she allows me. I know she has my back here, telling Adam she noticed how happy I'd been, but when we're around my father, it's a totally different story. She's right about one thing; I need to just come clean and stand up to the man.

Adam picked Cailin up after school, and I told them I'd meet up with them later for trick-or-treating. I didn't tell him why, and thankfully, he didn't ask.

After changing quickly, I pull up to church. Before I can second-guess myself, I head straight to my dad's office.

When I open the door, he glances up. The face that normally smiles sweetly when he sees me is completely gone. A glare in its place makes my stomach turn as he tosses his pencil on the desk and leans back.

"I had a visit from a parent of a student in your class," he says, hiding none of the anger in his voice.

"A parent of mine?" I ask, confused. "Who?"

"Mrs. Everson stopped by to express her concerns about who you're hanging out with and your influence on her daughter."

I want to scream. *The gall of that woman.*

She knew going to my father would be more impactful than going to Principal McAllister. I just don't understand people who want to interfere in someone else's life.

I'm done though. I'm sick of people judging me, judging Adam for no reason other than what they perceive.

I step toward his desk, not backing down. "Did she tell you he's a father of another student?"

"Yes, actually, she did. I'm guessing this is the *friend* you spoke of that you were up with at Mix Canyon too. I looked into it and found out he'd been hiding her for years. What kind of father does that? Poor girl was raised by nannies on the road while I'm sure he was on drugs, too high to actually take care of her."

He pushes me over the edge, and I can't hold back anymore. "No! That's nothing like what happened. You're assuming that, but you know nothing about how much of an amazing father he's been the entire time. He only kept her a secret to protect her."

He pushes back and stands up to face my same stance. "Exactly, Sarah. To protect his daughter from the awful lifestyle he leads. He didn't want what happened to you to happen to her."

I know he meant that as a slap in the face, but I'm over his words and how he uses them to hurt me to get what he wants.

"This is nowhere near the same thing."

"Yes, it is. You just can't see it because you're blinded by the glitz and glamour that's behind him."

Is that really what he thinks this is all about? Being famous? I wanted to touch people with my music. That has nothing to do with glitz and glamour.

"You're being ridiculous. Do you realize his daughter is the same little girl who sang on the stage with me a few weeks ago?"

His eyes waver, but he doesn't change his tone. "I guess she was lucky to have those nannies. At least he was smart enough to hire them to raise her."

Our SONG

This man is so frustrating. Will I ever get him to listen to what I'm saying?

"No, Dad, *he* raised her to be the little girl you saw. The nannies only watched her when he was onstage. Otherwise, he was by her side. He loves her more than anything. How can you judge him like that? Do you not practice what you preach? Matthew 7: *Do not judge, or you too will be judged. For in the same way you judge others, you will be judged, and with the measure you use, it will be measured to you.*"

"Don't use a Bible verse on me! I can judge him because that's who he is. I showed you the article in the paper about the riot they caused. I'm not judging because it's the truth."

I drop my shoulders, pleading with him to actually hear the words I'm saying. "No. If you actually read the entire article, you would have seen that they helped *stop* the riot, finished their entire performance, and then visited the few who had been injured in the hospital."

"Oh, how nice of them. They visited the people they'd injured. So, if David had visited you in the hospital after killing your friends and trying to kill you, it would have made it okay?"

My face drops. "How dare you compare the two things. You know they're two completely different situations."

"That's where you're wrong. They are not. God is looking down on you just as he was looking down on them, guiding them on the path to righteousness."

My blood boils as I clench my teeth and close my eyes. I know whatever I say won't make a difference. He made up his mind before I even walked through the door.

I decide to take the high road. "That's really sad, Dad. That you, a man of God, would not give another human being the chance to prove their worthiness before you toss them to the curb. But what about me? Your daughter. Doesn't my happiness mean anything to you? I've been living the life you wanted me to live, and yet I feel like I'm dying inside. The person I am here is not me. Adam has made me happy. Why don't you want me to live the life I want?"

I turn to leave, and he yells after me, "You tried that, remember? And someone tried to murder you for doing so. You will end this, Sarah. I forbid it."

I stop and stare him right in the eye. "Well then, it's a good thing

I'm not a little girl anymore, and I get to live my life the way I choose. You have no say in the matter."

He holds up his hand. "God is watching you."

"I know. He's watching you too." I exit his church, not sure if I'll ever step foot in it again.

Chapter 27

Sarah

Once I'm able to breathe without fuming, I head to Adam's to take Cailin trick-or-treating.

Cailin comes running out of the house. "Yay! Let's go trick-or-treating!" She gives me a big hug, and it's the final thing I need to get me back to my happy place, away from my dad and his close-mindedness.

Adam steps out of the house to join us on the front porch. "She's been bouncing off the walls, waiting for you." He leans in to kiss me and stops short. "Everything okay?"

I thought I'd be able to hide my emotions, but I guess my puffy eyes gave it away. I smile and lean in to kiss him. "Everything's fine. We can talk later, but don't worry." I place my hand on Cailin's shoulder. "Do you have your bag ready?"

She grabs it from the front step and holds it up high. "Right here! Now, let's go."

She runs toward Adam's truck. We're going to our downtown where they offer a stroll for the kids to get candy from the businesses and show off their costumes to the community.

Adam wraps his arm around my back and pulls me into him. He doesn't say anything, but his touch is soothing and exactly what I need.

After we park, Adam hops out of the car with his hat pulled low. At the zoo in a bigger city, the hat worked well to disguise him, but in this small country town, he sticks out like a sore thumb.

I've heard whispers of people asking if they've seen him yet or wondering if the rumors are true, but there's no stopping the gossip wheel now.

As we head down the block, people gawk as we walk by, and I notice others across the street pulling out their phones to take pictures. A few ask to shake Adam's hand, and more than one gives us dirty looks.

Adam's sole focus is on his daughter and the fact that he's finally able to take her trick-or-treating without hiding behind a costume, so no one knows who he is. His only role in life at this moment is being a father, and he's loving every second.

I'm in awe that he can ignore the comments, looks, and everything that's happening around him.

After we hit up every business in town, we head to a new part of our city where the streets are fully lit, so she can do some real trick-or-treating at people's houses. Adam and I stay back as she approaches each house, ready to show off her gown to the people who open the door.

I love seeing her joy as she runs from house to house with a group of kids we ended up hooking up with. She doesn't know them, but their common quest for candy was all they needed to welcome her into their fun.

I notice one of the parents who attends our church.

"Sarah, is that you?" she says, covering her eyes from the overhead streetlight to see me better.

"Hi, Danielle. Is that Joey in the baseball uniform?"

She smiles with pride. "Sure is. I guess it saves money if he wants to wear his uniform as his costume." She laughs as she shrugs.

"Hey, take it. Costumes can be expensive."

She walks closer, and I pause, feeling weird not introducing her to Adam, but not sure if he wants to be introduced. I don't even know what the protocol is when it comes to someone like him. I know he likes being just Adam Tyler in these situations, but what if she wants to meet Adam Jacobson?

Thankfully, she doesn't even give him a second glance as she puts her hand on my arm. "I just wanted to tell you how amazing your performance was last week at church."

I'm speechless. "Oh, um, well, thank you very much."

"Really, it blew me away. I knew you could sing, but wow, not like that." She turns to Adam and smiles. "She might even put you to shame, rock star."

A harsh laugh escapes my lips for two reasons. I can't believe she just tried to show him up like that, but I also love that she was so nonchalant about who he was, not afraid to say anything and not treating him any differently than a normal person.

"Maybe I'll get her to sing with me sometime," Adam quickly returns.

My body freezes. *He can't be serious. There's no way in hell.*

"Now, that's a show I'd want to see." She turns after her son calls her name. "Bye, you two." She waves, and just as easy as she arrived, she's gone, leaving me stunned.

Adam starts to walk, and it takes me a second to catch up, but when I hear his question, I wish I had stayed behind.

"So, tell me about this song."

I chuckle under my breath. "Oh, it was nothing." I try to blow off the subject.

He pulls me closer to him. "Obviously, she was impressed. How was it different than your other songs?"

I shrug. "Let's just say, it's a newer age song, so the tempo was more her wavelength."

"I'd love to hear you sing it."

Memories of my conversation with my dad come pouring back, making my body tense. I'm thankful when Cailin comes running up with a bag so full that she can hardly carry it.

"Dad, here. I can't even hold this." She lugs it up to him.

"I'd say it's time to go then."

Cailin says goodbye to her newly made friends, and we make our way to his truck.

Once we're at his house and Cailin gets a few pieces of candy, we get her ready for bed and promise to go through the rest of it, so she can attack it in the upcoming days.

After putting her down to bed, Adam stands at the kitchen counter, holding up two pieces of candy. "Kit Kat or Snickers?"

I rummage through the bag. "I'm more of a peanut M&M's kind of gal."

He takes both and opens the Snickers first. "Your loss. I'll have both."

"Should we feel bad for stealing her candy?"

He gives me a deadpan expression. "Seriously? Have you seen the loot she got? We're saving her teeth and a future dental bill. I'll slowly toss it out, and she won't even notice."

I playfully hit his stomach. "You wouldn't."

After popping the last bite of the mini Snickers in his mouth, he says, "Watch me."

I shake my head, laughing under my breath as I pull out the M&M's and pop one in my mouth.

"So, now that you have chocolate, want to talk about what happened today?" He lowers his head to catch my eyes with the most inviting smile I've seen all day.

I can't help the grin that follows even though I don't want to bring back the memories from today.

When I don't say anything, he steps closer and grabs my hands in his. "Please tell me it wasn't because of me. I wondered what would happen after meeting your mom today. Did she tell your dad we're dating?"

I shake my head, still in disbelief. "No, actually, a mom from my class went to him."

His eyes squint in confusion. "What? Why would she do that?"

I drop my shoulders and sigh into the air below me, trying to figure out how to help Adam understand the dynamics of this town. "This mom already came to me, saying she was unhappy about me seeing you."

"And you didn't tell me?" His eyes widen, making me feel guilty for not telling him sooner. "Sarah, why would you keep something like that from me?"

"I thought I had handled it. I didn't want to worry you about me or Cailin at school."

"This is more than just us. This is my daughter's school. Sarah, you can't keep this kind of stuff from me. I need to know what's going on with Cailin and you." His eyebrows rise, and I can tell he's serious.

My stomach feels like it's in my throat. I didn't think he'd get so upset. I also wasn't thinking about Cailin.

"I put her in her place, and she never went to the principal like she threatened. I saw her there today though. She knew how to get me back even worse than going to my boss."

"By going to your dad? What is this, high school?"

I laugh out loud. "Some things never change in small towns. My dad might only be the pastor, but he runs this town. The mayor, the city council members, even the police chief turn to him for guidance. It's like we're stuck in the olden days."

"Then, what did he say?"

"Don't worry about it. I'm an adult. God is watching him just as much as he says he's watching me."

"Sarah." He leans down to meet my eyes, making sure he has my attention. "You can't keep doing this. You have to let me in. I've watched you do this a few times, and I don't like it, especially when it involves my daughter. I'm asking you, what did he say?"

"He said he forbids me from seeing you," I shout louder than I should. I shouldn't take my frustrations out on him, but I'm sick of having to lie and hide to save everyone else's feelings.

He flinches back but narrows his eyes. "He can't be serious."

I stand up, reaching for my purse. "Yes, Adam, he's very serious. You don't understand my father."

He grabs my wrist, keeping me there so I can't run away. "Then, what did you say?"

"I told him he had no say in the matter, and there was nothing he could do to stop me."

He places his hand on my cheek, forcing my eyes to him. "I don't want to come between you and your dad. I'm a dad, remember? I'd die if some guy stole Cailin away from me."

"What am I to do, Adam? He won't even take the time to get to know you."

We stare into each other's eyes. I know he's torn, but this is a completely different situation that he and Cailin would never be in. He needs to understand that. He'll never be like my dad. He's going to want her to follow her dreams, and he'll always listen to her first before jumping to conclusions.

"I'll do right by him. I promise," he says.

I shake my head, sighing. I love his ambition of even wanting to try. It's a hopeless cause, but I don't want to tell him that right now.

Chapter 28

Adam

I'm sitting at the kitchen table, working on lyrics that were so strong in my head that I had to get them down on paper, when a car pulls up to our front gate. I walk to the camera system and smile when I see Jack on his motorcycle out front.

I press the code to let him in and step out onto the front porch to wait his arrival.

"What's up, bro?" We slap hands as he steps up to my house. "How the hell are you?"

"Same old shit, just another day. Wanted to go for a ride, so I thought I'd stop by, see how things are going."

"Cool. Yeah, come on in."

We head toward the kitchen.

"Want something to drink?"

He eyes me. "I know you don't have beer—lame ass—so what do you have?"

I laugh out loud. They always give me shit for not drinking, but I know they're just teasing. "Water, Coke, or a juice box." I playfully hold up the juice box.

"Don't give me that shit." He reaches in and grabs the Coke, and I place the juice box back in the fridge. "Any word on Max?"

"Nah, they said to keep the contact down for a few weeks while

Our SONG

he goes through detox. No news is good news, I guess. They said we can email him, but I haven't checked in yet, wanted to give him some time."

He pulls out the stool at my kitchen counter and picks up the paper I was working on. "What's this? New lyrics?" He reads them over.

"Just an idea I'm playing with."

Ever since I met Sarah, I've been writing slower, more romantic songs. I know they aren't for my band, but I had to get them out anyway. After hearing about the song she sang the other day, ideas have been swarming my brain, and they all include her.

"These have to do with your new girl?"

I eye him. Not because of the way he just said that, but because I can tell he's got something to add, and I wait for him to do so.

"Look, I knew she looked familiar the other day, and I finally put it together."

I stop him as their two stories from the past collide in my head. "New York."

"So, it is her?"

He's never talked about why he left New York. He just said the music scene had some shit go down, and I never cared enough to ask. Now, everything is coming together.

"It is. She just filled me in the other day."

He leans back against the counter. "Fuck. That was some fucked up shit. Glad to hear she's okay. I was good friends with Donnie, the drummer from her band. Honestly, I thought she died too. After the accident, I never heard her name again."

Realization that I never asked her stage name hits me. "She moved back home after the accident and hasn't been in the industry at all ever since."

He grabs his phone from his back pocket, scrolling like he's looking for something. "That's really why I came by. I wasn't sure what to think of it when I put it together. It's kind of an odd coincidence that she's in your life this way—with Cailin and all. In this world, it's hard to make sure people are on the up and up."

I laugh out loud. "Believe me, there's nothing fishy going on with Sarah. If it's an odd coincidence, then that's because it was meant to be. She's been through some crazy shit, and she is still dealing with it.

186

I came unannounced into her life, not the other way around."

He pulls up an article and hands me the phone where a headline turns my stomach.

Two Members of Band Killed, One on Life Support.

I read the article, reading the same accounts of what Sarah shared with me. I see the man who did it and read that Sarah used the last name of Hart. Jack stays quiet as I take in everything my girl went through.

At the end, I inhale a deep breath and hand it back to him. "Sorry you lost your friend."

He sighs and grabs the phone. "He was a decent guy. He and I shared a place for a few months when I first got to New York, before he hooked up with her." He clicks on his phone to something else and hands it back to me. "This was him, on the right."

The picture is of Sarah with guys on either side of her. Her outfit is edgy with short shorts and over-the-knee boots. Her tight top covers enough to make it sexy but not slutty. Her hair was darker then. I like her hair now, but I'm digging the way this looks on her.

Seeing my girl like this gives me an instant hard-on. All day, I've been working on songs to sing with her. Imagining her next to me onstage, looking like this, would be a fucking dream.

"It took me a while to find this shot, but it was driving me nuts. I knew I recognized her from somewhere."

"Did you ever see her perform?"

His eyebrows curve in as he nods. "*Hell yes*, is all I have to say about that. She was something special. She's why I left New York. When I thought someone with her talent died because of a jealous douche bag, I knew I didn't want to be in that scene anymore." He picks up the lyrics I'm working on again. "Is she planning on singing again?"

"If I can get her to."

His eyes open wide. "Seriously?"

"We haven't spoken about it, but you're not the first person to say she has an amazing voice."

"You haven't heard her sing yet?"

My laughter catches him off guard. "I've heard her sing *Jesus Loves Me* with Cailin, but I get the feeling that's a little different than what you've heard."

"Why would she sing that with Cailin?"

"Her dad's a pastor of the local church. She sings there every Sunday. While I was gone, they sang it together."

"No shit? She's a churchgoing girl?"

I sigh. "Yep, but I guess her dad has some issues with her seeing me."

"Ha! If he only knew how straight your ass really was. Are you going to set him straight?"

I stand tall. "If he'll let me. First things first though. Help me with these lyrics."

Jack and I are so lost in polishing the song that we completely lose track of time until Cailin comes running in the house.

"Daddy, Daddy, Daddy. I got invited to a birthday party in a few weeks. Can I go? Pleeeaasssse?" She places her hands under her chin in a begging form that I'm such a sucker for.

"You're so screwed with that one." Jack chuckles under his breath as he slaps my shoulder with the back of his hand before he sits up to get another drink.

When Sarah enters the house behind her, I raise my eyebrows in question of this invitation, and she nods her approval.

"Okay. I'll have to meet her parents and make sure it's okay if one of us hangs out the entire party, but if Sarah says it's okay, then you can go."

"Yes!" Cailin jumps up, throwing her fist in the air. "Thanks, Sarah!" She runs to give her a hug.

I stand to get my hug next. "How was your day, dear?" I tease, making her laugh as I kiss her lips.

When we turn the corner to the kitchen, Sarah is surprised to see Jack standing there. "Oh, sorry. I didn't mean to interrupt. What are you guys working on?" She points to papers spread all over the table.

"It's for you actually," I say, gauging her response.

"For me?" She picks up a sheet, reading, "*Hear me now.*"

"Isn't that what you were working on the other day?" Cailin asks as she climbs up onto the stool.

"Yeah, Jack was helping me finalize it and a few others."

"They're songs?" Sarah asks, glancing at the other sheets of paper. "How are they for me?"

My eyes meet Jack's, and he grins before giving his attention back to Sarah.

"I've heard you sing before," he says, making Sarah drop the sheet she was holding. Her statue-like stature makes Jack and I glance at each other. "I was friends with Donnie."

Her face goes white as her baby blues shine. "You were?" She slowly sits as she takes in the conversation.

"Yeah. I came to see you perform a few times. You have talent, and with these songs, I think you and Adam could knock it out of the park."

"Me and Adam?" She jerks toward me. "I'm not coming in between you and your band." She holds up her hands in defeat, making me laugh.

"Of course you're not. But there's nothing that says I can't have a side project. Something a little different, a little softer." I place my hand on hers as she stares up at me.

Sarah slowly shakes her head from side to side, more in disbelief than in denial. Her eyes are open wide, and I question if she's taken a breath.

"Well, that's my cue to head out," Jack says as he stands up and grabs his things.

Sarah stays silent as I walk my friend out.

"Thanks for your help today. I'm digging what we have going." I slap hands with him.

"Yeah, man. Her voice can carry some of that shit. It's got me excited too. Keep me posted. You guys are welcome to come to the studio when you're ready."

"Okay. I'll let you know."

He leaves, and I head back to Cailin, who's moved into the living room, watching cartoons.

"Have you finished your homework?"

"It's Friday, Dad. I don't have any homework," she deadpans, giving me a silly expression.

I rub her hair, messing it up for sassing me. "Doesn't mean I can't make sure."

She pushes me away as she laughs.

"We'll be in the kitchen if you need anything."

"Okie dokie, artichokie." She holds her thumb up, giving her attention back to the screen.

When I enter the kitchen again, Sarah looks like she's about to be sick.

She shakes her head at me. "No, Adam, I can't. These songs, they can't be for me, for us. I've already tried this. It didn't work out, remember? I had my shot already. I'm not singing like this anymore. No, I can't. What if people don't like it? I can't put myself out there again, only to live through the disappointment when—"

I pick up her hands in mine and stare straight into her eyes. "Take a deep breath." I inhale and exhale with her. "I'm not saying we need to head out on tour tomorrow. You've lit something inside me, and these lyrics were the result. We won't do anything you don't want to, but I'd love to hear you sing them with me. Even if it's only for us."

"It's just … Adam … I …"

I lean in to kiss her, trying to calm her nerves. I tightly hold her in my arms as I take everything I want from her, hopefully giving her all of me as well.

When I pull back, her eyes are full of tears. "I just can't. I'm sorry."

She grabs her purse and walks out my back door. I watch through the windows as she makes her way around my house, avoiding having to say good-bye to Cailin as she gets in her car and drives away.

Having to explain to Cailin why Sarah left without saying goodbye was interesting. It's not often that I have adult-type conversations with her, and I didn't want to tell her about Sarah's past, so I was left in a bit of a quagmire.

She asked if she could call Sarah, but I wanted to give her some time, so I told her we would in the morning.

After putting Cailin down for bed, I walk down the stairs just as Sarah's car pulls up to my gate. She has a code, but I watch as she sits at the gate for a few minutes, obviously still struggling with whatever is going on in her head.

I question if I should go to her, but whatever it is, she needs to work through it on her own. When her hand sticks out the window to push the gate code, I inhale and make my way to the door, glad she's taking those last steps to have this conversation instead of running away like I feel she has many times before.

I open my front door and step down to the driveway. For a moment, she sits in her car, staring up at me before she puts it in park and exits.

Her lips rub together as she nervously makes her way toward me.

When she's in front of me, her hand reaches out to touch mine. I stay silent, waiting for her to speak first.

"I'm sorry for leaving," she says, barely above a whisper.

I curl my fingers with hers, letting her know it's okay but waiting for her to speak more.

"I panicked. It's all just happening so fast. I finally came to terms with having you in my life and then had that fight with my father. Knowing you're in the music industry was hard enough for me to deal with. I never thought I would go down that road again."

I can't keep silent any more. "But why not?"

She wraps her arms around my waist, pulling me into her and burying her head on my chest. I let her, sensing she needs strength right now. I'm thankful she wants it from me instead of pushing me away again.

"I wanted your life so bad. I wanted to be the one onstage, having people sing my lyrics and screaming when they heard me perform them live. I was so close; I could taste it. Then, in the blink of an eye, it was gone. It took me over a year to recover from my injuries, having to have multiple surgeries. By then, everyone had moved on, so I did too. Especially with my father threatening to disown me. I'm terrified I won't be able to make it through if it doesn't work out again. I can only be crushed like that once in my lifetime."

I wrap my arms around her tighter, holding her for as long as she needs. When I feel her body calm, I pull back, placing my forehead to hers. "It's okay, Sarah. You don't have to do anything today or even next month. You have talent, and I'd hate for you not to follow your dreams. I believe in you. I wouldn't be standing here if I didn't. Just be open to the idea; that's all I ask."

She nods her head ever so slightly.

"Come on. Let's grab a blanket and go sit by the fire."

She takes a deep breath and nods as we step inside to get the blanket before heading out back. As she cuddles into my side, I play with her hair.

I'm dying to talk about the songs I wrote, but I don't want to push her. I'm happy she came back and that I didn't have to hunt her down, begging for her to sing them with me.

It's been a long time since a song I wrote has gripped me like this one has. There's a feeling I get deep in my gut that proves what I'm doing is exactly what I should be doing, and this song is dead on. Even Jack was surprised I'd gotten as far as I did in the short amount of time.

When lyrics fly like that, you can't deny their magic.

To my surprise, she brings it up first. "So, tell me about these songs." Her sight stays glued on the fire and not on me.

"I started working on them the first night you came over." I try to act nonchalant about them as I continue to play with her hair. "Every album I've put out is a little different as I evolve in my own life. After meeting you, I felt a new direction coming."

"But, Adam, your fans are pretty hard core. It's not smart to change your sound like that."

I place my hand on hers. "I'm not. I'll still have Devil's Breed. Max is going to need a break, especially from touring. And, now that Cailin's in school, I think I will too. I've been trying to figure out what my next move is for a while. When I met you, things started making sense, and that was when I had no clue about your past. It wasn't until the other day that I thought about actually doing something with you. Jack only came over today because he remembered where he'd seen you before."

"Donnie was such a good guy," she says more to herself than me.

I rub my thumb over hers. "He said the same thing. I knew things went down in New York, but he never talked about it until today. When I told him about the songs I was writing with you in mind, he was on board. He says you have a true talent. I'd love to hear you for real."

She laughs. "My dad would really love that," she says under her breath.

"Is this your life or your dad's?" I sit up to look at her.

"It's not that simple."

"You said you've already told him what you want. So, let's help him see what's possible. I told you I'd do right by him. Let me try."

She bites her bottom lip as her gaze leaves me and goes back to the fire. The truth is written all over her face. She still has the want, the desire to follow her dreams.

I'm going to be the one to make it happen.

"Hold that thought." I stand up and head back into the house to get the song Jack and I just finished.

When I come back, I hand it to her. "This is the one I was working on the first night you came over. I knew something was missing. It was you. I've never done a ballad with another singer. I've never wanted to. Until now."

She tilts her head and stares up at me. "Did you really just say ballad? Adam, your fans will laugh. They'll be wondering what I did to you if you come out with some cheesy love ballad."

A hard laugh escapes my mouth. "You're right. That's why it's not. It's my version of a love song. It's our song. It's how I've felt since I met you, just in my own way. Read it. Offer your input. Make it yours."

I stay silent as she takes it in.

I can't believe she thought I'd write a sappy love song for us. I don't think I have it in me to write something like that. I wrote my version of it, which is full of hidden meanings that I'm hoping she'll understand.

It's hard for me to express the feelings that have been running through me lately. Anger, hurt, disappointment—I've written all of that in the past. Love, like what I'm feeling for her, is all new to me.

"I like how you say, *You just want to be something.*" She points to the line.

"I added that today. After hearing your story, it made me think of you. I know you want more out of life. I want you to have that."

Her eyes meet mine, and I see all the pain she's lived through by not being able to follow her dreams. She was so close to making it big, only to have it ripped all away. I remember those days. I was living them while she was losing hers.

It wasn't until we added Jack that things really took off. To think we only got him because of what had happened to her makes my head spin. It's funny how life can twist and turn in certain ways, then bring you right back to where you belong.

"How fast or slow are you envisioning this?" she asks.

"Wanna hear?" I grin, tilting my head back to the house.

"Now?" Her eyes open wide.

"We've worked a little of it out on the piano. Then, Jack will come in with the guitar and drums, of course, but I can show you the beginning."

She stands and holds her hand out to mine. The beauty radiating off her right now is almost blinding. Knowing that I'll be able to share my passion, my music with her pretty much seals the deal.

This girl was made for me.

We walk to the house and the back room where the piano is. I practice a few chords to remember the keys and then start the song.

The first three notes are fast, and then some are slow. Then, it repeats as I start the song. My eyes close as I let the words take over, pouring all of the emotion I've felt for her these last few weeks into my actions.

I open them and see she's holding the lyrics, following along. I sing the next verse where I wanted our voices to meld together, and when she blends her words with mine, tingles take over my entire body.

Magic. Nothing but pure magic fills the air as we sing in tune for the first time together.

It takes everything in my power not to stop and make love to her right here on this piano. The way her body flows with the words turns me on like nothing I've ever imagined.

And her voice? Pure perfection. When I heard her sing the song with Cailin, it was different, lighter. Now, it has emotions. Feelings from her soul pour out of her body, and I see for myself what Jack was talking about.

She has it. She has that *something* special, and I'm so honored to get to be a part of it.

I continue with the chorus, and when it comes to her part, I give her the floor, encouraging her to continue. My heart pounds as she belts out the lyrics I've worked with her in mind.

Her eyes never leave mine as she moves on, singing the chorus, and I let her, loving the mixture of her doing it this round. When her voice deepens, really getting into the sound I'm going for, it really hits me.

We were made for this.

The end of the song has us repeating certain lyrics, and when I finish, I stand to wrap her in my arms. Not able to hold anything back as I show her how much that meant to me.

Chapter 29

Sarah

Waking up in Adam's arms is more than a dream come true; it's my heaven. I gave up on my dreams so long ago, but now, I'm filled with so much hope that I don't know what to do with myself.

I felt the way our voices came together so deep in my soul. This is what I've been missing. He's filled this hole that I thought would forever be empty.

I run my fingers through his, stirring him awake. The sleepy grin he gives me in return makes my heart sing. This man is becoming my everything, and singing with him last night was one of the most amazing moments in my life.

"Morning," he whispers as he leans down to kiss my forehead.

I hold him tighter, laying my head on his bare chest as memories of him making love to me last night run through my mind. It wasn't until he wrapped me in his arms, carrying me upstairs, that I realized we had been downstairs. I was so lost in the moment, not having a care in the world but him.

And I loved it.

"You'd better watch it." He chuckles under his breath. "You're giving me a chub, and Cailin will be awake any minute now."

I kiss his chest and push off of him just as I hear Cailin opening her bedroom door and calling for her dad.

"Come on in, sweetheart," he yells to her once I have his shirt slipped over my head.

"Yay, you came back!" she says as she skips over to his bed, climbing up to join us. "I slept great! How about you guys?"

I giggle to myself as I curl back up against Adam, who's got his arm tucked under his head to slightly prop himself up. I slept great, no thanks to her dad here.

He grins my way before saying, "We slept good. Why don't you give us some time to get up, and we'll get breakfast going?"

"Can I turn on the TV to watch cartoons?" Cailin asks, jumping off the bed.

"If that will buy me ten minutes," Adam whispers to me as he slides his hand down my torso under the covers. I jerk, shocked he'd do such a thing, and he has to bite his lip not to laugh out loud before he says, "Sure. We'll be right there."

Once we're alone, he throws me back, kissing my neck, as I fall into a fit of giggles, trying to fight him off.

We hear Cailin call for us from the kitchen, and he sighs, hopping off the bed in nothing but his boxers. Seeing his tall, fit, tattooed body stirs me even more, and I have to take a deep breath before getting up myself to slide on my pants.

Reaching for my phone, I see I missed calls from my sister and my mom last night. Closing my eyes, I take a deep breath and tuck the phone back in my purse. I don't know whose side they'll be on, and right now, I don't care. I don't want them to ruin my high I'm finally feeling after all this time. So, I push the thoughts away and finish getting my clothes on.

We head downstairs where I help Cailin, and Adam starts the coffee.

"So, what's the plan for today?" Cailin asks when Adam joins us in the living room.

"What do you think about going to the studio?" Adam asks.

I turn to him in surprise. "Seriously?"

"Oh, yes. Can we, Daddy?"

I look back to Cailin. "You like going to the studio?"

"It's super fun! They have all these buttons and sliding things that they let me play with to make funny sounds, and I get to sing into the microphone."

Our SONG

Her joy brings so much light into this world on a constant basis.

"What do you think?" Adam asks, placing his hand on mine.

"I-I mean … I've never been to one. Where is it? Don't you have to book and pay for it in advance?"

The guys from my band in New York and I were in the process of setting some time up at a studio when everything happened. It was expensive, and we were just about able to finally pay for it.

"Jack has one in his house. Most of our stuff has been recorded there. He lives about an hour away in the Oakland Hills."

"You think he'd be up for it?" I ask.

Adam nods. "Oh, yeah. He was digging what we were doing last night. Kept saying he'd love to hear it in the studio. I'll give him a call in a few. He doesn't have the early girl alarm clock that we do." He playfully rubs his hand over Cailin's head, making her giggle as she pushes him away.

I'm in absolute awe as we walk down to Jack's basement and enter the studio set up in his house. The wooden walls and foam-coated boards bring me both happiness and sadness.

My bandmates and I dreamed of being in a place like this someday. The studio we were saving up for was nothing compared to this.

Sound booths sit in each corner, and in between them, a drum set is set up with guitars sitting on their stands, just waiting to be picked up.

"Welcome to my humble abode," Jack says as he opens his arms wide.

"This is amazing." I sit at the mixing board, mesmerized by all the knobs and sliders, taking in what each one does.

Cailin climbs up on a high stool that's tucked in the corner. When I look closer, I see right next to it is a sign that says *Cailin's Seat Only*.

"So, I can't sit there?" I ask, teasing.

Jack swoops up next to her, crossing his arms in front of his chest like a bouncer would to intimidate someone. "Nope. This is Cailin's spot, and I'll have to escort you out if you try to do anything funny," he states in a deeper voice.

198

She mimics his motions and his tone. "Yeah, this is my spot."

Adam leans down to whisper to me, "See, it's not just me she has wrapped around her little finger."

I grin to Adam, and he winks as he steps into the sound booth.

"Is this thing on?" He taps the microphone, and Cailin holds up her thumb.

"So, you went over the lyrics?" Jack asks me.

"Yeah, and she sang a few parts that we weren't thinking she would, so I want to give that a try," Adam responds.

"Nice." Jack nods his head to me like he's proud of my work.

"What are you guys thinking for this? I mean, he played the piano for it, but what else do you want to add?"

Jack goes over how he wants it to start low, building the tempo until the beat drops and the song takes on more of the hardness their fans are used to.

I pick up the lyrics that Adam placed on the table as we walked in and go over them a few more times.

The song is a perfect love ballad for his genre of music. It doesn't use the words or slow pace that people are used to. It's not cheesy, and to some, it might even be confusing, but that's what relationships are—a mixture of emotions that flow like the ocean.

He's acting as if a relationship were as simple as asking someone if they could come over to his house. He wants to hang out, but it's more than just for the night.

He wants to take the place of the random people around her, and this is his way of showing it. Asking if she can hear him is his way of asking if she understands what he's trying to say, but he can't get the words out.

Saying he's only a little ways away shows he's ready now; she just has to invite him in.

It's everything I've always loved about Adam's music. There's so much meaning to the words that are spoken; you just have to care enough to listen to them.

"Did I hear we're bringing a chick in to sing with us?" Noah throws the door open, announcing his presence in a way only he can.

"Yeah, and if you lay a hand on her, I'll kick your ass," Adam says through the microphone from the sound booth.

Noah walks straight up to me, wrapping his arm around me and dipping me back, pretending to kiss me, whispering, "You'll learn I like to fuck with him a lot. Watch, he'll be here in—" We're ripped apart by Adam, and Noah falls back on the couch in a laughing fit. "Told ya," he says.

I lean up to kiss Adam. "He was just messing with you. No one could take your place."

The grin he gives me is priceless, and his crystal-blue eyes radiate back at me, filling my life with pure happiness for him. It's more than this moment. It truly is him that's putting my life back together when I thought it was lost forever.

"So, let's hear it. What you got?" Noah asks like he's asking me what I have to offer him to drink and not for me to sing in a sound booth for the first time.

I know, for him, this is an everyday event, but for me, this is an opportunity I was sure I'd lost. I glance around the room, not sure where to go and what to do.

Adam takes me by my hand into the sound booth, so it's just the two of us. "Don't be nervous. We'll practice a few times, and I'll be right here for you." He tilts his head, and I can't help but lean up to kiss him.

We get slightly carried away, and I hear Jack clear his throat over the loudspeaker. "Um, hello? There's a child here," he teases.

I turn in shock of what Cailin just saw and realize she's not even in the room.

"Just kidding," Jack says. "She went to get water. Just wanted to fuck with you. We're here to make music, not more babies."

Adam grabs the headphones and puts them over my head before picking up his pair. "We'll practice a few times. Don't worry about anything if you mess up. We have all the time in the world." Adam's voice is so reassuring and helps calm my nerves.

"What about the music? I'm not sure I can sing to nothing. How do I get the beat?" I ask.

"Don't worry. Jack laid down the piano track last night."

"Seriously?" I ask, surprised.

"Yeah. Once he gets on something, it's hard for him to stop. That's why he built this studio. It drove him nuts to have to quit and go home for the night when the place would kick us out." Then, Adam says to Jack, "Play the track, so she can hear it."

He nods, and a few seconds later, I hear the piano through my headphones. My eyes light up, and I can't help the biggest smile that covers my face.

This is seriously happening.

Adam leans in to softly kiss me. "Let's do this." He smiles and raises his eyebrows to me.

I nod, and Adam heads to his spot next to me with a microphone in front of him as well.

We listen to the beginning a few times, practicing where he'll come in and where our voices will merge together.

"Okay, let's try this for real this time," he says to Jack and then turns to me. "If you want to continue to your verse, go ahead, or we can stop and practice that a little more too."

I nod and hold my hand to my ear, ready to feel the beat straight to my soul.

Adam's voice begins, and chills run through my entire body. It's so powerful, so manly, so … Adam.

I sing my quick portion with him, which is more harmonizing than actual lyrics.

To my surprise, I look over to see Noah right as he pounds out a beat on the drums when Adam's voice drops, and he belts out the chorus. The growl-like inflection he does as he emphasizes certain words fits perfectly with the rhythmic beat.

It's been years since I've been with a group of guys who just fit together like this. My band was the same way. One member could join in, creating a sound no one had predicted but was pure magic.

Thinking of my band both breaks my heart and heals it at the same time. I know they wouldn't want me to live the way I've been living.

This is for them.

I place my hand over my heart, saying a silent prayer, knowing they're smiling down on me.

The chorus is coming to a close, so I take the motivation I'm feeling from their memory and belt out the lyrics that Adam wrote.

Cailin cheering behind the mixing board brings a tear to my eye, but I blink it away as I take in the moment.

My moment that I feel like I've waited a lifetime for.

We haven't practiced after that portion, so Jack stops the tape, and Adam jumps to his feet, picking me up and swinging me around. His excitement is the exact emotion flooding me right now, and I love that he feels the same way.

"That's my teacher!" I hear Cailin yell through the speaker system, making me laugh.

"That's my girl," Adam whispers right before kissing me.

They're both right, but I'm also so much more. I'm just finally able to show everyone else too.

Chapter 30

Sarah

Today has been the most amazing day ever! We spent all day working, perfecting, and redoing the song until it was perfect. No matter if we only do this one song, it will forever be *our* song, the first one we recorded together.

I love that Cailin's been here for every step. I can't think of many kids her age who would have lasted so long, but they include her, ask her opinion, and show her how every button or knob works.

Thinking back to those first days of school where she would sing constantly makes so much more sense now. This has been her life and all she knows.

How special that Adam includes her in everything.

We're listening to the final cut when Cailin says, "Do we still get to celebrate like we normally do even though Uncle Max isn't here?"

My heart stops. Max. I've been so focused on my dreams that I completely forgot about Max and the fact that he's not here.

Adam picks her up. "I called and left him a message after lunch because he still can't have phone calls, just to give him an update. What do you think we should do?"

She places her hand on her chest, acting overly dramatic. "I," she drawls out, "think we should still do it and take video that we can show him later, so he's still a part of it."

"What does this celebration entail?" I ask.

Cailin wiggles out of her dad's arms and runs up to me. "It's so much fun!" Her excitement is palpable.

"Wait, wait, wait," Jack yells. "I have to cover the equipment."

Jack places covers over the mixing boards while Adam grabs a few water bottles from the mini fridge and hands them out.

"What are we going to do?" I ask Cailin.

"You crack the top and place your thumb over it, like this." She shows me, and I look to Adam for reassurance.

I raise my eyebrows at him, asking if she's serious.

He laughs and begins the countdown, "Three, two, one."

Before I know it, water is being flung everywhere as Cailin, Adam, and Jack jump around, hooting and hollering. I turn to Noah, who's filming the event.

"Uh-oh," Noah says. "You guys, I think Sarah needs a little motivation."

In no time flat, both Adam and Cailin are on me, soaking me with their sprays. I shake the bottle, only letting a little water out of the top at a time to repay the favor.

Fits of giggles surround the room as the celebration comes to a conclusion due to our bottles being empty.

Adam wraps his arms around me, wiping the water from my forehead before he kisses it and brings me to his chest. My cheeks hurt from smiling so much.

"Everyone say good-bye," Noah says.

We all wave to the camera, and Cailin runs closer to it.

"We miss you, Uncle Max!" She kisses into the screen right before Noah shuts the video off.

I look up into Adam's amazing blues, happier than I've ever been.

"Welcome to the club, baby," he whispers only to me.

I lean up to kiss him. Hearing him call me baby does things to me that I shouldn't be feeling with everyone around us like this.

"See? That was so much fun, huh?" Cailin asks.

"So much fun!" I respond. "Do you guys do that after every song?"

Adam chuckles, throwing his head back. "No, I think Jack would have a fit. Only after the first and the last."

"Yes, he would," Jack says as he starts to wipe everything dry. "I'm down for some fun, but that's a lot of cleaning up." He laughs.

I help wipe things with a towel he threw to me. When we're finished, I sit on the couch with Adam. "How do you think Max will react? I don't want him to feel like we're doing something without him."

He places his hand on my knee. "Don't worry. I emailed him once Jack and I started working on the song. I wanted him to know he'd always be part of the band and that this was a side thing going on that he was welcome to jump in on whenever he was ready. He emailed back this morning, saying it was a cool idea. We're not sure yet how long he'll be gone for or what his next move will be. He said this took a lot of pressure off of him, knowing we're not sitting idle while he's there. He's the best guitarist around, and he knows we could never replace him."

I lay my head on his shoulder, absolutely content with life. When my phone rings, I get up to answer it. A cheesy smile covers my face when I see it's Maggie FaceTiming me.

"Oh, girl! You're never going to believe where I am and what I'm doing right now," I answer as I turn to an empty wall, so that's all she sees.

Her face scrunches. "If you tell me I interrupted you and Adam, I'm not sure if I'll scream from excitement or be weirded out because, you know, that's a little TMI on FaceTime." Adam laughs out loud, and she hears him. "OMG, I did." She bites her bottom lip in question. "Oh God, show me him. Wait, no. Sorry, that's weird. Never mind." She's waving her hand in front of her face.

I laugh out loud as I flip the camera to Adam. "Maggie, I'd like to officially introduce you to Adam. Adam, say hi to Maggie."

She yelps into the phone as Adam stands to head toward me. He waves before stepping next to me, so I flip the view back to me.

"Hot damn, you're tall," Maggie states with a slight laugh.

"Maggie's my bestie from New York," I say to Adam.

"Yeah, you can thank me later for helping her become the badass she is today." Maggie tilts her head with a shrug to her shoulder. "But, okay, you haven't told me where you are."

I glance to Adam, who grins my way, saying, "Show her."

I flip the camera again and show off the room.

"No. Fucking. Shit. You're at a recording studio!" she yells.

205

"And they just recorded a song together!" Cailin jumps up in the view of the camera, so I point it directly at her.

"Are you serious right now?" Maggie screams in shock.

Cailin dramatically nods her head. "Yes! They did. And it's sooooo good."

I turn the camera back to me, dying to see her reaction, but I can't through all the tears filling my eyes. I blink them away, but more come. I knew this was the best day of my life, but being able to share it with Maggie, who's been by my side for all these years, has pushed me over the edge.

"Oh, sweetie. Don't cry!" Maggie says.

I wipe my eyes. "I don't know why I'm crying."

"You're crying because you're finally getting what you've deserved all this time," she says.

"Damn straight." Adam pops into view, so Maggie can see him. "She's a natural talent."

"I'm so fucking excited for you! I can't wait to hear it. When can I?" she asks.

"It's finished. If Sarah trusts you, so do I. Let us make a digital copy, and we'll send you one soon."

She does a little happy dance. "Can't wait."

Adam laughs as he walks away, leaving me more alone with Maggie. We stare at each other, both not needing to say a word. She knows how big this is for me, how long I've wanted it.

Another tear slips down my cheek when she says, "Love you, girl."

I blow her a kiss. "Love you too."

"Go back to your rock-star hottie. Call me later."

"I will."

We hang up, and I inhale a deep breath, trying to calm the absolute glee running through me.

Adam wraps me in his arms, tightly holding me. "I'm proud of you," he whispers with his lips pressed against my forehead.

I bury my head in his shoulder, holding him tighter. "Thank you for doing this. Thank you for including me. You have no idea what this means to me."

His hand runs down my hair. "But I do. Music has been my healing too. I've felt those same feelings. Allow yourself to enjoy it."

"What happens now? Are we going to actually do something with it?" I ask, making him chuckle under his breath.

"Of course we are. I'll send it to my record label, get their feedback on what we have going here, and hopefully, they'll press for more. Jack and I have a few other songs we worked on that day."

My glee fades instantly when reality comes back full force. I close my eyes, trying to remember why I'm here, why I'm doing this.

I have to have faith …

I wince when I ask, but I need to know, "What if they don't like it?"

"Then, we put it out anyway on social media and YouTube. Let the fans tell us themselves what they want."

I pull back to meet his eyes. "Seriously?"

His shit-eating grin tells me all I need to know. "Hell yeah, I'm serious. Do you know how many views our songs get daily on YouTube? We don't need the record company to help us. It's just a courtesy really at this point. At least, that's what my manager said."

I step back, surprised to be hearing this. "You already talked to your manager about me?"

He pulls me back into his chest, and I feel it shake with his laughter. "Yes, I've done this a time or two before. The only difference this go-around is you."

"That's a big difference though." I try to pull back, but he keeps me up against him.

"Nah. They'll love it. Just like I do."

I give in, holding him tighter, letting the moment sink in for just a little longer.

I've been floating high ever since we got back to his place. That is, until I heard a ring over the intercom of his front gate. I glance at the camera system, and when I see my sister's car parked out front, I almost drop the glass I'm carrying.

Adam turns to me, concern written all over his face when he sees my reaction. "I take it, you know who this is?"

I inhale and set the glass down. Of course she would show up. I've been ignoring her calls, but I never thought she'd have the nerve to show up at his place like this. I know she's here to try to make peace, but some things just can't be obtained. It's time I be the person I want to be.

I close my eyes, inhaling, readying myself to be on the defensive. "Yes. Give me a second."

Adam presses the button to open the gate as I head out to the driveway. When Emily steps out of her car, I walk to meet her there.

"I hope you don't mind me showing up like this. I've tried your phone, but you haven't been answering," she says as she waddles up, holding her belly.

"Let me guess … you've been speaking with our father? How'd you know where Adam lived?"

She eyes me like she can't believe I just asked that. "Everyone knows that he lives here. It'll be the talk of the town for months, if not years."

I sigh, not really wanting to have this conversation and ready for it to be done with. "Look, I've had a really good day, and if you're here to talk to me about Dad, I'd rather not." I cross my arms, letting her know I'm not going to budge on this.

I love my sister, I do, but we couldn't be more different. She's always fit in here, with my father's way of thinking, since the day she was born. I never have. I've always wanted more. I've wanted to live outside their narrow-minded box.

"Mom's worried about you. Are you coming to church tomorrow?" she says, sagging her shoulders.

I know she doesn't want to be here any more than I want her here. I hate having her stuck in the middle. I can only imagine my mom bugging her to come talk to me.

Knowing my mom won't come here herself lights a fire so deep in my belly that I have to breathe out before it explodes inside me. That's so typical. My mom has always lived for my father, not for herself.

He's mad about my choices, so she has to follow his lead. She'll never step out of his shadow. It both breaks my heart and pisses me off.

But, mostly, it fuels my desire for more. I don't want my mom's life. This life. I tried to come back here and do what they wanted me to do, but I was never truly happy. Not like I've been these past few weeks.

Adam has brought that out in me, and I'm not going to stop.

"No, actually, I'm not," I say with more gusto than I planned.

"Sarah …"

"Emily …" I wave my hands around, mocking her, and then take a deep breath. It's not her fault this is happening, and I shouldn't take it out on her. "I know you think you're here to help, but you're not. I'm a big girl, and I can make my own choices. If Dad doesn't like it, then that's his fault."

She sighs, glancing behind me to see if Adam is around. Thankfully, he stayed inside. "I just don't want you to regret anything."

"Regret anything? I regret giving up on my dreams. I was really making a name for myself in New York. Yes, what happened to me was awful, but Dad saying it was God's way of getting back at me was fucked up, and you know it. Adam is lighting something within me that I've missed for years. I'm singing the songs *I* want to sing. We're singing them together. It's what I've wanted, and it's finally happening. So, either you're standing beside me or you're not. I'm not stopping though."

She places her hands under her belly to help hold the weight, sorrow shining in her eyes. "You know I want you to be happy. I just hope you know what you're doing. My babies need their aunt, you know?"

I place my hand on her stomach, feeling the bulge of what I assume is my nephew's little behind. "And I will be, except I'll actually be me, living the life that I want, that I've always dreamed of. Don't you want that for me?"

Her arms wrap around me in a tight hug. "I do. Believe me, I do." She lets me go and backs up just a bit, appraising me. "You do look happy. Tell Adam I'm grateful he's helping you follow your dreams."

I grin, thankful she's not fighting me more on this, and I help her back into her car.

Adam steps out of the house as she drives away. "Everything okay?"

I lean up to kiss him. "Yes, things couldn't be better."

Chapter 31

Adam

After putting Cailin to bed, Sarah leans into my shoulder, lying with me on the couch. "So, what other songs were you guys working on?"

"Already anxious to get back in the studio?" I tease her.

She smiles shyly. "Maybe."

"We can go again tomorrow. I was working on a few different ideas and probably have enough that we could hash them out."

"Seriously?" She leans back to look me in the eye.

"Jack's always down to play in the studio. I know he'll be up for it."

She curls back into me, playing with my fingers. "Aren't you nervous about what people are going to think?"

"Nah. I'm still the same person. With every album, things have gotten calmer. I've grown with my music. I think this is a good next step. It might have Jack and Noah on the line, but this is more our thing. We won't release it as Devil's Breed, so they won't expect that."

"Are the other songs duets too?"

"I thought it would be cool to have a few with just you, a few with just me, and then a few together. Really show the mixture between the two of us."

I feel her tense slightly beneath me. "By myself?"

I sit up and turn her, so I can see her better. "Don't be afraid.

We'll work on it together." I softly kiss her, leaning back again before smirking and going in for more.

Sliding down, I pull her on top of me, running my fingers under her shirt.

She tries to stop me. "Adam, Cailin's only been in bed for a few minutes. What if she comes down?"

I chuckle under my breath. "Come on. Sneak around with me."

She giggles and pushes back and off of me. "You'll have to keep it in your pants for just a little while longer."

She's lucky I know I won't have to wait long, or I might have just taken her into my truck.

"So, which song's on the schedule for today?" Jack asks as we all enter the studio.

I purposely didn't tell either Sarah or Cailin what I was working on because I wanted it to be a surprise. I hand it to Jack, raising my eyebrows so he knows to keep it quiet.

He nods and starts to get things ready. I pick up the guitar, practicing the notes I've been playing with.

Sarah enters the booth, sitting next to me. "I like that."

"Yeah, it kind of goes with the happiness of the song."

"Did Adam Jacobson just say his song is happy?" she says, pulling her head back in surprise.

I laugh out loud. "Yeah, this is definitely a happy song." I tilt my head toward the reason I live, perched on her stool at the mixing board. "It's about her."

Sarah's eyes brighten. "Really?"

"It's one I've been working on for a while. I wanted it to be my way to introduce her to the world."

"Does she know?"

I glance back at her with a huge grin covering my face. "Nope."

"What are you calling it?"

"*Cailin,*" I say without hesitation.

She laughs out loud. "So, there's no doubt who it's about?"

I kiss her before heading to the other booth. "Hey, Cailin," I yell

Our SONG

since I know nothing's on yet. "Turn on the mic in here."

She gives me a thumbs-up as she reaches over on the mixing board, doing as I asked.

"Testing, testing," I say.

She hits the button that allows them to talk to me in here. "You're on, Daddy."

Daddy … the best word I'll ever hear coming out of her mouth.

I've waited for this moment—to share the song I wrote only for her.

I don't actually sing her name until the very end, so to test the mic, I sing the lyric about having my own Cailin before saying how much I love her.

I watch as Cailin's eyes go from me to Jack to Sarah and then back to me. Sarah is wiping her eyes as she laughs.

She hits the talk button. "Did you just say my name in that verse?"

"Sure did. How about we sing a song about you this time?"

She jumps up, clapping her hands together. "Seriously, Daddy? About me?"

I let out a joyous laugh. "Yes, about you."

She jumps off the stool and runs into the booth. "Let me see! Let me see!"

I show her the lyrics, and we go over them together. I'm so impressed on how much she can read. I have to help her with only a few words, but she's mainly able to say them all on her own.

"Are you okay with me singing a song about you?" I ask.

"Are you kidding? I love it!" She wraps her arms around me. "Thank you so much, Chestnut!"

I hug her with all my might. "I love you, Sugarplum."

She releases her hold and starts to walk back to the mixing board. "Let's get this show on the road. We have a song to sing that's about ME!" She celebrates with a little happy dance, making us all laugh.

Chapter 32

Adam

While my girls are at school, I decide to work on more song ideas. I get so in the zone when I'm working on music that I don't even notice I left my phone in my bedroom until it's almost time for them to be home.

I run to grab it, excited to shoot Jack a text about the new stuff I'm working on when I see I have multiple missed calls and texts from my manager, Bruce.

I don't bother to listen to the voice mail or read the texts and just dial.

"Goddamn, you're hard to get ahold of!" he yells into the phone as his greeting. "I was about to send Jack to get your ass since I'm still in New York."

"Why are you blowing me up?"

"Seriously? Let's talk about the damn record company blowing *me* up. They fucking loved that song. They're dying to talk to Sarah. I guess they already knew who she was."

"No shit?"

"Yes shit. They want to put it out on YouTube like you suggested, but they want video of you two singing it together. I'm working up the contracts now. We'll need her to sign everything before we get going."

Our SONG

"Wait, they want a music video? That's a lot to put together for a song that hasn't even released yet."

"They don't want your standard video. They want the two of you in the studio, like you're recording it for the first time. More natural. No special effects or big production."

I nod slowly as a grin covers my face. "I like it."

It's a perfect idea. What a great way to introduce Sarah to the world. This record is about us, so having a video that shows just that will be the cherry on top to this amazing song.

"I knew you would. Now, when can we make this happen? With Max in rehab, they want to focus on you two to help take pressure off of him."

I glance at my watch. "They'll be home shortly. I'll talk to her then. Find out when the video crew can come, and we'll make it happen. Oh, but it has to be after school or on the weekend. She's a kindergarten teacher."

He chuckles into the phone. "Not for long, she's not."

We hang up, and I throw my hands in the air. I knew the song was amazing, but hearing how much they loved it, too, just solidifies everything. We're going to make this happen.

Twenty minutes later, Cailin comes running through the door, and I step outside to meet Sarah.

"You're never going to believe this!" I say, wrapping my arms around her waist and pulling her into me. I place a quick kiss to her lips before I let her say anything.

"Mmm," she sighs into my kiss. "Give me another one and then tell me."

I grin, kissing her again before saying, "They loved it."

"Who's they?"

I lower my head to stare into her eyes, waiting for it to sink in.

Her eyes widen when it does. "The song?"

I pick her up to swing her around. "Yes, the song. They fucking loved it! They want to release it right away on YouTube but with a music video to go with it."

She pauses as her hands grip my arms. "A music video?"

I can sense the internal panic brewing and lean in to kiss her worry away. "It's going to be okay. They just want us in the studio. Nothing over the top. Just us recording the song and showing the process."

She bites her bottom lip. I pull it out with my thumb.

"Don't be nervous. It will be amazing, just like you. I know it."

I pull her in for a hug again, hoping to stop the thoughts in her head because there should be none. This is her time, and I want her to enjoy it. The fact that I get to stand by her side, saying she's mine, makes me so fucking proud.

We enter Jack's studio on Saturday, ready to record the music video.

Sarah has been so cute all week. We went shopping multiple times with Maggie on FaceTime to find the perfect outfit. After ten different outfits, she finally settled on the sexiest one we'd found. And not because it shows off her body, but because it doesn't. The small black jacket hides the sexy crop top shirt she has on underneath, and we get the slightest peek every once in a while, but it leaves the rest up to imagination.

What surprised me the most was that she wanted to color her hair back to darker brown like she'd had it when she lived in New York. She loved it that way but said it was too hard to look in the mirror because she wasn't able to be that girl anymore. When she had brunette hair, she was the rocker she always wanted to be.

When she shared with me that she'd been having her hair cut by her sister for the last seven years to avoid people seeing her scar, I finally got what a big deal this really was, and it made me even more excited for her.

Jack gives her a hug before asking, "You ready to show the world who you are?"

Seeing the camera crew makes her stop in her tracks.

"Let it shine, girl. You've got something special. Own it. Rock it." He sticks out his tongue and holds up his rock-star fingers.

His antics put a smile on her face and ease the moment as I introduce her to everyone.

Cailin jumps up to her spot. We even bought her a new dress for the occasion. Bruce wasn't sure if it was a good idea to have her in the video, but I insisted. She was just as big a part of the original recording, and she needs to be here now.

Our SONG

I've kept her from the limelight, but it's time people know she exists. No matter how many times I thought about letting the secret out, I never could have imagined it would include me dating someone at the same time. The world can be cruel, but knowing I also have a woman in my life has seemed to soften the blow.

We go over where the cameras will be, making sure one angle isn't seen in the other's view frame. I've done this time and time again, but when I glance over to Sarah, I see the apprehension written all over her face.

After walking up to her, I kiss her forehead and wrap my arm around her. "Just be yourself. Once they're set up, they won't move, so you'll forget they're here."

She lets out a sarcastic laugh. "Easy for you to say."

"Okay, all set up," the lead cameraman says. "We're just going to hit record and let you guys do your thing. We'll edit it all together in post."

I turn to Sarah, smiling. "See? Simple."

She laughs nervously. "So, I just have to act natural? How is that even possible, knowing I'm recording something that the entire world will one day see?" She bites her lip as she takes in the cameras around her.

I hold out my hand to her, leading her to our spot in the booth. She comes willingly, and when we're behind closed doors, I take advantage and push her up against the wall where I know Cailin can't see us.

Her head tilts up, meeting my eyes. With one hand above her head against the wall, I slowly raise my other hand, moving her hair away from her face. My finger slides down her cheek to her neck and down her cleavage.

I keep my vision locked to hers. When her lips part, I grip my hand around her right hip, bringing it against me.

I tilt my head, lowering just slightly so I can brush my lips against hers. Grinding into her again, I whisper, "Just breathe. I got you. I promise."

I kiss her again, letting her take what she needs from me in this moment so she can relax and be herself.

My hand reaches around to her backside, and I pick her up, swinging her legs around my waist and pushing her against the wall.

Her fingers run through my hair before pulling softly.

When my dick gets harder than I intended, I pull away just enough to inhale a deep breath. I place my forehead to hers, trying to calm the fire burning within me. "The things you do to me, Sarah," I whisper.

"Um, can we actually get this thing going, or are you two going to hide in the corner the entire time?" Jack asks over the loudspeaker.

We both chuckle under our breath, and I release my hold, letting her feet slide down to the floor.

Our eyes meet one last time, and she rises to her tiptoes to give me a sweet peck, quietly thanking me for calming her nerves.

With my cock as hard as a rock and a grin covering my face from ear to ear, I turn to see the red light on the camera glaring back at me. I wonder for a quick second if they caught our little tryst, but then I hope they did. This is a love song, and I want the world to know it was not written with just anybody in mind.

Only her.

With the music track running, Sarah and I are going to sing into the microphones just like we would if we were recording it for real. You don't get the same passion and expression when lip-syncing, and we want this to be as real as possible.

The song begins with my portion, and when Sarah joins in, the feedback from our original recording rings in her ears, catching her off guard when she hears her own voice.

She covers her mouth in horror, and I rush over to her, picking her up and swinging her around. I want to make this experience as fun as possible for her because that's what this is all about.

Following your dreams is hard work, but it's also fun. We've done the hard work already, creating the song. This is the reward we get.

Showing our mess-ups and the fun we have together—that's what this video is all about. I want people to see us, the real us. We had a good time recording it the first time, but things were more serious as we made sure every note, every lyric was right. Now, we're more relaxed, more comfortable, and just having a good time.

After a few takes, she relaxes and even starts to have some fun herself.

On the second verse, I close my eyes, holding the headphones to one ear, lost in the moment, and when I open them, I see she's out of her seat. Quickly, she covers my eyes and leans around to kiss my cheek, completely messing up my lyrics. As fast as I can, I swing my arm around her, pulling her to my lap, and kiss her, almost making both of us fall off the chair. I steady myself and hold on to her tightly as she drops her head back, laughing at the entire scene.

Seeing her like this is a dream. She's floating on cloud nine, and knowing I had something to do with that makes me feel good inside.

I've never made a music video like this. With Devil's Breed, it was big productions, tons of setup, and recording the same lines twenty times to get different angles. This is just about the song—no show, no lights, just lyrics and us.

Once we make it through the song, we get a few shots of Noah on the drums as well as Jack and Cailin at the mixing board, going over things and high-fiving each other. Seeing them together, like they always are but knowing the rest of the world will see this, too, makes me such a proud dad. My little girl is something else, and I want everyone to know it.

When the cameraman suggests she pretend to play the drums, she jumps at the chance. Her little face lights up when Noah hands her the sticks and puts the earphones on her. If the song doesn't go viral on its own, it will just for the takes of her in it.

Seeing the smiles that cover both my girls' faces is all I need to make it the perfect day.

Sarah

"Sarah, will you read me a book tonight?" Cailin asks after we get dinner cleaned up.

"What am I? Chopped liver? I wrote a song about you, remember? What did she do?" Adam teases, making Cailin giggle.

She wraps her little arms around her dad's neck. "I love you, Daddy. Thank you for the song."

"Love you too, baby girl. Sweet dreams."

I grab her hand and head upstairs. She picks out a book, and we read it together. When it's finished, I kiss her forehead and walk toward the light when she stops me.

LAUREN RUNOW

"I'm really happy you're here, Sarah."

I turn, a sudden weightlessness overcoming me. Hearing her say that means more than she could ever know. I give her a hug. "I'm happy I'm here too."

"My daddy has always been fun, but he's happier with you around. I can just tell."

Yes, that's the sound of my heart doing the biggest, happiest dance it's ever done. If it got any fuller, it would explode.

"That really means a lot to hear you say that."

She smiles big. "Nighty-night."

"Nighty-night, sweet girl."

I exit her room and head back down to Adam with a grin covering my face.

I hear Adam on the piano and get an idea. If we're releasing this song on YouTube, we should have some other content ready to go with it, stuff that shows him truly being himself.

If he's ready to show off his daughter, I want people to also see the man I'm falling in love with.

I grab my phone and sneak into the back room. The simple tune of "Turn the Page" begins, and I start recording. It's not the same without the saxophone, but when his voice starts, my body melts into his soothing tone.

I sit in hiding while he pours his heart into the song that means so much to him. There are no lights, no fire, no other instruments, just him putting his soul out there when he thinks no one's watching.

From behind, you can see how he sings with his entire body. The passion is unmatched by anything I've ever seen. Chills cover my body as he hits every note with ease. The man is beyond talented, and I pray he allows me to show the world what I'm seeing now.

He finishes the last note, and I hoot and holler in celebration, walking up to him with the camera still running.

I sit next to him and hold the phone out, so I'm in the frame with him. "Yes, you heard that right. That wonderful rendition was *the* Adam Jacobson singing in his den when he thought he was alone. I know you think it was amazing too. If you didn't already love this man, I know you do now. Just like me."

I beam in his direction, and he instantly leans in, kissing me so passionately that I have to grip the phone so I don't drop it.

219

Our SONG

His forehead falls to mine as he whispers, "I love you too, Sarah."

My eyes widen as I take in what I said first and then what he said back.

I turn to the camera, smiling so big that I think my cheeks are going to crack. I laugh as I say, "And that's a wrap."

I press the red button to turn off the camera and wrap my arms around him, kissing him with everything I have.

Chapter 33

Sarah

Adam's record company wants to keep everything very hush-hush before we release the song, but I've still been living in a whirlwind the past few days.

Since we're releasing it on YouTube, they've decided to create a channel just for us to keep things separate from Devil's Breed.

I would have thought YouTube was no big deal, but I've quickly learned how much money can be made on the channel and how that will be handled. These YouTubers are raking in the dough! Thank God Adam has been here to guide me through the contracts and how everything will work.

I've had PR people combing through my Facebook and Instagram accounts, making sure everything is in line. I had no idea how much of an invasion of privacy this life can be.

Today's the day though. At five o'clock tonight, the song will release, and a massive social media push will happen.

Maggie's been texting and calling about it every day, and I finally broke down and called my sister a few days ago. The fear of her being on my dad's side was almost enough for me not to say anything, but I want my family to know. I want their support.

She was more excited than I could have ever imagined. She even told me she was proud of me for standing up for what I wanted out of life.

Our SONG

There's no going back now. In a few short hours, I won't be Sarah Russo, daughter of Pastor Russo and a kindergarten teacher from a small town no one's ever heard of. Very soon I'll make my mark on the music industry. Whether I fall flat on my face or stand high on a pedestal is in the hands of millions of people I'll never meet.

Knowing I have Adam by my side to pick me up if this fails is the only thing getting me through the day.

As we sat in class, I tried to ignore the looming video premiere and went about my day, but the nerves rolling around in my belly were almost too much to handle. Cailin was good at keeping our secret. I was very thankful whenever she noticed my internal struggles and popped up to give me a hug throughout the day.

Now, I'm at Adam's place, wiping the counter for the fifth time from the sticky lasagna I made in the oven.

Adam steps up behind me, wrapping his arms around my center. "It's going to be fine," he whispers in my ear.

I drop my head back on his chest. "I'm sorry I'm such a spaz."

His laughter tickles my ear. "I kind of like it actually." He grips me tighter. "Seeing you all worked up is getting me all worked up."

He tries to slip his hand under my shirt, and I swat him away. "Down, boy. Cailin doesn't go to bed for a few hours."

His lips trail kisses around my neck, sending chills throughout my body and creating an urge I didn't have three seconds ago.

In the blink of an eye, he grabs my hand and yanks me away from the kitchen and upstairs. I close my hand over my mouth to hide my laughter, peeking to where Cailin and Linda are playing a board game.

"They'll hear us," I say once we're in his room.

He closes the door before turning to me and seductively removing his shirt. "Then, you'll have to be quiet." His eyes twinkle with mischief.

I giggle and cover my mouth again, shaking my head.

His smirk is sexier than ever when he yanks my shirt over my head. "Then, they'll know what we're doing, and I'll blame it all on you, saying you couldn't keep your hands off me one second longer."

"Adam!" I gasp, playfully hitting his chest.

His lips meet mine as he slides my pants and panties down my legs in one fell swoop.

222

When his boxers go next, his cock springs free, and all worries I had of us being heard fly out the door as I lie down and grip the pillow next to me, practicing my screams into it.

Adam's shoulders bounce as he climbs on top of me. "You'd better keep that right there, sweetheart."

He slams into me, and I pull the pillow halfway over me as he has his way with my body. He's super playful, yet his thrusts are punishing. We've never had a quickie, but hot damn, if this is what I've been missing, we need to sneak away more often.

Adam runs his fingers under my neck, tightly holding me as he pounds quickly into me. I catch his arms in my eyesight, his muscles pulling tightly and his biceps bulging as he uses my body for the workout of a lifetime.

When he slows his pace and grinds into my clit, I officially lose my shit and grip the pillow as my orgasm races through me, clenching around his shaft and releasing throughout my entire body.

He's quick to follow, and when we're both sated, he falls on me, trying to catch his breath as I lie like a wet noodle underneath him.

My mind is completely empty as I enjoy the release he just supplied me. His laughter brings me back to reality. When I feel his breath on my neck, my lips grow to a huge grin.

"I'm not sure I can move," he teases, trying to lift his chest off of me.

I grab him and hold him there. "No, not yet."

He kisses my cheek, staying there for a few breaths before pulling back. "So, you're okay that I attacked you that way?" He chuckles under his breath when he sees his pants are still wrapped around his legs.

"Okay? Please. I welcome anytime you want to do that." I slowly make my way up to a sitting position, not wanting the relaxation floating through me to end yet.

He leans down to softly kiss me. "So, it helped?"

I hold him there to get one more kiss. "Absolutely. Thank you."

"Ha! Being thanked for giving you an orgasm." He purses his lips and slightly nods his head. "That I could get used to."

I playfully hit his arm as I slide off the bed and reach for my clothes.

"Good, because guess what? It's five." His eyebrows rise up and down, making butterflies swarm instantly in my belly. "Come on. Let's go see the magic."

Adam saw the final cut but said he wanted me to wait until it released, so I could experience everything for the first time. He said the excitement dies when you can't share it with the people you love. He knew I'd want Maggie to see it, so we could celebrate together, and now that it's time, he couldn't be more right.

We get dressed and head back downstairs, hand in hand.

"You guys ready?" Adam announces our arrival.

Cailin jumps up. "It's time?"

"Yep. Let's do this." Adam turns on the screen and clicks the YouTube icon on his smart TV. He has to scroll a little since it's a new video, but when it comes into view, we see it already has over three thousand views.

"Is that right?" I sit next to him and ask. It's only been out for five minutes.

He grins my way, his blue eyes shining brightly. "Just wait. I bet it'll be hundreds of thousands by the end of the night."

He clicks the video, and it goes full screen on the wall-mounted television.

The screen flickers with the title "Hear Me Now" seconds before Adam appears, and the piano begins. When I see myself next to him, a flush covers me from head to toe.

He wraps his hand around my knee, leaning in to whisper, "You look absolutely breathtaking."

I tuck my hands under my legs as they start to shake from his words, from the emotions running through me, and from this moment. I've never been so happy in my life, and I feel like it's all going to burst out of me if I don't contain it somehow.

We watch as the video cuts between us singing and working on production. To my surprise, the camera caught our quick make-out session, but the way they cut it into the song totally works. It doesn't even make me blush because it's so obvious, the feelings we have for each other, and it fits perfectly with the song.

When Cailin appears on-screen, high-fiving Jack, we all cheer, and she jumps up to take a bow in front of us.

Everything about right now is perfect, and when my phone rings, showing Maggie calling, I feel like my world is complete.

I answer the FaceTime call to a lunatic Maggie screaming at the top of her lungs.

"Holy shit, girl! That was fucking fantastic."

Linda jumps to cover Cailin's ears, making us all laugh.

I can't talk because I feel like if I do, I might burst the dam I'm barely holding back. Instead, I just laugh, looking over to Adam, who's grinning from ear to ear.

Adam takes the phone from me and stares right into it. "We have a star on our hands."

"Hell yeah, we do! You guys are amazing together."

He leans over, kissing my lips and pulling me onto his lap. "You got that right."

"Oh my God, Sarah. I'm so fucking happy for you right now. Please tell me there will be more."

Adam glances to me and back to Maggie. "Only if she'll have me."

Maggie's eyes open wide. "Yes. I'm saying yes right now. She'll have you, and I'll kick her ass if she doesn't."

We all laugh, and I grab the phone from him, so I can talk to her better. "Thank you for watching it and calling."

"Are you kidding me? I'm pissed I'm not by your side right now to celebrate properly. Next time you have a life-changing event, try to remember I live on the opposite coast, and I can't get there with a week's notice."

I smile so hard that my cheeks hurt. The support I've gotten from her since day one is unreal. "You got it."

"Love you, girl. I'm so proud of you."

I blink away a tear. "Thank you."

I blow her a kiss, and we end the call.

Cailin runs over and wraps her arms around my waist. "You were so amazing. I think this is the best song yet."

Adam picks her up, so we can all hug together.

Linda holds up her phone. "Let me get a picture of you three."

We all smile big as we mark the moment with a picture taken of the three of us together.

Our SONG

I didn't get a wink of sleep last night. I was too happy to even try. Adam and I stayed up late, watching the numbers climb on views as well as the social media posts that followed.

I had expected the naysayers and the haters, but overall, the response has been amazing. People are loving seeing Adam finally in love and sharing his life with his fans. Girls keep saying how jealous they are of me, and I can't blame them one bit.

Hell, I'd be in their same shoes if this wasn't my actual life.

Our surprise made front-page news on a few music journals, and it's also mentioned on *Billboard Magazine*'s daily blog.

As we're drinking our morning coffee, still flying high from the night before, a buzz at his front gate makes us turn to see who's coming by for an early morning visit.

Visions of my mom's blue Honda come into view, and my face pales. I wanted so bad to call her last night but chose not to. I didn't want anything to ruin my high, and knowing she was next to my father, it was just too risky.

When Adam takes in my expression, he comes up to me, asking, "Is this someone you want to talk to?"

I inhale, setting my coffee cup down and standing up. "It's my mom."

He places his hands on my shoulders, leaning down to meet my eyes. "Don't let your mind go wild until you know why she's here. It's very possible she's here to congratulate you."

I nod, and he kisses me before hitting the button on the gate, letting her in.

Rubbing my hands together, I make my way to the door and down the stairs, awaiting her arrival.

Please be proud of me, Mom. Please don't ruin this for me.

She exits the car, and I have the answer to my prayers as soon as I see her eyes that are filled with tears.

She heads toward me, throwing her arms around my neck, pulling me in and hugging me harder than she ever has. "You were absolutely amazing, Sarah."

That's enough to break the dam I've been holding back for the past week, and I cry into her shoulder. Tears of joy, tears of relief, and tears of pure happiness flood my soul as I let go of all the stress I've had on my shoulders the past years.

"I'm so proud of you," she says, pulling back and wiping her face. "I must've watched the video a hundred times last night with your sister." She wipes my cheeks and hugs me again.

I inhale a deep breath. "Thank you, Mom," I try to say, but my voice cracks.

"Thank you, sweetheart. Thank you for continuing to follow your dreams. You will be such an inspiration to everyone around you." She laughs, wiping her eyes. "I didn't mean to make you cry."

"I know." I blink and look up to the sky, trying to stop more tears from coming. "I'm really glad you're here."

"Me too, honey. Me too."

"Please, come in."

We head back into the house where Adam is standing, waiting to make sure I'm okay. When Mom grabs Adam, engulfing him in a hug, he smiles and hugs her right back, winking at me.

"Thank you for bringing my daughter back to us," she says when they pull back. She's holding onto his hands, grinning up at him.

"Thank you for trusting me. Your daughter truly is something special. I just held her hand; she did the rest," he responds.

My mom pats the back of his hand. "Sometimes, that's all you need in life—to have someone who will hold your hand through anything."

I wrap my arm around his waist, never feeling so proud as I am right now to stand by his side and show that he's my man.

Adam leads us into the kitchen where he pours my mom a cup of coffee, and we go over the entire process and what's happening next. My mom's face lights up at every turn, and there's no question if she supports me. The way she keeps reaching for my hand, clasping it with the biggest smile across her face, is the most assurance I've ever needed.

When I notice my mom starting to sit back and pause, I look at her in question. "What's going through your mind?" I ask, praying it has nothing to do with my dad.

"I have a suggestion if you're up for it," she says nervously.

Adam and I glance at each other before encouraging her to go on.

"Now, I've already spoken to Principal McAllister, and he was okay with it, but obviously, I don't want to step on your toes, and it's absolutely up to you."

"What's up to me?"

"I'd be honored to help you by taking over your classroom, so you can focus on your music."

My eyes widen as I sit up straighter. "What was that again?" I must not be hearing things properly.

She places her hand on mine, giving me that motherly stare that comforts my soul, no matter what emotions are running through me. "This isn't your dream. I've seen that since the day I retired. I saw the passion in your eyes on that video. I want to see more of that in you. Besides, I miss those little rug rats. You know I can't stay away."

I place my other hand on hers. "But what about Dad?"

She blows me off. "Let me worry about him. I was made to be a teacher, not some sit-at-home, retired housewife. I've been going crazy and can't take it anymore, which he was going to eventually have to pay for, so he's going to have to be okay with it."

I pull her in for a hug. "Thank you, Mom."

"Thank you, sweetheart. You're following your dreams, and I'm not giving up on mine. You've taught me a lot these past few weeks. I should be thanking you."

I pull back to meet her eyes, sighing at her selflessness in this moment.

I lean in to kiss her cheek. "I love you, Mom."

"Love you too, sweetheart."

Chapter 34

Adam

Holy shit, things haven't stopped since that video released. Our social media accounts have been blowing up, and the record company hired someone to take them over, especially Sarah's.

She's not used to this world. Unfortunately, some haters have reared their ugly heads, but that was to be expected. Most of the feedback's been amazing, and people are begging for more.

She was a genius when she filmed me singing *Turn the Page* without me knowing. I would have never put that song out there, but with our song taking off so much, when they asked for more, she suggested the personal video, and they loved the idea.

I even got a call from the man himself, Rock and Roll Hall of Famer Bob Seger. Linda about died when I told her. You'd think she'd never met a rock star before. It was pretty cool to tell her I spoke to him though, and he promised he'd send me a signed album for her.

They want us to start on a music video for the song I wrote for Cailin, and Sarah and I are currently working on her solo song. She's titling it *Bring Me to Life*, and I'm fucking digging it. It's all about how I woke her up again and saved her from what she had been becoming.

Lying on my couch, she holds up the notebook to me that she's been writing in. "Right here, I think it'd be cool for you to come in and have a small piece."

"But this is your solo," I say, making sure she knows it doesn't have to include me.

She gives me a coy smile. "I know, but it's all about you bringing me back. I want you to have your spotlight in it too."

I lean in to kiss her as my phone dings. It's a text message from our publicist, saying they're setting up a photo shoot for tomorrow. I show Sarah, and her face goes pale.

"What kind of photo shoot?" she asks.

"One of us that they'll use as our promo shots."

She glances down at her outfit. "What am I supposed to wear?"

I scroll through my phone to the picture Jack showed me of her last band and hold it out to her. "Don't worry about it. They'll have stylists there, but just in case, please tell me you still have these shorts and these boots?" I raise my eyebrows to her, making her giggle.

"Yes, I still have them."

"Good. Then, it's done. Wear those and hopefully they don't have anything else that fits."

I wink, and she takes the phone from me to examine the picture closer as she sits up, crossing her legs underneath her. When she runs her finger over the two guys in the photo, I sit next to her, placing my hand on her knee.

"You know they're smiling down on you right now," I say, kissing her head.

She sighs and gives me a small grin. "Just doesn't seem fair."

"Life's not fair. I'll be the first one to admit that. But things come together. You have to move forward."

"You have to have faith …" she says, barely above a whisper.

"Nah, faith has nothing to do with it. You make your own destiny." I stand up, heading to the kitchen to grab a water.

She follows me. "You really don't believe in God or a higher power, do you?"

I take a swig of water, trying to think of how to answer this. I don't want to offend her, but I don't want to lie either. If I want to spend my life with her, I need to be forthcoming about my feelings on the matter.

I step closer and grab her hand. "Just like me being straight edge, I don't care if my friends drink around me. That's their business. I feel the same way about religion. But no, I don't believe. If there truly were a God, then why the hell would he have put me through the way I was raised? Believe me, no God I've heard of would have treated a child that way."

I feel her tense, so I step closer, putting my other hand on her cheek. "But just because I don't believe doesn't mean I think you're crazy that you do. If that's how you feel, I'd never fault you for that, just like I hope you wouldn't fault me for my feelings."

She takes a deep inhale and stares into my eyes. "It breaks my heart to hear you say this. Not for my beliefs though, but for you. You're right. No kid should have gone through that, and I hope, one day, you can forgive and open your heart."

"I don't need to forgive. My mom's dead. My life changed the day Cailin was born. She's my true angel, and now that I have you, my heart is full."

She grips my hand tighter, making sure I don't walk away. "If you believe a god punished you with an imperfect childhood, do you think you can also credit him with a perfect daughter? He gives life. He doesn't tell us how to love that life. That we do on our own. All you need is faith."

I take in what she said, thinking about her words and beliefs, but decide this is not a conversation we should have all at once. I've told her my feelings. Instead of stating them again, I kiss her forehead and turn to grab my water once more, hoping I didn't just upset her with my truth.

Linda agrees to watch Cailin after school, so we can head to the photo shoot. My eyes keep roaming to Sarah's legs in the seat next to me.

Those short shorts and high gray boots are officially my kryptonite, and I have to remind myself to keep my eyes on the road.

I run my fingers up her thigh, and she laughs, pushing me off her, knowing exactly what my intentions are.

When we arrive at the spot, I put the car in park and lean over, needing at least one taste of her before I exit.

Fuck, is that a mistake. Now, my cock is rock hard and pushing uncomfortably against my jeans.

I lean back only slightly to inhale a deep breath and about come in my pants when Sarah grabs my dick, rubbing softly up and down.

"I will fuck you in these boots tonight," I growl.

"Promise?" she teases, reaching up to bite my bottom lip.

I have to close my eyes to gain self-control before falling back in my seat and hating the fact that we're in a public parking lot and not somewhere I can take her in the backseat right now.

I hear her laugh as she opens the door. "Are you coming?"

"I was trying to!" I deadpan back to her.

Her giggle does nothing to help my libido right now.

When we enter the studio, I introduce her to everyone, and they instantly take her back to hair and makeup.

I follow them and whisper into her ear when she sits in the chair, "Enjoy being spoiled. You deserve it."

She grins from ear to ear before talking to the hairstylist and makeup artist about how she wants to look.

I lean back in the doorway of the room, crossing my arms as I take in the woman I love. She's beautiful without a drop of makeup, but I know this is the way the world works.

Sarah is absolutely radiant with one woman behind her curling her hair and the other standing in front of her, doing her makeup. I can see the glow she's radiating across the room.

Seeing her happy is the best feeling on earth.

When the artist starts to apply her lipstick, I have to leave the room. Seeing her pouty lips slightly sticking out makes my cock jump at the thought of them wrapped around me, and I just got the thing to finally go down.

The photographer is going over some ideas as Sarah enters the room. I glance in her direction, and my heart stops.

She looks fucking to die for.

I'd love to strip her of her clothes and fuck her right here, but I know I can't, so I drop to my knees at her side and playfully bite her shorts.

She laughs and tries to push me away as the photographer jumps to get his camera.

"Hold that pose!"

I gladly hold the pose and take full advantage by running my fingers up and down her leg.

Her laughter only makes me want to continue.

The photographer takes his shots. "Perfect! Love it. Okay, now, let's get some head shots and some together."

I rise to my feet and kiss her again, whispering, "Definitely fucking you in these boots for the next month. Get ready."

She eyes me, but I know she's dying like I am right now.

Chapter 35

Adam

"I hope you're sitting down," I announce as I enter the kitchen where Sarah and Cailin are fixing dinner.

Sarah is standing at the kitchen stove when she turns my way. "Uh-oh. Should I sit?"

I run up and grab her in my arms, swinging her around. "Guess who iHeartRadio wants to perform at their Thanksgiving concert to raise money for the Feed the Hunger benefit that's televised worldwide?"

Her eyes narrow. "They want Devil's Breed for that show?"

I laugh out loud. She's right to question that; it's not really our crowd. "No, silly." I set her down and tap my finger to her nose. "They want us. Me and you."

I watch as the white in her eyes gets bigger and bigger. "What?" she says in disbelief.

"Are you serious?" Cailin jumps off the stool and runs to me.

I pick her up and swing her around too.

"Yes, I'm serious. Whoever doesn't know us now will by the time December comes around."

Sarah turns back to the stove and is unusually quiet.

I put Cailin down and walk up behind her, placing my hands around her waist and my head on her shoulder. "You're excited, aren't you?"

She inhales and nods her head while she stirs the onions.

"How come I don't believe you?"

Her shoulders sag when she realizes I'm not buying the front she's putting on.

She sighs and steps away from me to the refrigerator. "At least now, I don't have to worry about not being with my family on Thanksgiving."

Her words are a knife to my gut. I didn't think about the upcoming holiday. I've always either been on the road or at Linda's house. Thanksgiving wasn't exactly a tradition for me until Linda, so I've never thought twice about the holiday. Hearing she is worried about her family does something I don't like to my stomach.

She hasn't spoken about her father since their fight. I know her mom took over her class, so I guess I just figured everything had smoothed over. With how busy we've been, I feel bad for not checking with her sooner.

I know she cares for her family, and I don't want to be the reason they're not talking. "I told you I'd make it right. And I'll keep my promise."

When her eyes meet mine, I see the trepidation. A quick nod is all I get as she heads to the counter.

Once all the plans are finalized for our performance, I set Sarah up with a spa day to help her relax and get pampered. I told her I was going shopping. It's the truth, but while I'm out, I'm also going to talk to her father.

Her mom and sister are already set to join us for the concert, and all I've been told is that her father isn't going to come.

This is definitely a situation I never thought I'd have to deal with, but here I go, heading to talk to the father of the girl I love and ready to fight for what's right.

I open the door of the church office to see an older lady with a pink sweater pulled over her shoulders, typing away at a computer.

I don't miss the way the woman's eyes widen as she looks me up and down. "May I help you?" she asks.

Our SONG

"I'm here to see Pastor Russo," I say, standing tall.

"Is he expecting you?"

"I'm sure in some way he is but not at this moment, no."

She stands. "Let me see if he's available."

A few minutes later, a tall man with graying hair and a small gut steps out of the back room. He removes his glasses to glare at me. With pursed lips, he stares without saying a word.

I step forward with my hand outstretched in greeting. "Mr. Russo. It's nice to meet you. I'm—"

"I know exactly who you are. What I don't know is why you're here."

I pull my hand back to my side and square my shoulders. "Sir, I'd like to have a few words with you."

"I don't believe I have anything to say to you."

"Please, I'm coming to you as a father myself. My daughter, Cailin, performed for your church with Sarah a few months ago. I'm only asking for a minute of your time."

He reluctantly steps back, allowing me to enter.

I nod my head. "Thank you."

He sits down at the large desk, and I take a spot on the opposite side. Family pictures of Sarah and her sister cover the dark wood from when they were little up until more current ones.

I smile at the little girl Sarah once was. I can only hope that, one day, Cailin turns out to be as amazing as Sarah is.

I look Pastor Russo directly in the eye. "I know you don't approve of me in Sarah's life, and I'm here to try to mend that relationship. I can only imagine how hard it is to raise a little girl and one day watch her leave to create a life of her own. I know you only want what's best for her. I do too."

"And you think you're what's best for her?" He eyes me up and down, disgust written all over his face.

I hold my head high. "It's not about what I look like on the outside. These tattoos are how I express myself. Every single one has meaning. What should matter is what's in here"—I place my hand on my heart—"on the inside. I know what love is. The day my daughter was born, it smacked me across the face. I wasn't lucky enough to have a father who cared for me like you do for Sarah. I want to stand by you, not in front of you. Sarah deserves the best life she can lead.

Music is what she wants. Music is what's healed her."

He stands up, his chair falling to the floor with the force of his movement. "Your kind of people and music are what almost killed her. You have no clue what we had to do to help with her recovery after the accident." His eyes widen as he clenches his teeth. "I *never* got my daughter back."

He inhales, taking a moment for what he said to sink in. Any hurt he just felt is removed, and anger sits firmly in its place. "Then, I found out she had been selling herself to the devil the entire time, performing in strip clubs and horrible bars. She was lying to us and would go weeks with only one meal a day. All of her money that *I* had been sending her was paying for the one thing that almost took her life."

He glances down, shaking his head. When he looks back up at me, his face is stern. "God has shown his path for her. He forgave her sins and gave her another chance."

"That is what you do when you're passionate about something. You should be proud your daughter has that kind of drive that she's willing to sacrifice for what she wants. If you can honestly say God has shown his path, then why am I here right now? Why did he bring Cailin into my life? Why did he bring Linda into my life, who gave me music and told me to enroll Cailin in your daughter's class?"

His body language relaxes, and I know he's hearing my words.

"I see the looks I get all over town, the way I'm not welcome here, but you know what? This is where I want to raise my daughter because of how highly Linda speaks of this town as a great place to raise a family. I'm willing to put my own feelings aside, so Cailin can have friends and someone who loves her like a grandma would, even though they share no blood relation. I don't want her to grow up in a big city. I want her to be able to ride her bike and go to the park where other families are as well."

He steps back slightly. Even though he's been against me this entire time, I'm thankful he's listening to what I'm actually saying.

"I'm not going to lie to you, sir. I'm not a religious man. I've never had someone show me the way of the Bible or what it feels like to believe in something higher than me. But if you think her injury was God punishing her, then please explain to me why he would bring me into her life. If you believe one, then you have to believe the other."

Our SONG

I pause, seeing if he has a response. When he doesn't, I hold my ground and never break my eye contact with him, giving him a second to let everything I said sink in.

"I'm in love with your daughter. I just want what's best for her. We're performing on Thanksgiving at the iHeartRadio benefit in San Francisco." I place a ticket to the event as well as our demo tape on the table. "As a father myself, there is *nothing* that would stop me from seeing my daughter shine the way Sarah does. Put everything you think of me and my type of music aside and listen for yourself. Your daughter has talent that no one can deny. I know it'd mean the world to her to have you there. But it's your choice."

I step back, waiting for a brief moment before saying, "Thank you for your time," and then I turn around to leave.

I said everything I had to say. If he comes to support his daughter or not is up to him.

Chapter 36

Sarah

"Breathe," Maggie says, placing her hands on either side of my head.

I might or might not be freaking out just a little. I made a huge mistake by looking out to the crowd. And that's not including the millions of people watching at home.

We've never performed the song live. Of course, we practiced, and we did a trial run onstage earlier today, but now that the time is here, my stomach is flipped so far upside down, you'd think it's riding the most insane roller coaster known to man.

I'm so glad Maggie was able to be here. My sister, mother, and Linda are in the seats. I love that they're here as well, supporting my dreams.

The only person missing is my father. I try to pretend that it doesn't matter, but every time I think about it, sadness washes over me. I just want to know what it feels like to truly have his support, something I've never had from him.

That's definitely not the case with Maggie. She's been there since day one, helping me find the guys in New York and giving me feedback on lyrics. I couldn't have done it without her.

Adam surprised me by flying her out for the show. I was beyond shocked when she showed up at Adam's front door a few days ago. He amazes me at every turn, and with every day, I fall for him more and more.

Our SONG

I look into her eyes and take a deep, cleansing breath. "I'm okay. It's okay," I say more to myself than to her.

She laughs and engulfs me in a hug. "Just keep saying that, and it will be."

Adam walks up to us. "Are we ready to show the world who's on top?"

Maggie laughs and hands me over to Adam, who allows me to curl into his arms.

"Don't be nervous." He rubs his hand down my hair before pushing me back to talk to me face-to-face. "There's nothing to worry about. You are one of the most phenomenal singers I've ever heard. I have absolute faith that you'll do wonderful. I wouldn't let this happen otherwise."

I inhale and nod. He pulls me in and kisses me with so much intensity that I forget who I am and where we are.

"I'd fuck you against the wall right now if I knew it wouldn't freak everyone in here out," he whispers in my ear while holding me close to him.

I laugh out loud. I know he said it so crudely because of where we actually are. The event is being held at the San Francisco Armory. The building was built for military purposes in 1912, but for the last fifteen years it was owned by Kink.com and was used as a pornography and BDSM lounge.

The new owners have turned it into a concert venue, but the upstairs rooms are still set up for the BDSM sets. The red velvet walls along with antique furniture and hooks on the ceilings are definitely a sight to see.

Adam smirks. "That's the laugh I was going for. Keep that feeling because we're on." He winks and grabs my hand, pulling me up to the curtain we're about to walk through.

I hear Maggie scream, and when I turn to her, she's jumping up and down, blowing me good-luck kisses.

I blow a kiss back before taking a deep breath. Ready to give it my all.

We take our place onstage while they announce us from the main stage to the right.

Adam squeezes my hand one more time, whispering, "I love you," before placing his hands on the piano and starting the first notes.

Screams erupt when the lights above us shine brightly, and I grab the microphone from the stand in front of me.

When Adam sings his first note, the crowd goes wild. It's so overwhelming as I watch the love of my life sing with such passion. His eyes are closed as the words flow from his lips and his hands glide over the keys.

When it's my turn, his eyes meet mine, and the smile and small tilt to his head are all I need to encourage me to dive in with both feet first.

The spotlight hits me, and I bring the microphone up to my lips and go for it. Singing the lyrics with everything I have.

The applause lifts me up, washing away every ounce of nerves I had and filling me with so much life that I feel like I can float away.

I glance out to the crowd, seeing people clapping, singing, and swaying to the love story we're telling. It's by far the most unbelievable, emotional, and uplifting moment of my life.

I never thought I'd be here again, yet I'm standing on the biggest stage of my life with the most wonderful man and singer I've ever known. My life is absolutely complete.

Before I know it, our moment is over, and I drop the microphone to my side, in absolute disbelief of what we just did. Adam picks me up, bringing his lips to mine as the crowd claps louder than I've ever heard.

They let us stand there for a few moments, letting the crowd show their love, before the lights are cut, and the show goes to commercial.

When we exit the stage, Maggie runs to us. "Oh my God!" she screams with her arms wide open to engulf both of us. "You guys fucking killed it!"

"She did, didn't she?" Adam says, kissing my forehead. "I'm so proud of you."

My cheeks hurt from smiling. I want to take this entire moment in and never forget this feeling.

We make our way down the hall to the green room, so I can grab my things before we go back out to the seats to join my sister and mom as well as Linda and Cailin.

Every person we pass gives us praise about how well we did and how much they enjoyed the performance. The high I'm experiencing is above anything in my entire life.

Our SONG

But everything stops when we turn the corner, and my father is standing at the door to our makeshift dressing room. I pause, not sure how or why he's here.

Adam leans down to kiss my forehead, encouraging me to move forward.

I glance in his direction, whispering, "How?"

He grins to my father and then back to me. "I told you I'd try to make it right."

Maggie rubs my shoulder, and I lean up to softly kiss Adam before slowly making my way to my father. The little girl in me who was always searching for his approval wants to jump into his arms and celebrate my success, but the scorned adult knows better.

"Hi, Dad."

His lips tug to a slight smile, and I can tell he's just as nervous as I am.

"How did you get back here?" I ask when he stays silent.

His eyes lift to Adam and Maggie and then back to me. "Adam came to see me. He had some pretty powerful thoughts to share."

I turn and smile at Adam, who's keeping his distance. I reach my hand out, wanting him by my side.

"It's good to have you back, Sarah," Dad says to my surprise. "I was blind to how much of you we had lost in New York. But, right now, with him, on that stage, I see it now. My little girl who I thought was gone forever."

His eyes tear up, and he quickly blinks them away as I rush into his arms.

"Oh, Daddy," I say, letting the tears fall freely. "You have no idea how much it means to me to hear you say that."

I pull back from him, keeping one hand wrapped around his waist as I wipe my eyes.

"You were amazing tonight." He holds his hand out to Adam. "I can't thank you enough for coming to talk to me and opening my eyes. You're right. She's pretty talented."

He glances down to me, and I curl up into his arms even more.

"I'm glad you were able to make it." Adam and my dad shake hands.

And I was lying before. Now, my life is complete.

The rest of the concert is a blur from the happiness, shock, and astonishment of where my life has come.

I hear the other singers and watch as lights flash across the screen, but I don't take any of it in. I'm in my own world, high above the clouds, with Adam by my side.

My sister keeps laughing when she sees me bouncing in my chair. She leans over and whispers, "Some things never change with you, do they?"

I cover my mouth before I burst out laughing from the memories of us having to sit still in church and me feeling like I was going to bust at the seams.

As the host closes the show, everyone claps, and I jump out of my seat, feeling like I'm ready to run a marathon.

Cailin dances around our group as we make our way out of the venue. Cameras flash from every direction while people yell to get our attention. Adam approaches a younger boy reaching out an album to have him sign it.

The boy's eyes grow wide as he stares up at Adam in awe. "Thank you so much," he says in disbelief. The boy's dad takes a photo of the two of them.

I hold Cailin close to me so she doesn't get lost in the shuffle of people screaming to get their idols' attention or news cameras wanting their next interview.

"Sarah, Sarah, over here," I hear someone yell from behind me.

I turn around to see a news camera pointed directly at me with a woman holding out a microphone. Adam grabs my hand, putting his other on Cailin, and walks us toward the two of them.

"Adam, Sarah, you guys were unreal in there. When will the entire album release?"

Adam stands with ease, talking to the woman without a care in the world. "We hope in the next few months."

"Will every song be a duet?"

"We'll have a mixture of both of us. Some solos, some duets."

"Sarah, when will your solo release?"

When I glance to Adam, his smile takes away all the nerves of giving my first on-the-spot camera interview.

"It's next in line. I'm excited for you all to hear it," I respond.

"Okay, move the line along," the security guard says.

Adam starts to pull me away, and I turn to wave to the woman.

"Thank you for the interview," she yells out.

Maggie grips my arm, her smile saying it all.

This is really happening.

When our limo pulls up, my poor sister has a hard time sliding across the seat with her pregnant belly, but once she's in, her face lights up. The opulence is not lost on her or my parents.

This is what I've always dreamed of. I wanted to be the person to give them this. To show them what I could do and treat them to a lavish lifestyle.

The hotel is only a few blocks away, and when we arrive, the chaos is no different than the place we left. Though there's no longer a red carpet, limos and taxis line the streets. Security tries to keep the fans at bay as celebrities pour out of every car that lines the entrance.

We wait our turn as people scream from behind the ropes the hotel set up.

"We love you, Adam," a group of girls screams when he rolls down the window to wave.

Maggie loves all of the excitement, but I can tell my parents are a little overwhelmed by the entire experience.

The limo comes to a stop, and the bellhop opens the door for us. Adam hops out first, only to be met with screams so loud that my dad covers his ears.

They're letting people out of their rides in rows of three, and we're the last ones in this batch, so we have the longest walk to the entrance. The hotel is handing out gift bags, and Cailin runs ahead to get one.

Adam and Linda jump to chase after her, but Linda calls over her shoulder, "I got her," so Adam backs off and pulls me close as everyone else exits the limo. Maggie is quick to smile and wave at everyone who looks her way.

People from all around are screaming Adam's name, begging for him to look their direction. He waves at a few before wrapping his arm around me to pose for a picture.

We continue our walk when I feel a firm hand grip my shoulder. When I turn, I see my father with his eyes soft and glistening in the lights that flash all around us.

His slight smile as he stares at me means more than any word he could say right now.

A camera crew runs our direction, holding a microphone out toward us after saying, "You must be Sarah's father. Tell us, how proud are you of your daughter?"

My dad blinks a few times, before glancing down at me and pulling me closer to him. "We couldn't be more proud of our little girl."

I lean in for a hug. "Thanks, Daddy."

"And this man right here." He reaches out his arm from around me to touch Adam's shoulder. "He's been a huge blessing in our lives, in more ways than one."

Seeing my dad welcome Adam into our family makes a tear slip down my face. I wipe it away, smiling big at the camera.

The woman's eyes crinkle at the sides as she gives me a closed mouth grin. "Congratulations, Sarah. You've made it."

I turn to my dad, then Adam. *Yeah, I finally have.*

Epilogue

Sarah
Seven Months Later

"Let's blow this popsicle stand!" Cailin shouts as we head toward the bus, ready to head to the next venue.

Life has been both a dream and a whirlwind since our song was released. The record label wanted us in the studio to create an album as soon as possible, and it was released two months ago.

With it being summer and Cailin out of school, we're on tour to promote the album, so we're living city to city, performing as much as possible and loving every minute.

Since the guys in Devil's Breed helped with the album, they are here, right alongside us, and play a few of their songs while we're onstage. Even Max has rejoined the guys and hangs out with us most nights.

The blend of our music has been a true blessing. People who love my and Adam's music have fallen for the craziness that is Devil's Breed and vice versa.

The best part is having Cailin by our side the entire time. She's no longer in the shadows, hiding from town to town. We still had to hire a nanny to watch her while we prepare and perform, but that nanny sits to the right of the stage with Cailin during the show, so she doesn't miss a thing.

As we enter the bus, I hear everyone scream, "Surprise!" making me halt in my footing.

I search around the bus to see my parents, my sister, and even Maggie as well as people from our record label. I turn to Adam to see what's going on. His grin tells me he was totally in on something and left me out of the loop.

"Look!" Cailin says, grabbing something from the label's publicist and bringing it to me. "It's a gold record!"

My eyes widen as they fill with tears. "Seriously?" I scream with joy before wrapping my arms around Adam.

His laughter just makes me cry more happy tears. "I wanted everyone to be here to join in on the celebration when you found out."

I quickly kiss him before running to my parents, giving them each a hug. "I'm so glad you're here," I say, trying not to be a blubbery mess.

"Us too, sweetheart," my dad says while rubbing my back.

I give my sister a hug and kiss my nephew, who is sleeping in her front baby carrier.

When I get to Maggie, we both scream and jump up and down in celebration.

"I'm so proud of you!" she says when she pulls me in for a hug. "And believe me, I tell everyone that you're my best friend and that I helped make you what you are today."

I laugh out loud, knowing she's teasing but also knowing it's the goddamn truth.

"Love you, girl." I tightly hug her.

"Shall we pop some champagne?" Bruce, our manager, says, holding up a bottle of Chandon.

"Oh! Can we, Daddy? Please, please, please?" Cailin bounces on her toes with her hands in front of her chin and her little lip sticking out.

I laugh out loud as I turn to my parents, who look a little shocked by what she just said. "After we finish every song in the recording studio, we spray each other with water, pretending it's champagne. She's always wanted to try it with the real stuff."

"Oh," my mom says, but my dad still looks unsure.

I grin while softly hitting his shoulder. "Don't worry, Pops. It will never happen."

Our SONG

I walk up to Adam and run my arm around his waist, bringing my head to his chest. My smile is so big that my cheeks hurt as I take in the people around me. It's hard to believe the path that led me here. I never gave up faith and knew God had a plan for me. In the end, it's exactly what it should be.

Playlist

Don't Need You – Bullet for my Valentine
Sarah listens to this when she turns on the car in the first chapter.

Riot – Three Days Grace
Inspiration for the Devil's Breed song that calms the riot.

All Star – Smash Mouth
The first song Cailin sings with the wrong lyrics.

Listen to the Music - The Doobie Brothers
When Linda is explaining who Cailin's dad is she sings the wrong lyrics to this song.

HandClap - Fitz and the Tantrums
Adam and Cailin sing the wrong lyrics during their first dinner home.

Tears Don't Fall – Bullet for my Valentine
Inspiration for the Devil's Breed they discuss while driving to the zoo

Like a Nightmare – Deadset Society
This plays on the radio as they drive to the zoo

Power - Elevation Worship
Sarah sings this in church when she has her breakthrough.

Turn the Page – Bob Segar
Adam sings this when he thinks no one's watching. He learned how to play it for Linda.

Hear Me Now – Bad Wolves featuring DIAMANTE
Inspiration for the song they sing together!

Bring Me To Life - Evanescence
Inspiration for the song she sings on her own.

Cailin – Unwritten Law
Inspiration for Adam's solo song for his daughter.

Acknowledgments

This book started in my real life three years ago when I was chastised for taking my kids to a Papa Roach concert. We got to hang out backstage (they are from my hometown) and someone grabbed me saying I should be taking my boys to Disneyland not rock concerts. With Jacoby (Papa Roach's lead singer) only a few feet away, I tried to defuse the situation saying this is our version of Disneyland and excuse myself from her presence.

I grew up going to concerts with my mom. It's still my favorite thing to do, and I love bringing my boys. I hate that rock music is looked down upon by some due to their loud beats or tattoo covered singers. I would much rather let my boys listen to the meaningful lyrics of rock music than the "popular" music out today.

And that's why the idea of this book was born.

Thank you to my boys, Mason and Leighton, for always rocking out with mom! And to Leighton, who was the inspiration for Cailin. He's always making up lyrics to songs and singing them every second of the day. I'm his Sugarplum and he's my Chestnut—nicknames he made up for us. Love you, Chestnut!

I published my first book, Unwritten, four years ago on September 15. The series was about a couple and their love of a little known band called Unwritten Law. It's so fitting that here I am, four years later almost to the day, releasing a book that I based off of Unwritten Law's song Cailin that's about the love of the lead singer's daughter. And yes, there was no doubt that I was going to name Adam's daughter Cailin.

It's amazing to think I've been writing for four years, and this is my thirteenth book. I wouldn't want to be in this author world without my bestie, Jeannine Colette. We met through the book world but have become so much more than co-authors. Being able to talk through a book with someone is HUGE and I'm so glad to have her in my life.

I'm a member of Private Party Book Club (join us on Facebook if you haven't already!) and am so thankful for the authors I've met there. When I put out a call to see if any of the authors had time for a beta read I was excited when Christi Barth offered to read Our Song. What she did for this book was SO MUCH MORE than I expected, and I'll forever be in debt to her!

Thank you to Stefanie Pace, my amazing beta reader and the one person I can count on to tell me straight up, "That's a crappy ending. Change it!" LOL.

Yes, it took me a few other beta readers before I listened to her but in the end, she was right and I changed the ending. Thank you to Cole Robitaille, Stacey Spence and Autumn Gantz for being those extra beta readers.

I have no clue what I would do without Autumn Gantz with Wordsmith Publicity. She keeps me in line, helps me plan things out and makes things happen. She was in the middle of Hurricane Dorian's path and planning this release out early just incase she lost power for a few days. Autumn, thank you for everything!!!

To my proofreaders, Grey Ditto and Allisia Wysong, thank you for helping an indie author out! The things you find are amazing!

And to all the blogs, readers and instagramers who signed up to help promote Our Song, THANK YOU! I was blown away by the support this book received! I normally have to send hundreds of review requests, but with this one the sign ups poured in all on their own. You have no idea how much that means to an Indie Author, thank you!

About the Author

Lauren Runow is the author of multiple Adult Contemporary Romance novels, some more dirty than others. When Lauren isn't writing, you'll find her listening to music, at her local CrossFit, reading, or at the baseball field with her boys. Her only vice is coffee, and she swears it makes her a better mom!

Lauren is a graduate from the Academy of Art in San Francisco and is the founder and co-owner of the community magazine she and her husband publish. She is a proud Rotarian, helps run a local non-profit kids science museum, and was awarded Woman of the Year from Congressman Garamendi. She lives in Northern California with her husband and two sons.

You can also stay in touch through the social media links below.
www.LaurenRunow.com

Check out her books on Amazon: http://amzn.to/1Tjw1jr

Check out her books on Goodreads: http://bit.ly/1Isw3Sv

Follow her on:
Facebook at https://www.facebook.com/laurenjrunow
Instagram at https://instagram.com/Lauren_Runow/
BookBub at https://www.bookbub.com/authors/lauren-runow
Twitter at https://twitter.com/LaurenRunow
BookandMain: https://bookandmainbites.com/LaurenRunow

Join her reader group: Lauren's Law Breakers

Sign up for her newsletter at http://eepurl.com/btD6j9
Make sure to enter your birthday for a free book on your special day!

Made in the USA
Lexington, KY
08 November 2019